THE REVENGE OF DRACULA

THE REVENGE OF DRACULA

Peter Tremayne

Walker and Company, New York

First published in the United States of America
in 1979 by the Walker Publishing Company, Inc.

ISBN: 0-8027-0634-7

Library of Congress Catalog Card Number: 79-64722

Printed in the United States of America

10 9 8 7 6 5 4 3 2 1

'You think to baffle me - you - with your pale faces all in a row, like sheep in a butcher's. You shall be sorry yet, each one of you! You think you have left me without a place to rest; but I have more. My revenge is just begun! I spread it over centuries, and time is on my side.'

- *Dracula* by Bram Stoker,
Constable, London, 1897.

For Ron and Hilary Colbert who would agree that if the only vampires on this Earth were like Dracula then it might be a happier place.

THE REVENGE OF DRACULA

INTRODUCTION

A writer receives many varied and often strange packages through his postbox. There are sometimes letters of praise for his work, sometimes abusive letters, copies of reviews to flatter his ego or make him rail at the wretches who dare call themselves critics and, less frequent but more welcome, are royalty cheques from beneficent publishers.

For me, the arrival of the morning mail is the high spot of my day and, depending on what is contained in the oddly assorted envelopes and packages that cascade each morning over my front door mat, my mood is established for the rest of the day. It is probably not a very mature reaction, but nothing puts me in a good work mood for the rest of the day than to receive some exciting titbit in the mail.

Not long after the publication of *Dracula Unborn*,* a book in which I edited and introduced Professor Abraham Van Helsing's translation of an amazing 15th Century manuscript written by Mircea, the youngest son of the evil Vlad Dracula, I received a rather bulky package which had been addressed to me care of my publishers and passed on by them. The package contained a lengthy manuscript written on ill-assorted sheets of paper, yellowing around the edges. The hand was a neat copperplate, executed in fading brown ink. The whole thing smacked of the Victorian era and a date, *1866*, written at the beginning of the manuscript confirmed this.

Now, as a writer, it has not been an unusual occurrence for me to receive ageing manuscripts, discovered in some family trunk or forgotten drawer, and passed on by some hopeful scion who felt it contained publishable material. Neither is it unusual for the manuscript to turn out to be some illiterate philosophical ramble written by a bored suburban parson with nothing better to do than

* In the U.S., *Bloodright*.

inflict his views of morality on an equally bored world.

With that vision in mind I was about to toss the manuscript aside when I observed a covering letter. The letter was addressed from a certain mental health clinic near Guildford in Surrey. Furthermore, it was from the psychiatrist in charge of the clinic. It was a rather un-flattering letter, somewhat curt in tone:

I am not in the habit of reading the type of lurid tales that writers of your ilk produce. Vampire stories have always seemed to me to be merely crude and sensational efforts to exploit people's genuinely-held fears and superstitions. While such stories, unfortunately, enjoy a vogue, they lack the charm and strangeness of genuine folk tradition.

I have read your book *Dracula Unborn* merely because some sections of the press have taken the work seriously. The *Bolton Evening News* of February 1, 1978, for example, devoted a lengthy article to the discussion of its historical merits. While I appreciate that it is an accepted literary custom for an author to pretend he has found a genuine manuscript which he is merely editing, I cannot help but say that *Dracula Unborn* was a very irresponsible book to write. Filled, as it is, with genuine historical detail, it gives the impression of a serious historical document which has fooled even some newspapers.

Do you realise that there is a serious psychiatric condition called lupomania or a 'werewolf complex'; that people of certain neurotic instability genuinely believe that they are victims of vampires and werewolves and, in some horrible cases, may believe they are the vampires themselves and have committed terrible acts in this belief? Your book and others like it, can only feed these fears.

As a psychiatrist, I take the strongest objection to such fiction. It can have an extremely harmful effect. Need I quote the recent bizarre case of the unfortunate man who died in Stoke-on-Trent in 1973? The cause of death was asphyxiation after the man had swallowed garlic which he had placed in his mouth as protection against vampires. I can refer you to a more recent case of a boy in Stafford in 1975 who killed himself because he believed he was changing into a werewolf.

2

And what of the mass hysteria in London during 1969/70 when people began to report visions of vampires in Highgate Cemetery in North London?

I believe that nothing illustrates my contention better than the enclosed manuscript and shows the suffering of the unstable mind when caught up in this vampire mythology. This manuscript was written by an inmate of this clinic when it was, unfortunately, termed a lunatic asylum in the 1860's. In those days an enlightened attitude towards the mentally handicapped had not permeated Western civilisation. The poor unfortunate who wrote this could, in all probability, have been easily cured in the light of modern psychiatric knowledge.

The writer of the manuscript, as you will see, suffered from classic symptoms of personality disassociation and delusions, believing that he was being persecuted by a vampire. The story, an imagining from his fear-crazed mind, is certainly the equal to any horror-fiction of today. There are several interesting parallels to your own *Dracula Unborn* and it seems obvious that the man had access to the same historical sources as yourself.

I hope a reading of the manuscript will serve as a salutory lesson that such tales can have a harmful effect on a person's mental stability.

It took me a while to recover from this rebuke to my literary endeavours but eventually, more out of curiosity than any real desire, I sat down and read the manuscript.

What I read electrified me!

The doctor was surely mistaken when he said that the story was just the "imagining of a fear-crazed mind." So many things fitted in with Mircea's manuscript which the 'lunatic' could have had no access to. I was convinced that the manuscript I now held was not a lunatic's ramblings but another terrifying chapter in the story of the attempts by that horrifying personification of evil - Dracula - to spread his blood lust throughout the world.

I wrote off immediately to the psychiatrist and asked for permission to publish the work. After all, he had sent it to me to read in support of his case so why not present it to the public and let them judge.?

At first he was reluctant and objected most strongly on the grounds that I would turn it into a fictional horror tale. Eventually, after some correspondence and a telephone call, he agreed to the publication on condition that I did not alter one word of the manuscript (a condition I was more than willing to meet); secondly, that I made it quite clear that the writer was a man named Upton Welsford who wrote the manuscript while he was in an asylum for the mentally ill, and undergoing treatment for delusions. This I promised to do. Thirdly, in addition to the foregoing conditions, I would allow the psychiatrist to append, as an afterword, a note on the mental condition which he, in the light of modern psychiatric learning, believed Upton Welsford to have suffered from. That, also, I willingly agreed to do.

Having fulfilled these three conditions, I now leave the story for you to read and decide whether indeed it is merely the ramblings of a lunatic or, if not, whether a great wrong was done to Upton Welsford when he returned from Romania in 1862...some thirty-five years before Bram Stoker collected the material to publish his great work *Dracula*.

Peter Tremayne

London, 1978.

CHAPTER ONE

They say I am mad.

And at times, mostly at night, as I stand peering through the small iron grille that blocks the window of my room, and staring at the ominous black clouds that scud across the death-white face of the moon, I find myself wishing that it *was* so, wishing that I were indeed mad. For at such times I experience an unearthly, chilling tingle that vibrates against my spine; I find my heart beats twice as fast; I feel the blood bursting hotly into my cheeks, roaring in my ears, and a mist begins to cloud my eyes. And through it all I hear *his* voice, mocking, sardonic, telling me that the time is coming... soon, soon!

Momentarily the swirling mists clear; I catch a glimpse of *him* - a tall, thin man, all in black. I see his face, that waxen face; the high aquiline nose, the parted red lips with the sharp teeth showing ivory-white between them; and the eyes - those black eyes ringed with red fire, flaming as if I were staring at the very sunset.

And the voice:

'Soon...*soon!*'

It is almost a caress.

I wish, indeed, I were mad as they say I am. I wish I *had* embarked on the impossible adventures of lunacy and merely encountered the monsters created of man's first morality which have ever vexed him into the spinning of fantasies by which to elude or do battle with them.

But I am sane; yes, I say it is so. I am sane even though I be committed to this brooding asylum filled with the tragic storage crypts of the unthinkable and the unrealisable deliriums of infantile man. I am suffering from no delirium, I am spinning no fantasy, for I have experienced the unthinkable, I have realised the unrealisable, I have suffered the torture of the damned and now know that soon... soon such a monstrous evil will burst forth upon the earth that the Horsemen of the Apocalypse will seem like the riding forth of Cherubim and Seraphim by comparison. Yet who can I warn? Who will believe me? Who will take seriously the ramblings of the mentally deranged?

They have, at last allowed me pen and paper. Smilingly (oh, how I hate their smiles of superior knowledge) they have told me to commit my fantasies and deliriums to paper. They say it will be therapeutic for me. As if there were some medical cure for a branded soul in torment! But, since I have pen and paper, I will write my story... my delirium, my fantasy... call it what you will. I will commit it to writing.

Alas, I can no longer hope that it will be believed... not now. But maybe one day the world will know the terrible truth of what I shall presently recount for I hear, whispering in my ears, that evil, sardonic sneering voice.... 'Soon... *soon!*'

It all began a few weeks before Christmas, in the early December of 1861. In fact it was the very day after my twenty-sixth birthday which I had celebrated with my father, a widower, the Reverend Mortimer Welsford, at Gisleham in Berkshire, in which village and county I had been born and received my rudimentary education before going to Oxford to take my degree. I recall that I had returned to London on the morning following my birthday, a Tuesday, or so I believe, because the next day I was due to attend an important meeting at the Foreign Office.

Straightway I must point out that I, Upton Welsford, served the British Government only in a minor capacity. I was personal secretary to Viscount Molesworth. Lord Molesworth's connection with the Foreign Office is such that I need not elaborate on this point. Ever since I had come down from Oxford and started a career in the Foreign Office, I had served under the patronage of Lord Molesworth, whose interest in my career and welfare was prompted by the fact that my father had once been chaplain to the Viscount's father. Therefore do not be deluded that I was in any way a person of great weight or importance. If the brutal truth be known, I was nothing more than a lowly clerk. Nevertheless, Lord Molesworth required my presence for that meeting and his summons caused me to hasten from rural Berkshire into the smoke-blackened mists of wintry London.

Having caught the Bristol-London stage before breakfast, I was in Westminster by midday and walked the length of Whitehall to my rooms by Charing Cross. Depositing my bags, I went out to lunch at a nearby tavern and then discovered that I had an entire afternoon to idle through.

My father, who is inclined to over-generosity on birthdays, had given me five guineas to celebrate my twenty-sixth year of life. The coins jangled comfortingly in my pocket as I strolled through the fog-bound streets that grey, comfortless afternoon. As I walked, my feet turned towards Petticoat Lane. I was in no hurry, so I did not summon a coasting hackney-carriage even though it was a fair measure to tread. Now I must confess that my one vice in life is the collection of unusual *objets d'art* and the reason my feet turned in the direction of Petticoat Lane was because of the collection of junk shops that were found in the area. Sometimes, among the piles of coloured bottles, cordage and dusty bric-a-brac, I have uncovered tiny porcelain figurines, statuettes and vases of such unusual quality that I have added them, one by one, into a modest collection that is the envy of my friends. Thus it was, with this idea of seeking yet another treasure to add to my collection, that I walked contentedly through the gloomy afternoon.

Would to God I had been beset by a gang of footpads and thieves; would to God I had been run down by a flying carriage in the foggy twilight of the city streets; would to God I had never reached my destination!

It was late afternoon when I came upon the shop. The sky had already blackened with the early dusk of winter. An old man in a thick, yellow woollen muffler - I recall him well - was shuffling along the street, lighting the gas lamps.

I recall that I had been staring into the grimy window of some shop, scarcely able to see through the twilight and the dirt of the window-pane, when the old man lit the gas-standard which stood opposite, letting a yellow beam of light play on the window. I was about to turn away when this light caught at something in the corner of the window, causing a myriad white pinpricks of light to dance

7

over its surface. I turned and tried to wipe the dirty pane with my sleeve, the better to see the object. It looked like a small statuette of some animal, some unusual animal.

Intrigued, I opened the door of the shop and entered into a musty interior to the accompaniment of a jangling bell.

Almost directly, a large, red-jowled man appeared from behind a curtain at the back of the shop. He bent to a hurricane lamp on a makeshift counter and turned up the wick, causing his dust-laden wares to be more clearly observed.

Two glistening blue eyes stared at me from a weather-beaten face. The man came forward and as he walked his rolling gait betrayed his former occupation: a sailor, without doubt.

'Ar'ernoon, cap'n,' his voice held the cheery accent of a true born Cockney. 'Wot can I do for yer? Sum'ink toikes yer fancy then?'

He gestured about the shop.

I nodded.

'There is a small statuette in your window. It's some kind of animal in black.'

'I knows the one,' replied the man, going to the window and reaching forward into the bric-a-brac. In a trice he had returned with a dusty object in his hand. He looked at it a moment, then pulled a dirty rag from his pocket and proceeded to dust it after a fashion.

''Ere y'are, cap'n,' he said, thrusting it into my hands.

The object was a figure of a dragon, its serpent-like neck arched and its wings spread out behind it. It was of excellent workmanship and carved from some dark green mineral. Its surface was smooth and cold to the touch. Although I was not by any means an expert, I had been collecting *objets d'art* long enough to recognise nephrite jade. It was a superb specimen.

'Where did you obtain this from?' I asked the man casually, trying not to let him see my greedy excitement.

'Howt heast, cap'n,' he said.

'Out east?' I repeated.

'Port o' Kowloon, cap'n. I served fifteen years afore the mast 'fore planting me stumps ashore. Picked this up on one o' me last trips.'

'Chinese, is it?'

I held up the small carving. It was about six inches long and some three inches high. There was no question that it was a fine piece. The carving had been lovingly carried out and the face of the dragon seemed to bear a malevolent smile, menacing yet triumphant. There was no way to indicate the date of its creation. It could have been a few years old... or it could have been a few centuries old.

There was no doubting, however, the quality of the nephrite: that much I did know. I also knew that a great many other coloured minerals have been mistaken for jade and I once knew a colleague who paid an enormous sum for a jade vase only to find out that it was made of serpentine. To be on the safe side I walked to the window of the shop and held it up to the rays of the gaslight which seeped in from outside. I did not dare conduct my experiment by the hurricane lamp in case the seaman-cum-shopkeeper guessed at my knowledge. Carefully removing my cravat pin, without being observed, I drew its point along the smooth green-black surface. Had it been serpentine, or, indeed, verdite, which is a deep green micaceous rock, there would have been a scratch on the surface. Both minerals are softer than jade and liable to scratching. Nor could the mineral have been saussurite, another mineral with jade-like qualities, because the colouring of the piece would have been greyish green and not black green. It was nephrite jade right enough and therefore valuable.

The junk dealer stood looking at me expectantly.

'How much do you want for it?' I asked.

He shuffled his feet and gazed into the distance before replying, a sign by which I deduced that he had not been in his present calling for long.

'Why, cap'n, 1 was 'oping to 'ave two guineas fer it.'

Two guineas!

I felt a momentary surge of triumph for I knew that certain dealers would have demanded no less than ten guineas for such a piece, even if it were only a few years old.

'I'll take it then,' I said without preamble.

'Aye, aye, cap'n.!

The man was as enthusiastic as I was. He ducked behind a small counter and emerged with a piece of yellowing newspaper. Taking the statuette from my hands, he wrapped it carefully and handed it

9

back. Meanwhile, I removed from my pocket two of my father's golden guineas and laid them in his palm.

'Thank'ee, cap'n, thank'ee kindly,' nodded the man, finger to a vanished forelock.

With the jade statuette under my arm, I bade him a good day and left the shop.

Ah, the proud vanity of man. I strutted home like some vain turkey-cock, delighted in my dealings and sparing no thought of remorse for the man I had, through his ignorance, cheated. Cheated? My mind did not even contemplate the concept. That was business. But had I known then what I know now I would have dashed that little carving into the Thames, taken a mallet and splintered it into fragments, or paid ten times two guineas to be rid of the accursed thing.

For that innocuous little statuette, about which I felt so triumphant, was to be the source of the evils into which I was about to be unwillingly drawn.

I was not aware of having a nightmare. All I know is that I started from my sleep with my heart lurching wildly within me. I felt cold and yet, at the same time, my body was wreathed in perspiration as if I were ill with some fever. I lay for a moment feeling my body beyond the control of my mind, my hands and feet trembling with a curious and indescribable sensation. Slowly I drew myself together and sat up, shaking my head to clear it.

A pain, sharp and unexpected, caught at my brows so suddenly that I jerked forward in the bed, head to my knees, and groaned aloud in agony. I placed my hands upon my temples and massaged them fiercely in order to try to dispel the exquisite agony that seared along my throbbing nerves.

Curiously, too, I suddenly became aware of a smell, a fragrance that was both sweet and sickly. It seemed to fill my bedroom so that my lungs heaved against its odour and I coughed several times.

I reached out of my bed for a match and lit the lamp. A glance at the clock showed it to be nearly two o'clock in the morning.

With strange pains throbbing through my head, I tumbled out of bed and went first to the windows, throwing them open to dispel the sickly sweet smell that pervaded the room. Then I went to the room

I used as a sitting-room in order to obtain some powders for my headache.

To my surprise, the smell in my sitting-room was just as strong as it had been in my bedroom. I opened the windows here as well. I swallowed the headache powders with a glass of water and sat in a chair waiting for them to work. Although a slight breeze was blowing in through the windows, causing the ingress of the cold night air, the smell remained all-powerful.

The thought crossed my mind that Mrs. Dobson the landlady, who also cleaned my rooms daily, must have put some strange plant in my rooms which emitted the disagreeable odour. I knew Mrs. Dobson was keen on potted plants and seemed to collect them from all corners of the world.

I peered round to find the source of my discomfiture but the only potted plant I could see was a sulky aspidistra which I had reluctantly inherited from the previous tenant and which stood on a china pedestal to one side of the fireplace in my sitting-room.

Puzzled, I made a thorough search of the rooms. I could find no explanation of the smell which, I had reasoned, must have produced the terrible migraine which assailed my temples. Having completed my search, I suddenly realised that both smell and headache had disappeared and was acutely aware of the December chills which were rustling through the curtains at the windows.

I closed the windows and returned to the warmth of my bed, perplexed at the reasons for my troubled night.

CHAPTER TWO

Next morning, having breakfasted, I decided to walk from my rooms along Whitehall to the Foreign Office. Although my headache had gone, I had a strange feeling of exhaustion and a hot irritation seemed to ring my eyes. I felt as if I had been denied sleep for several nights. The brisk walk through the cold morning air had no effect in reviving me.

Viscount Molesworth was already in the office, standing with his back to a newly-lit fire, hands clasped behind him. He was a big florid-faced man with sandy hair and watery blue eyes, which twinkled humorously from his fleshy face. His face, however, rarely mirrored his emotions and assumed a permanent expression of melancholy. I believed him to be unfortunate in his physical appearance in that his chin receded under his fleshy cheeks and his top teeth protruded over thin, bloodless lips. He never seemed to care about his appearance and his clothes always looked as if they had been slept in the night before.

It was a stupid man who judged Molesworth by his appearance. His mind was like a rapier in spite of its outward covering. He was an excellent chess player and this probably stood him in good stead in his role at the Foreign Office for he had been responsible for several successful negotiations on behalf of Her Brittanic Majesty's Government. Molesworth was a generous friend but an unremitting enemy.

His eyes narrowed as I entered the suite of rooms we used as offices.

'Morning, Welsford,' he said languidly. It was one of his poses to assert a listlessness and boredom when, in reality, his eyes never ceased to observe and interpret. 'You look deuced tired this morning.'

I nodded agreement.

'I've had a bad night, m'lord,' I replied. 'Seemed to have had a migraine.'

He raised his eyebrows as if surprised.

'Better now, I trust?' he asked and then, without waiting for a reply, continued, 'The Foreign Secretary is due here in a moment. He seems to have some sort of job for me.'

That much I had guessed and it would be foolish of me not to admit that I had pondered a long time, during my journey from Gisleham to London, on what sort of commission the Foreign Secretary had in mind for our department. For those of short memory, the year 1861 had been especially busy for the Foreign Office and our missions abroad. A state of civil war had broken out in the United States of America and, while Britain tended to display a bias towards the seccessionist states of the South, it was our job to convince the world of our neutrality. We had been forced to send troops to the American continent, however, with France and Spain, in order to exact payment of financial debts from Mexico. In Africa, the ever troublesome Boers - the Dutch settlers - had moved out of the British colonies in the south and formed an independent republic called the Transvaal. The Foreign Office and the Colonial Office were not sure under whose jurisdiction the matter fell. Closer to home, in Europe, the Italian states were causing concern having, with the exception of Rome and Venice, been united as one Kingdom under Victor Emmanuel of Savoy. Britain was inclined to be slightly suspicious of Victor Emmanuel's political aspirations. Prussia needed watching, for a new Kaiser, Wilhelm I, had succeeded to the throne. Finally, Russia had amazed and confounded her critics when Tsar Alexander II abolished serfdom throughout her empire.

What sphere would our assignment fall in?

I was not to be kept in doubt for long. Hardly had I seated myself at my desk and gathered the papers for the meeting when the door was opened and the Foreign Secretary, Lord Clarendon, was announced.

George Frederick William, the fourth Earl of Clarendon, was not an impressive man. Distinguished, yes; but not impressive. He still had the sprightliness of youth in his lean, handsome figure. His curly hair still fell in profusion over a broad, intelligent forehead.

But his dimpled chin and wide eyes, set in a well-shaped head, were more in keeping with a ladies' man than a distinguished, sober, Whig politician and one of the Empire's great statesmen.

As he entered the room and shook Molesworth warmly by the hand, I had a definite feeling of 'presence'. The Foreign Secretary cast a quizzical glance in my direction.

Molesworth extended an arm towards me.

'Allow me to present my personal secretary, Mr. Upton Welsford.'

'Delighted, Welsford,' there was a distant tone in the Foreign Secretary's voice.

I did not see the look of inquiry which passed between Clarendon and Molesworth but Molesworth, as if in answer to an unspoken question, said: 'Mr. Welsford has my complete confidence in all matters pertaining to my office.'

Clarendon seated himself while Molesworth offered him a glass of port. He then waved me to draw up a chair and indicated I should take notes.

'And now, my lord?' prompted Molesworth gently.

Clarendon put down his glass and leant back in his chair.

'Briefly, the Government want you to undertake a mission to Romania.'

'Romania?' echoed Molesworth.

I confess that, though I prided myself on geography, I had never heard of the place.

'Romania is yet to come into existence officially,' explained Clarendon. 'It is the name by which the united principalities of Moldavia and Wallachia are to become known, following their independence from the Turkish Empire.'

He paused and toyed with his glass of port.

'To put you briefly in the picture, I'd best sketch in some history. You may recall that in the summer of 1853 Moldavia and Wallachia were occupied by the Russian armies. England and France formed an alliance with the Turkish Empire, which has ruled those provinces or principalities since the 15th Century. The following year saw the outbreak of a war between Turkey and her allies, ourselves, and Russia. The theatre of war was in the Crimea. What grew evident in the conflict was that the people of Wallachia and

Moldavia - who, by the way, are more Latin than Slavic in origin - wanted neither Russian nor Turkish rule.

'It occurred to Britain that should these provinces be united as an independent state under native rulers, it would have a distinct influence on the balance of power in Europe. We began to investigate possibilities with the local nationalist movement. We realised, although she was our ally, that the Turkish Ottoman empire was rather unstable. Russia certainly wanted to pick up the strategic parts of the Turkish Empire afforded by Moldavia and Wallachia. So also did the Austrians, who came into the war on Turkey's side. France, as well.'

He paused while Molesworth replenished his empty glass.

'From Moldavia and Wallachia, Russia could secure a good toehold to Europe and dominate vital trading routes to the Middle East.

'However, when the Crimean War ended in 1856, the peace treaty was so designed that it placed Moldavia and Wallachia under the protection of the European Powers. A Paris Peace Congress was set up to decide what was to be done. The nationalists, led by a man with some outlandish name - Grigore Alexandru Ghica - demanded that the protecting powers recognise the right of these principalities to break away from the Turkish Empire and form one united country called Romania.'

'Why Romania?' asked Molesworth curiously, lighting a cheroot.

Clarendon waved a hand in the air.

'On account of the natives believing they are descendents of the ancient Romans. The Romans did settle the area and called it Dacia or some such name.'

He paused to recollect his thoughts.

'Now, the British Government was in agreement with the establishment of an independent Romanian state. As one of its sponsors we would be able to maintain a presence in the area and secure favourable trading links. On the other hand we were supposed to be allies of the Turks. So we pretended to play a middle game while, by agreement, the French put pressure on the Turkish Sultan Abdul Mejid and his Porte - er, parliament, that is - to allow the principalities to hold a referendum on the matter. The result was that both principalities voted for independence and their union into a single state, with an invitation to a foreign prince from one of the ruling families of Europe to become its titular head.

'The idea was endorsed at the Paris Convention. But in 1859 Moldavia's elected assembly decided to depose its ruling prince and elect, unanimously, I may add, a Colonel Alexandru Iona Cuza as ruling prince. Cuza was the leader of the 1848 insurrection against the Turks. Within a few days Wallachia also elected him as their ruling prince. This election of a prince was rather heady stuff but the British Government decided to go along with it and acknowledge Cuza as ruler.

'He seems a pretty impressive fellow - set to work immediately on organising common laws and institutions for both principalities. The Romanian language, a rather odd mixture of Latin and Slavic, was proclaimed legal - it had been suppressed by the Turks - and the country seems to be heading for an industrial reorganisation. Why, it is even starting to export refined oil for the first time this year.

'Now a few days ago Cuza, who is officially know as Prince Alexandru, issued a proclamation to the effect that the union of Moldavia and Wallachia had been achieved and that Romanian nationality had been established.

'The British Government's attitude is to welcome this new European State and to give it aid and advice - but with caution. I say "caution" because its political future is far from clear and there are certain dangerous radical elements near the seat of power. The Prime Minister is particularly anxious to establish a full diplomatic mission in Romania but we must obtain some first-hand accounts of the exact situation in the country before we proceed further.

'For example, Austria has become extremely worried by the situation. The Romanian people are not confined to the principalities of Moldavia and Wallachia. They also populate another principality, a rather large one, called Transylvania, which was a province of Hungary.'

'Was?' queried Molesworth. 'I was under the impression that it still is.'

Clarendon waved an expressive hand.

'Last October the Austrian Emperor, Franz Joseph, promulgated a constitutional document..'

Molesworth interrupted:

'Yes, I know. It's called the October Diploma which puts an end to the Austro-Hungarian absolutist system and opens up a constitutional rule more in keeping with our style of democracy.'

'Then you should also know, Molesworth, that the same document allows Transylvania to become an autonomous state within the Habsburg Empire. However, there is a strong liberationist movement in Transylvania which wants the principality to unify with Moldavia and Wallachia into Romania - a movement called Astra, I believe. It was to take the sting out of this nationalist movement that Franz Joseph issued his decree of autonomous self - government within the empire.'

Clarendon leant back and smiled at Molesworth.

'In brief, Molesworth,' he said, 'the British Government desire that you, together with a small staff, go to Romania in the New Year. You are to reach there by the end of January when Cuza is dissolving the separate assemblies of Moldavia and Wallachia and instituting the first National Assembly of Romania. Naturally, many European states will have representatives attending the ceremonies that will go with the official declaration of the new state. We are sending an official embassy...'

'Then what will be my position?' interrupted Molesworth.

'A special embassy,' replied Clarendon. 'You and your staff will concentrate on building up an exact picture of the political situation in the country. Test out the strength of all the parties and political groups. Also, try to find out what the aspirations of Transylvania are... whether the people desire union with Romania or not. You will present a detailed report of how you see the developing role of Romania in Europe. Will you accept that mission?'

Molesworth was quiet for a moment, seeming to contemplate the task before him. Then he inclined his head.

'Very well, my lord,' he said, simply.

'Excellent! Excellent!'

Clarendon stood up and stubbed out his cheroot in a glass ashtray. 'I shall report your acceptance to Lord Palmerston at our Cabinet meeting this afternoon. The Prime Minister will be pleased. In the meantime, I advise you to collect as much background information as you can about the country. Interpreters may be necessary, but on no account are the natives of the principality to be taken into your confidence.'

After a limp handshake with Molesworth and a curt nod towards me, the Foreign Secretary bore down upon the door like some battleship under full sail with Molesworth, like a frigate, trailing in his wake.

'We shall have several briefings before you leave,' Clarendon was saying over his shoulder. 'I suggest the first week in January would be an excellent time for your departure. If there is anything you require, let my office know.'

Molesworth paused a moment by the door, looking thoughtfully after the disappearing Earl.

Then, decisively, he shut the door.

'So, Welsford,' he returned to me with a ghost of a smile puckering his lugubrious features, 'we seem to be in for an interesting journey.'

He took out some maps of Europe and spread them across his desk, tracing the countries' boundaries with a forefinger.

'Moldavia... Wallachia...' he peered curiously at the map, 'and here is Transylvania... H'm, come and see, Welsford. There they are, to the north-east of Greece. Well, we'd better see what we can find out about the area. See what you can dig up from the libraries while I'll try to find if there are any natives from the country living in London.'

'Very well, my lord.'

'Compile a dossier giving a sketch of the history, geography, industrial and mineral wealth and recent political developments. But you'd better not be too long about it. We shall want time to digest it and form a plan of campaign this side of Christmas if we are to set out in the New Year.'

A feeling of excitement began to grow in me as I examined the prospects of the journey to a new and strange sounding country.

CHAPTER THREE

The next few days would make very boring reading if I rendered them into my account. I spent most of my time at Smirke's rather splended new buildings which now house the British Museum. The museum has an awe-inspiring collection of books through which I browsed, collecting and collating much invaluable data on the principalities which comprised the new state of Romania. There were also several briefing sessions with Lord Clarendon over the next few days in which he advised Lord Molesworth as to what particular information the British Government desired.

The important thing as far as my narrative is concerned was the developement of migraine which always seemed to manifest itself at night, causing me to awake with the most excruciating headaches. And then there was that smell, that curious sickly sweet smell that almost caused me to suffocate in the night. I cannot count the times that I staggered from my bed, chest heaving, head burning, to fling open my windows to escape from that terrible, terrifying odour.

For five consecutive days I was haunted by that smell and cursed by those terrible head pains. There came great hollows under my eyes and my friends remarked on the blackish marks that encircled them.

Things became so intolerable that I consulted a doctor who had rooms in Soho. He was a good natured but bumbling sort of man who gave me some strong powders to be taken for the relief of the headaches. Then he gave me a homily on the stupidity of overwork and the need for relaxation, with plenty of fresh air and exercise, before presenting me with a bill for one florin.

I promised to call back if the insomnia continued but I confess that I had little faith in the good doctor's remedies.

And the insomnia did continue.

It was on the fifth day, when I was feeling very depressed and

19

ready to resign from my work, that I bumped into my old university friend, Dennis Yorke. After an unsatisfactory morning at the British Museum studying columns of meaningless figures on Romania's potential trade in imports and exports, I had turned down Holborn into Chancery Lane and made my way to a favourite restaurant of mine. If I was not going to sleep, I was determined that I was not going to starve as well.

And there it was that I bumped into Yorke.

He was several years older than me, the third son of an Earl, although he was not inclined to discuss his family with anyone. We shared the same rooms at Oxford while he was studying philosophy and theology and other esoteric subjects. He was very much involved with occult matters such as the new and growing fad of spiritualism.

Yorke was a tall man, with black curly hair and a long pale face whose sensitive qualities would have won it a place in a Renaissance painting of the disciples of Christ. He usually puffed at a pipe containing some strange eastern weed and he was given to strange practices such as meditation and the exercise of the body, which practices he called Yoga and which, he told me, originated in the east. I seldom saw him these days for he had a private income and devoted himself to his theosophical studies.

Yorke was, in fact, just paying off his hansom cab as I came up.

'By Jove, old fellow,' he cried, clapping me on the back in that expansive way he has, 'you look as if you haven't slept for a century.'

I nodded miserably for, being a trifle vain, I usually took pride in my appearance.

'I'm afraid I haven't been sleeping too well of late, Yorke,' I replied. 'Headaches and all that sort of thing.'

'Well, a good luncheon will set us up, eh? Come and share my table,' he said, propelling me into the restaurant.

It was as we came through the doors that I reeled as if I had been hit.

That smell! That same sickly sweet smell that pervaded my rooms at night; that haunted my sleeping and waking hours! Was I going insane?

I looked wildly around, my nostrils twitching to ensure the

20

evidence of my senses.

'What's up, old fellow?' demanded Yorke. 'You look definitely unwell.'

'Do....do you smell anything unusual?' I gasped.

He sniffed suspiciously.

'Not really - oh, you mean that beastly plant smell - some potted plant they have in the foyer, I suppose.'

At least, then, I was not imagining the smell this time.

The manager came up to conduct us to a table.

'That smell,' I demanded of him. 'That smell, what is it?'

The man looked a trifle disconcerted at the wild look that must have flared in my eyes.

'Smell, sir?' He paused and sniffed loudly. 'You mean the flowers, sir?'

'Whatever it is,' I gasped. 'What is it?'

The manager smiled politely.

'A genus of oleaceous shrub, if I may say so sir. I am something of an amateur horticulturist.'

I looked at him blankly.

'A genus of what?'

'Oleaceous shrub - jasmine, sir. Jasmine flowers. Perhaps a trifle oriental for some tastes, sir. But they are quite decorative...'

I interrupted him rudely.

'Give us a table as far away from the damned things as possible. I can't stand the smell.'

The manager pursed his lips in annoyance, and with one arched eyebrow, conveying what he thought of my taste in flowers, he conducted us to a select corner of the restaurant, wished us 'bon appetit' and clicked his fingers to a hovering waiter to bring us the menus.

Yorke regarded me over the top of the menu with a bemused expression on his face.

'You really do seem pretty grim, old man,' he said gently. 'What's up?'

'Why should anything be up?' I almost snapped.

'You tell me, old fellow?' he replied, not in the least perturbed by my rudeness.

I suddenly realised that I was being rather silly. After all, it was

21

not Yorke's fault that I was suffering from insomnia.

I unbent and confided in him the details of my sleepless nights, the terrifying headaches and the strange smell.

'You always smell the same odour each night?' he asked when I had finished my story.

'Always. I did not know what odour it was until the manager told me just now. It is always the scent of jasmine, which is strange because I am sure I have never encountered jasmine flowers before.'

Yorke scratched the side of his long nose.

'Have you seen a doctor?'

'Yes,' I replied, 'but so far it doesn't seem to have done me much good.'

'Well,' said Yorke, 'if you should feel no better and would like me to suggest a means whereby you might be alleviated from the condition, I might be able to help you.'

At the time I thought Yorke meant that he would be able to recommend some of the strange eastern drugs I knew him to be experimenting with. Not being interested in such things and, if the truth be known, being a little afraid of them, I said no more and we fell to attacking our meal.

That night came the first of the strange, terrifying dreams!

CHAPTER FOUR

I was walking through a garden.

The smell, that sickly sweet smell of jasmine, was overpowering. It was oppessive in its intensity and caused my temples to throb against my head like a regular slow beat on a drum. I was aware of a curious black velvet-like shroud that hung across the gardens and yet... and yet I was fully aware of the tall dark trees and shrubs that hemmed me into a narrow way, a small path, which I traversed.

A part of my mind rebelled against the illusion, indeed, told me it *was* an illusion. I was not walking through some exotic garden; I was home in bed in my rooms in Charing Cross. Yet my senses: sight sound and smell, rejected this logic.

Abruptly, as if I had stepped through some hidden veil, I came to the entrance of a tall marble structure. Pillars soared to dizzy heights towards the heavens and were lost in the blackness of a night sky. On the steps that led to this edifice there stood a statue on a marble plinth.

The statue was that of the dragon: an exact replica of the one I had bought in the junk shop.

Even now I can see every detail from that vision. Its surface was smooth, green-black, shining now and then as a rebellious moonbeam glanced through the moving black clouds. I can see its hideous face, the eyes wide and staring, a forked tongue protruding grotesquely between evil, canine teeth. The face, which evoked strange terrors, bore a menacing yet triumphant expression.

And while I looked on I became aware of the monotonous beating, the drumming which grew in strength and volume, seeming to join as one with the throbbing in my temples.

I reached a hand to my head and groaned in my anguish.

Then, above the drumming, I distinguished human voices, chanting, chanting to the very beat of the drum, joining and mingling until voices and drum were indistinguishable.

I knew not what they chanted; all I knew was that their voices filled me with such fear that I stood trembling in the shade of the great dragon-beast, unable to move or speak.

Suddenly, as if materialised from elemental dust, I was aware of a figure standing with its back towards me. It was a small, boyish figure, draped from head to feet in a startling white robe, contrasting vividly with the blackness of its surroundings. Two white arms were raised in supplication towards the malignant dragon statue, two pale hands, palm outwards, paid homage to the beast.

Like the tinkling of crystal in a gentle breeze came a voice, unreal, ethereal, speaking in some timeless tongue which I knew was not my native English but which I understood as clearly.

'I come from the Isle of Fire, having filled my body with the blood of Ur-Hekau, Mighty One of the Enchantments. I come before thee, Draco. I worship thee Draco, Fire-breather from the Great Deep. You are my Lord and I am of thy blood.'

Then the chanting ceased, died with such abruptness that the silence was like some physical blow to my ears.

The tiny figure before me bowed to the image.

'The time is come when the world must be filled with that which it has not known, when you, great Draco, must come into the world and fill it with abundance. Take then this offering which we, the children of thy blood, give you freely - blood of our blood, life of our life!'

I could see, with sudden dread, a silver glitter in the right hand of the figure, the waning rays of the moon glinting on the blade of a knife.

Like a mouse before a cat, I stood still and trembled, with a dawning awareness of the ordeal to come.

The figure turned slowly towards me, arm raised once more towards the sky, wielding the knife that I knew was about to taste my blood.

I raised my eyes to the face of that figure...

My breath caught in my throat. Never have I seen such a serenely beautiful countenance. The pale, heart shaped face, the wide-set, deep green eyes, surmounted by raven black locks which tumbled in profusion from the drapes that covered her figure. The red lips were parted slightly showing perfect white teeth.

The eyes peered into mine and, for a moment, were full of tenderness and sorrow. Tears welled from them and trickled down that perfect skin.

'Prepare...' the words were but a whisper scarcely heard. 'Prepare... for this is the way of Draco which is thorny and hard and we mere mortals must obey his will even though sorrow be our lot and despair our inheritance.'

The knife was beginning to descend.

I knew that it was all wrong. I tried to tell her. Tried to open my mouth.

I could feel the point of the knife biting into my flesh and I screamed....

I thought at first it was the wild beating of the drums. Then I became aware that the noise was a banging on my door.

I lay in my darkened bedroom wrapped in a twisted profusion of bed linen and blankets, sodden with sweat. My mouth was dry and I felt cold and sick.

'Mister Welsford! Mister Welsford! Can you hear me? Are you alright?'

It was the voice of Mrs Dobson, my landlady, accompanied by another resounding tattoo on my door.

There were other voices outside the door, some raised in annoyance.

Crying to them to wait a moment, I struggled from my bed into a dressing gown and went to open the door.

Mrs Dobson and two gentlemen, I believe they shared adjacent apartments to mine, stood outside wrapped in dressing gowns and bearing annoyed expressions on their faces.

'What is it, Mrs Dobson?' I murmured, my tongue rasping dryly in my throat.

Mrs Dobson was a large, raw-boned woman. She stood like a pugilist awaiting the bell, feet slightly apart, hands on hips, jaw stuck out aggressively.

'What is it?' she repeated, as if she had not heard me properly. 'Why, there have been cries and bangs coming from your room these past fifteen minutes. You have woken up two of my gentlemen,' she jerked her thumb at my two agitated neighbours.

'I say, old boy,' the voice was a near whine from a pimple-faced young man who, I believed, worked as a clerk in the City, 'can't a fellow rest and all that?'

'I'm...I'm sorry,' I mumbled, wanting to return to my bed, 'I had a nightmare, a bad dream...haven't slept too well lately. Sorry about the noise.'

Mrs Dobson pursed her lips.

'Well, I can't have it, Mister Welsford. This is a respectable house. My gentlemen must have their rest.'

'I'm truly sorry, Mrs Dobson,' was all I could say, repeating the phrase as if it were some magic charm against Mrs Dobson's wrath.

Muttering to themselves, Mrs Dobson's two gentlemen retired to their own rooms and I made to close my door.

'Are you alright?' Mrs Dobson was reluctant to go without a proper inquest into the matter.

'I'll be fine,' I reassured her. 'It was just a bad dream. A bad dream, that's all.'

The bad dream returned, however. It returned the next night and the night after. It was so vivid; each time I dreamed it the scene took on many new details but always, always ended at the same horrific point. That serene, beautiful face, the welling tears, the soft gaze of compassion, the steeling against something which is distasteful but which has to be done, haunted me in my waking hours. The face of that sweet girl grew more vivid and real to me than the face of any girl I had known.

Yet so fearful did I become of those dreams that I became too frightened to go to bed at night, preferring to pace my rooms, to read or write, catching up on my Foreign Office work until exhaustion overtook me and I fell asleep where I sat. Even so, exhaustion did not prevent the grotesque nightmare from returning. I even became afraid to fall asleep during the day lest the vision haunt me still.

My work began to suffer.

Lord Molesworth, thinking I was pressing myself too hard, warned me to ease up and suggested I take a long weekend's holiday. He did so even though he was being pressured by Lord

Clarendon to conclude the arrangements for the trip to Romania which was now a mere few weeks away. Naturally, I protested that I would be fine and returned to the doctor I had consulted. Alas, he did little more than prescribe a stronger sleeping draught and headache powders. He even suggested that I dose myself nightly with tincture of opium or laudanum. Against this I protested most strongly and so the doctor dismissed me with a sigh.

In my desperation for sleep I sought out my friend Yorke and reminded him of his offer to help me if the doctor was unable to cure my insomnia.

'What shall I do, Yorke?' I cried in desperation. 'I simply cannot continue in this fashion. I shall kill myself with exhaustion if I do. I shall be in no condition to accompany Molesworth to Romania nor to complete the detailed study I am doing for him. That would mean that my career in the Foreign Office would be ended.'

Yorke sat in his red smoking jacket, puffing some obnoxious weed in his pipe. He stroked his aquiline nose with a lean forefinger, a trick he has when pondering a problem.

'I can suggest something which might be a solution and yet... yet I hesitate to do so because you are the son of the Reverend Mortimer Welsford.'

I frowned.

'What has my father to do with this?' I demanded.

'Your father, old chap, is an excellent minister of the Anglican faith and has more than once lectured against dealings in the occult.'

'What do you mean? What are you suggesting?'

'Well, when conventional medicines fail, I have been impressed by those people who are described as psychic-healers.'

I stared at Yorke in amazement. Yorke, as I have already explained, was interested in matters appertaining to the occult. He had even written a monograph on witchcraft which was strongly decried by my father, who had suggested that my friendship with my old university colleague should cease forthwith. But I knew Yorke to be a level-headed fellow and not given to fantasising. He had a tremendous wealth of knowledge on occult matters and pursued his subject as a science. If he found the matter interesting, then it was his affair. As for myself, I never was greatly interested in religions one way way or another.

27

I gave Yorke a wry smile.

'I confess, old man, I don't think an old lady waving a magic wand around my head will bring back my sleep.'

Yorke pursed his lips in annoyance.

'That isn't exactly what a psychic-healer does. I can tell you that I have seen people cured, yes, actually cured, of many ailments over which doctors have given up in despair. You've tried a doctor, so why not give this a try?'

I was sceptical and yet I was also desperate and in desperation men do many things which are not generally in their nature to do. Yorke pressed his advantage and, in a fit of weakness, I agreed to compromise and accompany him to a meeting which he called a séance. I would go merely in order to see what the business was all about. There would be no attempt at psychic-healing at the meeting but, if I found the meeting agreeable, Yorke would take me to a meeting where I could be healed.

I must confess that after I left Yorke I felt all kinds of a fool and was half inclined to send a message round to his rooms cancelling the arrangements that I had made for that night. But as the day wore on and I began to build up a fear of the coming night, I was seized with a desperate hope that Yorke might be offering me salvation... perhaps I could be helped. I wanted so desperately to sleep and yet my fear of the dark shadows of the night caused me to almost torture myself in my efforts to keep awake.

CHAPTER FIVE

The Hansom deposited us outside a terraced artisan's house in a winding street just south of Hampstead Heath. I believe the road was called Fleet Road, although I am not too sure. There was really nothing remarkable about the street or the house and I have only a vague recollection of the name because Yorke told me that the River Fleet, which rises on the Heath, ran through the sewerways under the road on its underground journey through London down to the Thames.

The paint-peeling door was opened to Yorke's imperious knockings by a homely-looking woman who was as unremarkable as the house. She welcomed us in the flat accents which I always associate with south-eastern England and said that 'Madam' was in the front-room. She quickly corrected 'front-room' to 'sitting-room' and took our outdoor coats and hats from us, then bade us follow her.

A door leading into a small, overcrowded room was opened. Most of the room appeared to be shrouded in gloom, a lamp spluttered dimly from the centre of a green baize covered table. In its glow were ringed six expectant faces, while the figure of a large, and very stout, woman stood in the shadows of one corner. The homely woman who had answered the door to us motioned us into vacant chairs.

'Is that the lot, dearie?' came a shrill Cockney voice.

For a moment I could not place it and then realised that it was the stout woman in the shadows who had asked the question.

The homely woman almost curtseyed.

'Yes, mum... er, Madam Bing. That's the lot.'

'Roight ow, luv. We can begin.'

I cast a quizzical look at Yorke, but he had lowered his eyes to the green baize table top. A quick look at the circle showed the rest of

29

the participants had done the same. The homely woman had taken a seat by the door; she was seated slightly forward on the chair's edge with arms folded across her bosom. The stout woman, who had not yet stepped forward into the circle of light, shifted her position slightly.

'Now' (it was almost 'naw') 'fer those wot aint bin before, me nyme's Madam Bing. I fink ternoight will be a good 'un if we get sympathetic (this came out as('symper-fetick') vibrations. But don't hexpect miracles, dearies... I don't produce hectoplasm or do hany of that stuff.'

She was interrupted by a loud stage whisper from the homely woman.

'Madam means an emanation of bodily appearance.'

It sounded as if she had learnt some lesson by heart.

'Quite so, dearie,' breathed the stout woman heavily. 'Quite so. I don't go in fer hactual physical manifestation...' She laboured the words and I could almost see her shoot a look of triumph at the homely woman, 'not hactual physical manifestation.' she savoured the words again, 'but we gets messages from the hother side none-the-less.'

There was a pause.

Someone coughed.

'Roight. Let's begin.'

'Er... what shall we do, madam?'

It was a small, slightly balding man sitting to the left of me who ventured the question.

'Do, dearie?'

Madam Bing's voice was slightly querulous.

'Some mediums request we sing,' explained the balding man apologetically.

'Not in my séances, you don't!' snapped Madam Bing. 'Now' she clapped her hands loudly so that several at the table jumped. 'Just sit still, think of yer departed loved ones who 'ave crossed hover... concentrate... concentrate...'

She started to walk around the circle at the table, humming softly to herself.

After a while she stopped, opened a book, and began to read from it under her breath. It sounded like a volume of psalms.

'Is there anyone here whose name begins with J?'

The question came abruptly.

There was a brief pause then the balding man nodded eagerly.

'Me. My name begins with J.'

I fancied I heard a sigh of relief.

'J,' continued Madam Bing in strident tones. 'J, is the name John?'

The balding man shook his head.

'It's Jo ...'

Madam Bing gave a shriek which cut out the last syllable.

'I 'ave it. Joe! Joseph, that's it, ain't it?'

'No, Madam. It's Jodocus.'

'Well, yer family call you Jo, don't they?' demanded her querulous voice.

'I wish they did,' confessed the balding man. 'It's always been Jodocus.'

There came an annoyed exhalation of breath.

'Ah, I'm losing contact ... losing contact ... Wait. Is there anyone here whose name begins with the letter A?'

A woman who had just been wiping her nose with a handkerchief on which the name 'Nancy' was prominently emblazoned, nodded slowly.

Madam Bing moved to the side of the table facing the woman, a pale-faced creature of middle age who looked like a nursery governess.

'The letter A that I am getting is fer a first name,' went on Madam Bing.

The pale faced creature nodded miserably.

I could almost feel Madam Bing smile.

'Yes, yes. A first name... your name... it is Amalia, no... Adela... no, no... it's coming clearly now... Agnes. That's it. Your name is Agnes, isn't it?'

The pale faced creature grimaced.

'That's it,' she admitted in a whisper.

A tiny gasp of amazement went round the table.

'Yer don't loike ter be called Agnes, do yer, dearie?' demanded Madam Bing. 'There's a spirit 'ere, a spirit hentity wot tells me yer don't loike ter be called Agnes.'

31

The woman shook her head again.

'Yer prefer ter be called Nancy, don't yer? That's wot this 'ere spirit tells me.'

'Please,' a look of hope came into the woman's yes. 'Please, is it my mother - she passed over three years ago. Is it her?'

'That's roight, dearie. It's yer mum,' consoled Madam Bing. 'She says she's very 'appy where she is and don't worry. It's a lovely life on the other side and she's far 'appier than when she was in this life, no disrespect intended to yer.'

The pale creature gave a gulp, which was suspiciously like a sob.

'Dear mother,' she whispered 'Can you ask her...'

'Contact is gone,' thundered Madam Bing. 'Alas, our time is short. Now then, now then... is there somebody here...'

I shook my head incredulously and tried to catch Yorke's eye.

I wondered how far such people could be taken in by such an old charlatan. Nancy is, of course, a diminutive of Ann or Agnes and it was easy to see how Madam Bing worked up to her revelation. I did not know whether to be amused or annoyed by the whole thing. What perturbed me was that Yorke was apparently taken in by a pack of rogues. And these were the very people he suggested might cure my insomnia.

Madam Bing was rambling on.

She had just assured one earnest-looking youth that she had a message for him from his great grandfather who was 'in spirit'; that his great grandfather was happy in the other world, was leading a life full of greater happiness and fulfilment than life in this world and that his offspring must not worry... everything would come right and be resolved as it should. Each message seemed to me to be basically the same. The deceased were happier in the other world than they had been in this one and those they had left behind should not worry. I fell to wondering whether the messages had some central design and origin in our collective subconscious to allay man's primordial fear of death.

I was wondering how much longer I would have to put up with this nonsense when Madam Bing suddenly started and gave a little scream.

I do not know whether it was a stage-effect managed by the homely woman who was still sitting on her seat by the door, but suddenly a window blew open and extinguished the flickering lamp. There were several exclamations but the voice of Madam Bing called us to silence from the darkness.

'I... I am in contact... in contact...' her voice was strangely contorted, and I silently congratulated her on her performance.

'There is one among us who is sceptical... and yet he is the most vulnerable of us all. He must seek protection of the inner circle or doom will be his lot, evil his inheritance.'

Her voice was rather uncanny in the darkness and seemed to have lost its earthy, Cockney roughness.

'Who is it, Madam?' came the stage whisper of the homely woman.

'*He* knows that I mean *him*. His ancestors were born where the well stands beside the ford of a river.'

A peculiar sensation overcame me. I felt a sudden chill in the room and shuddered violently. I had told no-one my name and, although Madam Bing did not mention it as Welsford, yet surely she had given an accurate derivation of that name?

As if in answer to my thoughts, Madam Bing continued with a triumphant ring to her voice.

'Yes... you know, do you not? You know that I am talking to you... I have a message for you, a message... it is difficult... there are others... other spirits trying to prevent it coming through... trying to prevent it... no, it is coming now, it is strong.'

I sat rooted.

'You are soon to cross the water... do not do so. Beware of the land beyond the forest. Beware of the land of mountains.'

I frowned in bewilderment.

'Beware of *the land beyond the forest!*'

Madame Bing's voice rose to a cry of desperation.

Abruptly there came a thud of something falling. One of the women in the circle screamed.

There was a fumbling and somebody struck a match, I think it was Yorke, and soon the lamp was relit.

Madam Bing lay crumpled in a corner of the room.

The homely woman sprang across the room with a cry of horror.

Yorke was there before her and bent over the prostrate woman, checked her respiration and thumbed back her eyelids.

'I should go and make a cup of tea, madam,' he suggested gently to the homely woman who stood with fluttering hands. 'Madam Bing has merely fainted, that is all.'

'Goodness me, it's never happened before,' mumbled the woman as she disappeared, presumably in the direction of the kitchen.

There was a groan from the inert figure on the floor. Yorke helped the stout woman into a sitting position.

It was the first time I had seen her features in the light of the lamp, which Yorke had turned up. She was a large, moon-faced woman with lustreless eyes and a big, slack mouth.

''Ere,' she demanded petulantly, ''ere wot's going on?'

'You passed out, Madam Bing,' replied Yorke in tones of gentle reassurance.

She stared at him blankly.

'I did?'

'You did,' affirmed Yorke, accompanied by a chorus of agreement from the rest of the circle.

'Strewth!' exclaimed Madam Bing softly, sitting upright and adjusting her hat, which had been knocked askew.

Yorke turned to the rest of the company.

'I suggest we leave Madam Bing to recover...'

There was a murmur of general assent and, with the exception of Yorke and me, the rest of the company moved hesitantly towards the door, dropping florins into a cardboard shoebox that stood on a small table near the door. As the last of them left, the homely woman re-entered with a pot of tea on a tray.

'Crikey, luv,' said Madam Bing, 'I don't 'alf need that.'

'Where have the others gone?' asked the homely woman.

I sent them away.' explained Yorke. 'I thought Madam Bing needed some peace and quiet to recover by.'

'Too true, dearie. Don't I just?'

The moon-faced woman was already tucking into a piece of fruit cake and throwing back her second cup of tea.

The homely woman had immediately gone to the shoebox and counted the florins, then gave a piercing glance towards Yorke and myself. With a blush of embarrassment, I hastily took out a florin and placed it in her box, which a moment later was added to by Yorke.

At this the homely woman smiled and nodded.

Yorke turned back to Madam Bing.

'Are you alright now?'

It was a superfluous question for the woman was on her third slice of fruit cake.

'Bit exhausted, dearie. Bit exhausted. Never passed out before.'

'Madam Bing, what did you mean by "the land beyond the forest"?' I suddenly blurted out.

The moon-faced woman looked at me vacantly.

'Wot dearie?'

'You told me to beware of the land beyond the forest. What did you mean?'

The woman shook her head ponderously.

'Not me, dearie, not me. Wot the spirits say I only repeats, don't I? I don't know wot they're on about, do I?'

'Madam is merely a medium, Mr... er...? the homely woman looked curiously at me.

Yorke cleared his throat.

'Well, old chap, we must be going.'

The homely woman shepherded us out into the hallway and gave us our hats and coats.

'Thanks for coming, ever so lovely to see you.'

Her meaningless words followed us down the street.

We walked in silence for a while before I turned to Yorke.

'Well?' I demanded.

He looked at me and raised an eyebrow but said nothing.

'Hang it all, Yorke,' I insisted, 'the woman was off her head... a charlatan... even I could see how she did it.'

'Could you?' Yorke let a smile pass across his face.

We walked across South End Green to the South Hampstead railway station.

'Even a child could see that,' I said, exasperated by his mysterious attitude.

'And tell me, my child,' he said with a sardonic note in his voice, 'could you see how she contrived to blow out the lamp, know your name and give you a warning not to go abroad, which I know you are planning to do?'

I bit my lip.

'She must have found out from somewhere,' I said lamely. 'You're surely not trying to suggest that she was genuine?'

'Welsford, old man, I've been studying this sort of thing for quite a while. Now it is perfectly true, as you have observed, that the major part of Madam Bing's séance is merely a performance. She does her 'messages' as a conscious act and you have seen some of the tricks she uses. But now and again, in spite of herself, something seems to come over her, seems to take control of her and a genuine occult experience occurs. She is definitely what is called psychic but she does not give herself a chance to develop her powers... she prefers the easy way.'

I gaped at him in disbelief.

'You're trying to say that the old charlatan has moments of genuine psychic manifestation in spite of herself?'

He nodded.

'That's about the size of it, old fellow. I've been trying to get to all her séances to catch any patterns that may occur. It's for a monograph I'm writing on unwilling or unknowing mediums.' he added.

'Well,' I said hotly, 'if she is an example of your so-called psychic-healers, I am not impressed.'

It was then I realised that I had not once thought about my frightful headaches or terrifying nightmares, the very reason I had been persuaded to go to Madam Bing's performance.

Yorke grinned.

'I didn't mean you to be impressed, old fellow. I just wanted you to see the sort of thing that happens at a séance.'

Just then the train came in and we climbed aboard. It was fairly late in the evening and there were few people on the train as it trundled towards Gospel Oak and swung southwards to Kentish Town.

I had sat in silence for some minutes.

'Well, having seen a séance, and even received a message, do you want to come with me to a more genuine meeting?' asked Yorke.

'Of course not,' I retorted. 'I have never seen so much chicanery in all my life.'

Yorke shook his head sadly.

'You're rather a narrow fellow, I declare,' he said, musingly. 'But never mind. I'll not press you at this moment.'

I retreated into silence.

Somehow I felt affronted that he - a doctor of philosophy from St. John's College, Oxford - should suggest that such a person as Madam Bing, or some confederate of hers, could possibly cure me of insomnia when a fully qualified doctor of medicine had failed. What I had seen was pure skulduggery... except, except I puzzled over Madam Bing's revelation. It even crossed my mind that Yorke might have fed her the information, but I dismissed the thought almost at once. Yorke was not that sort of fellow.

When we reached our destination, I bade a rather stiff farewell to Yorke and hailed a Hansom.

As I climbed in, slamming the door behind me, Yorke's voice caused me to peer down at him from the window.

He was staring up at me with a look of concern on his face.

'I say, Welsford... do not take that warning too lightly, will you? Beware of the land beyond the forest!'

Then he disappeared among the crowds mingling in front of the railway terminus.

Confused, I ordered the cabman to drop me before my rooms at Charing Cross.

CHAPTER SIX

The nightmares continued without respite. They always centred around the jade statuette and, in my spare moments, I sat in my rooms holding the damnable thing in my hands, peering at it curiously this way and that in a futile attempt to fathom the secret of its connection with my dreams. Finally, I resolved to take it to an acquaintance of mine, Professor Masterton, who was an expert in ancient oriental art at the British Museum. Perhaps he would be able to tell me something more about the little dragon which, in my nightmares, I had heard called Draco.

Masterton seemed pleased to see me when I called on him before lunch the next day. I told him the story of my purchase of the statuette from the former sailor who had bought it in Kowloon but I left out all mention of my strange nightmares and its connection with them. I told him that I merely wanted the statuette dated, if that were possible, and would appreciate any other information he could give me of its origins.

Masterton turned the statuette over several times in his big, boney hands and then asked me if I would mind returning after lunch.

When I returned to the museum two hours later I was immediately shown into Masterton's *sanctum sanctorum*. He jumped up as I entered and was clearly excited. Seizing me by the hand, he dragged me to his desk and pointed dramatically at the grinning dragon.

'So you think it is Chinese, eh?'

His voice trembled with excitement.

'Well,' he went on, barely giving me time to give my opinion, 'well let me tell you that you are mistaken... totally mistaken.'

I looked at him in puzzlement.

He nodded in violent affirmation of his conclusion.

'I have had two colleagues examine it in order to confirm my observations.'

'What is it then?' I asked.

'My dear boy, my dear boy...' the words seemed to fail him. He paused, steadied himself and walked to a cabinet.

'A sherry? A port?' he asked, pouring a rather liberal glass of port for himself and a more modest sherry, on my instructions, for myself.

'You are clearly excited by something, professor,' I said, in order to prompt him.

'Excited? The statuette you have brought me is Egyptian.'

'Egyptian?'

'Indeed, my boy. Egyptian, dating back to the Thirteenth Dynasty.'

I held up my hand in protest.

'Professor I am not at all conversant with ancient history. Can you tell me what it means - the Thirteenth Dynasty?'

He gestured to me to sit down.

'What you have here, my dear Welsford, is an ancient Egyptian statuette dating back to the reign of Queen Sebek-nefer-Ra of the Thirteenth Egyptian Dynasty which is, roughly, about three thousand years before the birth of Christ.'

I was astounded.

'You mean to tell me that this little piece of jade is nearly five thousand years old?'

'I do,' he said emphatically. Furthermore, I can even tell you what the statuette represents - it is a likeness of the Egyptian god Draco - the Fire Snake or dragon.'

I felt the blood turn to ice in my veins.

Draco! I could hear the words of the priestess, for such she must be, echoing through my troubled sleep. 'I come before thee, Draco. I worship thee Draco, Fire-breather from the Great Deep. You are my Lord and I am of thy blood.' Yet how could I possibly have known that the statuette was of the god Draco? I had surely never heard the name before, apart from in my dreams; I had believed the jade to be a Chinese carving until Masterton had informed me otherwise. How, then, could my subconscious relate that fact into my troubled sleep?

39

Professor Masterton leaned forward and peered at me anxiously. 'Are you alright, Welsford? Are you feeling faint?'

I made a negative gesture.

'It...it is just a surprise to learn my statuette is so ancient.'

'Indeed, indeed,' Masterton picked up the green-black jade and caressed it lovingly. 'It is of beautiful workmanship. Beautiful.'

'Tell me something about Draco,' I urged him. 'I really know nothing about ancient Egypt.'

I had no need to ask Masterton twice. He reached for a pipe and, having lit it, he sprawled in his leather padded chair, his eyes taking on a faraway expression as he summoned up his store of knowledge.

'Thousands of years before the birth of Christ, a religion - or perhaps we'd best describe it as a primitive science - flowered in ancient Egypt. This religion became known as the Cult of Draco; the cult of the Fire Snake or dragon. The cult was the first systemised form of the primitive mysteries and natural sciences of Africa and the Egyptians elaborated it into a highly specialised system of occultism which spread across the world and flourished in the tantras of India, in Mongolia, in Tibet and in China.

'The cult was evolved from the concentration of knowledge of carefully observed physical phenomena extending over enormous cycles of time. The knowledge gained was based upon intercourse with manifestations of the occult and spirits said to be seen clairvoyantly.

'Life after death was observed as a natural fact; the Draconians believed it was not only possible to free the spirit for the next world but to free the body as well - in other words to make the earthly body immortal. They called such a freed body *ka* or *sekhem*. The body retained all the characteristics of the original mortal being; it was, in fact, the normal earthly body of the man or woman. The Draconians studied ways of releasing the *ka* in this world - of gaining immortality for themselves and there are references to what are claimed to be successful experiments in which the Draconians created living men and women whom they called the Undead.'

I shuddered.

'It sounds horrible.'

The professor, interrupted in his academic discourse, shot me a look of disapproval.

'No more so than other primitive religions.' he observed. 'Man struggles towards knowledge by his fear of ignorance, but sometimes his fear causes him to act as the animal he undoubtedly is.'

Two years previously, in 1859, a scientist named Charles Darwin had published a very contentious book called *The Origin of the Species* which claimed that man was, in reality, a species of animal descended from the apes and not created by God at all. The argument still rages furiously and while I keep an open mind on such matters, I knew that Professor Masterton was a keen supporter of the Darwinian theory, as it is now called.

'Where was I? Ah yes, the cult of Draco flourished for many centuries, becoming exceedingly prominent in the Sixth Dynasty. But it was a rather controversial cult which, so I believe, relied on great blood sacrifices. During the Eleventh Dynasty the ordinary people of Egypt were turning to the worship of more liberal gods, solar worship which was perhaps more beneficial to them, gods such as Osiris and Ammon. Under the leadership of the priests of the new liberal religion, the people rose up and drove out the followers of Draco.'

He paused and relit his pipe.

'And was that the end of the Draconian cult?'

Masterton shook his head.

'Queen Sebek-nefer-Ra commenced her reign in the Thirteenth Dynasty, nearly three thousand years before the birth of Christ. She suppressed the worship of Osiris and Ammon and made a blood bath of their followers. She brought back Draco as the official state religion. She was an initiate of the inner circle of the most profound mysteries of the cult and was known to her followers as the Great Mother. During her reign the cult obtained its maximum power, spreading through the known world and especially into Asia. It was during her reign that the priests of the Draco cult were accused of creating Undead monsters in their efforts to prolong life.

'From the Seventeenth Dynasty, about 2410 BC, the temporal power of the cult went into a decline and was finally extinguished when the Pharaoh Apophis, the last of the Typhonian rulers of the city of Avaris, was overthrown.

'From that time on the cult was vigorously persecuted and

suppressed by the Osirians, who accused its priests of bestial practices, of blasphemies and so forth. All the scientific knowledge gained by the Draconians was lost to mankind, which now returned to the more primitive worship of the sun!'*

I frowned.

'You sound as if you are disappointed that the Draconian Cult was overthrown, professor?'

Professor Masterton pursed his lips.

'I am a scientist, my boy. I disapprove of the loss of any scientific knowledge. Perhaps mankind would have been better off with the wealth of knowledge of natural science gathered by the Draconians, rather than expending its efforts in propitiating primitive fears by doing homage to a ball of gaseous fire in the sky.'

'And are you sure that my statuette dates back to...?'

I paused because I had lost my way through the maze of his historical lecture.

'It dates back to the Thirteenth Dynasty; to Queen Sebek-nefer-Ra when the Draconian Cult flourished.'

He took up the statuette from the table with one hand and took a magnifying glass in the other.

'I take it that you have not observed the base of the statuette too closely?'

I confessed that I had not.

'Take a look, then.'

I took the statuette and the magnifying glass from him and peered at the base. There were some mysterious symbols on it from which I could make out no sense at all.

'What does it mean?'

Hieroglyphics, my dear boy,' murmured the professor. 'Thanks to the works of Thomas Young of England and Champollion of France, we can now translate that ancient Egyptian writing.'

---

* *According to Mircea or Michelino, the son of Vlad Dracula, his father claimed descent from the High Priests of the Egyptian Cult of Draco, from whose ancient rites he had managed to perform the ceremony which bestowed on him immortal life. Dracula further claimed that his name derived from Draco, the Dragon god itself.*

Tremayne.

42

'And?' I asked, not liking mysteries.

'One of the symbols, that within the oval, is the royal seal of Sebek-nefer-Ra; the other is a short inscription which I would translate as "all power is found in Draco".'

Fascinating and perplexing as the professor's explanations were, it did not really solve the problem of my nightmares but merely added mystery to them. The solution to the frightening nightmares and sleeplessness was certainly not to be found in the dry tomes of the British Museum.

I picked up the statuette and placed it into my case while profusely thanking Professor Masterton for his help.

'Wait!' he cried, 'I have discussed the matter with my colleagues and we are prepared, that is, the Museum is prepared to purchase the statuette from you for the Department of Antiquities - we will meet any reasonable sum you ask for.'

Even the old scholar could not hide the touch of envious greed that flitted in his eyes as they dropped on the case wherein I had placed the carved animal.

I smiled.

'It's not for sale, professor. I did not want to give you that impression.'

His face twitched.

'It is a rare piece...we have few monuments that go back to that particular period.'

I shook my head.

'Consider an offer, my boy,' he pressed agitatedly. 'At least consider an offer.'

'Professor, you have been a great help to me and I am most truly grateful. The statuette is not for sale - at least, not at this time. But I will make this assurance - should I ever want to sell it, you shall have first offer.'

I shook the hand of a disappointed and frustrated man and turned out of the museum with his voice still ringing in my ears: '... any reasonable sum, mind you. We will meet any reasonable sum.'

I returned to my rooms to ponder on my perplexity.

Would to God I had accepted the professor's offer there and then.

CHAPTER SEVEN

Having spent another exhausting, sleepless night, I arrived in my office about ten o'clock and tried to struggle through a pile of newspaper cuttings on Romanian industrial development as visualised by some French correspondent. I had not been at my task long when Lord Molesworth entered with a rather self-satisfied look on his face. Behind him strode a short, stocky man with distinctly foreign features - high cheekbones, a broad Slavic face and hair the colour of jet.

'This is my personal secretary, Mister Upton Welsford,' he began as I struggled to my feet.

The stocky gentleman bowed stiffly from the waist.

'Welsford, I want you to meet Mister Ion Ghica. We are, indeed, fortunate in finding this gentleman who is spending a few days in our country. Mister Ghica is from Bucharest, in Romania.'

I murmured the customary formula of greeting.

Molesworth waved us all into his suite and ushered us before the fire and, as if by magic, Molesworth's servant appeared with a tray of drinks.

Ion Ghica proved to be a very talkative gentleman, especially where his own country was concerned. He was widely travelled. He had been educated at the Sorbonne and then taken ship to America where he had spent five years and where he had learnt to speak a peculiar form of English. He was more invaluable than a guide book. From him we learned much of the country to which we were to journey in the New Year. It turned out that Ghica was a prospective member of the Romanian National Assembly and sailed under the political colours of a 'progressive'. He had much to say on the need for the Romanian parliament to make its first task the emancipation of the peasants and the granting to them of smallholdings, which they could use upon some payment to the former feudal landowners as compensation. Serfdom was still prevalent in the Romanian principalities, although in some areas there lived groups of peasants who were free and called *mosneni*.

He was a veritable encyclopaedia of information and dispensed it in an entertaining manner. We gathered that Romania was unique, lying in the heartland of Slavonic Europe but totally different from other Slavic countries. The Romans had bequeathed the Latin language to Romania which had been the most remote easterly outpost of the great Roman Empire. The Romans, in so far as one could judge from Ion Ghica, seemed to have bequeathed much more than language to the Romanians. Not only the close Latin similarities of their language and culture could be heard, but the affinity of character, the sparkle and even the physical appearances can be discerned so that there seemed little difference between a Romanian and an Italian from the plains of Lombardy or the Tuscan mountains.

But Ion Ghica also presented a picture of a tragic country.

Throughout the centuries his country had been overrun by the Celts, the Romans, the Goths, Huns, Avars, Slavs and Persians, all of whom had fought across its mountainous countryside. Charlemagne and his Franks had tried to conquer and failed; Khan Krum and his Bulgars did not succeed either, nor did Arpad and the seven tribes of Hungary. Magyars, Vlachs, Vzes and Kumars also swept in their war bands over the unhappy land.

Ghica seemed rather proud of that bloody history.

And, no sooner had all these nations gone into the melting pot to create the Romanian people, than the Turks were moving in force across the Danube, incorporating Moldavia and Wallachia into their Ottoman Empire while Transylvania fell to the Austrians.

Ghica assured us that now the people of all three principalities wanted to unite into a common Romanian state. They wanted no more Turkish overlordship nor Austrian overlordship.

'And one day, one day soon,' he said in his accented English, 'I tell you, my friends, that it will be so. The people of the land beyond the forest shall unite with us in Moldavia and Wallachia.'

I was so startled that I dropped my sherry glass on the floor.

With a mumbled apology I bent to pick it up, confused thoughts tumbling through my mind.

'What did you mean, Mister Ghica?' I asked after I had deposited the fragments of my glass in a tray. 'What did you mean just now by the phrase - the land beyond the forest?'

He frowned.

'Mean?'

'Yes. What is the land beyond the forest?'

'Oh,' he smiled. 'It is - how do you call it now - a translation of the name Transylvania.'

It was with a feeling of growing unease and apprehension that I bade the stocky Romanian farewell as Lord Molesworth ushered him off to luncheon at his club while I returned to my paperwork. Try as I would, I could not concentrate. My head pounded with voices.

The squeaky tones of Madam Bing:

'Beware, beware of the land beyond the forest!'

The heavily accented tones of Ion Ghica:

'The land beyond the forest is a translation of Transylvania!'

The voices echoed in my brain with an ebb and flow like the sound of waves cascading over the rocky seashore.

At last I threw down my pen in disgust and began to pace my office wondering what it all meant. I rationalised that the whole thing must be some preposterous coincidence.

I realised that I had become so agitated that I had not noticed the passing of time. It was already six o'clock and the winter's night was heavy and black. I drew on my coat and muffler and made my way into the great thoroughfare of Whitehall where I hailed a cab to take me to the tavern in the Strand where I usually took my evening meal.

Sunk in gloomy thoughts, I hunched back in the cab as the driver sent his horses trotting along Whitehall and through the great square which is dedicated to Lord Nelson's famous victory at Cape Trafalgar. We were passing into the Strand when we happened to halt sharply. I was jolted from my reverie and, from my seat, saw that a large hackney carriage had turned in front of us, momentarily blocking the road and we would have plunged into it had it not been for the sharp reaction of my driver. The drivers exchanged courtesies which are impossible to set down in this record.

While the exchange was taking place my eye was caught by the comely figure of a woman walking rapidly along the pavement near the cab. Although she walked rapidly, I detected some nervousness and indecision in her manner. Once she halted and turned, looking back the way she had come, and then hastened on again. My cab had stopped by a lamp which threw a pale yellow light through the evening mist across the pavement.

The woman walked into the circle of light.

My mind registered that she was wearing a blue costume of some light texture and carrying a matching parasol. A large blue hat of a darker hue hid her head entirely. But I saw that her figure was young, graceful, and mentally argued that she could not be more than twenty. Then, as she stood under the lamp, she suddenly threw back her head and paused, as if to listen.

My heart beat a wild tattoo and leapt to my throat.

I knew her face well. It was the face of the girl in my grim nightmares. The pale-faced girl with the compassionate gaze, the same whose upraised knife plunged into my breast.

Before I could recover my wits the girl had hurried by.

By the time my paralysis had vanished my cab was moving off at a quick trot.

Standing up, so that I nearly toppled out of the cab, I hammered on the communication hatch and cried to the cabby to halt a minute. He had scarcely done so when I leapt from the vehicle and ran back towards the lamp standard under which she had stood. There was no sign of her. I paused and listened. The mist swirled thick, yellow and cold in the night air. No tell-tale footsteps echoed out of the gloom. I hurried foward a few paces but almost at once I realised the hopelessness of spotting the young woman.

Stunned, I retraced my footsteps.

The cabby seemed rather relieved to see me, perhaps believing that I was merely trying to avoid payment.

At the tavern I ate my meal automatically, neither seeing nor tasting the food that I shovelled into my mouth.

My mind was in a complete whirl. Firstly, I had discovered that there was such a place called 'the land beyond the forest' and that I was shortly to go on a journey there when a medium had warned me against going to that place even before I realised its existence. Secondly, I had been told that a creature, Draco, not only had an existence in my nightmares but in ancient history and that I possessed a statuette of that creature. Thirdly, that a girl whom I thought I had dreamt up in some exotic fantasy had an existence in reality.

What madness was this that was seizing my mind?

I awoke from a semi-doze about seven o'clock next morning and, feeling in the worst physical condition that I had ever felt, I plunged my head under the cold water tap in order to shake myself into some sort of semblance of wakefulness. I had come to the end of my tether; there was nothing I could do, no one I could turn to. Night had become a period of terror for me and yet, in daytime as well, my whole being was seized by the most acute anxiety which caused my heart to race erratically and my limbs to take on a life of their own.

In my despair I sat down on my bed and wept. Yes, a grown man... I wept helplessly, not knowing what next to do.

It still lacked half-an-hour to eight o'clock when I finally drew myself together, washed for a second time, dressed and went out into the crisp winter morning. I did not know where I was going; I let my feet take me eastwards into the Strand and then north towards Bloomsbury.

Yorke opened the door to my knocking, sleep still causing his eyes to squint in the morning light as he tried to fasten a dressing gown about his lean frame.

'Good Lord! Welsford! But its only...'

He gave me a searching look and then silently stood aside as I brushed by him into the hallway of his tiny apartment. He closed the door, yawning away his sleep (blessed sleep!) and turned to regard me with a frown.

'You look pretty tuckered out, old boy.'

I slumped into a chair by the smouldering embers of the previous evening's fire.

'I am desperate, Yorke,' I said simply. 'I cannot go on much longer. The dreams... the nightmares... they continue. I cannot take it any more.'

Yorke must have detected the hysteria which edged my words.

'Let me put the kettle on for some tea,' he said and stirred up the embers in the hearth to a partial blaze on which he deposited fresh wood. It seemed only a few minutes before a black iron kettle was singing merrily on the hearth and a delicious hot, sweet liquid was scalding my throat.

'What do you want of me Welsford?' asked Yorke after a while.

'I need help,' I said heavily. 'I'll try anything...'

Yorke put up a long forefinger and stroked the side of his nose reflectively.

'So you're prepared to try my suggestion - psychic-healing?'

'Anything!' I said abruptly.

'Even though you don't believe in clairvoyance? In mediums?'

'I'm desperate, Yorke.' I repeated. 'I'll tell you straight that I don't believe in all that mumbo-jumbo but I am prepared to accept that you believe that there are people who might be able to help me. People who can, perhaps, harness natural forces in some way which can be of help to me. I do not believe in miracles... but I believe the basis of a miracle lies in natural causes which we have yet to understand; that a person might be cured simply by the strength of his mind believing in the cure.'

Yorke smiled, perhaps a trifle cynically.

'You think you'll believe in a cure?'

'I'll try anything' I affirmed.

'I can't say I applaud your motive or your views but I appreciate your desperation. I am, as you know, an occultist, a scientific observer of natural forces which have become suppressed or distorted as our civilisation gets more pretentiously sophisticated. But I believe there might be a chance you may be helped by the method I have suggested.'

'Then you'll take me to a proper medium?' I asked eagerly.

'Tonight there is a séance in the East End. Professor De Paolo is the medium. Not only is he an excellent fellow as a medium but he is one of the foremost psychic-healers.'

I held out my cup for Yorke to refill it with his delicious brew.

'What time is the séance?' I asked.

'Not until six o'clock.'

I bit my lip.

'Would you mind terribly if I stayed here for the rest of the day?' I asked. 'I associate my rooms so closely with the nightmares that I feel uneasy about going back to them. I am sure to fall asleep and every time I do...'

'Of course you can stay here,' Yorke assured me. 'I have some work to do at the British Museum but I shall return about one o'clock for lunch. Treat the place as your home, there are plenty of books to read.' He indicated his well stocked bookshelves.

Yorke cooked a delicious breakfast of crisp bacon and eggs which reminded me of our carefree days at Oxford when we shared the same rooms and ate many such breakfasts together. After he had gone, I walked about his rooms, my eyelids heavy and drooping, but trying to prevent myself from falling into that dread sleep. I picked a book from the shelf - I can even remember its title and author. It was a new book, a mystery novel by a writer called Wilkie Collins entitled *The Woman in White*. I tried to concentrate on it, sitting in the chair by the roaring, open fire. My eyelids kept drooping, however, and I experienced a kind of resigned despair as I knew I could not force myself to keep awake any longer. The next thing I knew was that someone was shaking me by the shoulder.

I started up.

Yorke was grinning at me.

'It's nearly four-thirty,' he said.

I gaped at him in astonishment and looked at the ornate, wooden cased clock ticking away on the mantle-shelf. It confirmed his statement.

I suddenly realised that I had slept and felt refreshed.

'Jove, Yorke!' I cried, springing to my feet. 'I've been asleep... asleep and I haven't dreamed.'

Yorke nodded.

'I came in at one o'clock and found you snoring merrily before the fire. You were obviously so peaceful that I decided to leave you to sleep a while longer. How do you feel?'

I paused to consider.

'I've had the best sleep I've ever had. I feel really rested. The dream has gone... gone entirely.'

Yorke reflected: 'I must say you look a little better than you did first thing this morning, old chap.'

I felt exuberant.

'I really feel rested,' I said again.

'I've prepared some tea,' said Yorke, indicating a table on which was a magnificent spread of hot buttered scones, some cakes and a pot of tea. 'It's just a snack before we go the séance, after which we can go out and have dinner.'

I frowned, my natural reticence returning now that my need was no longer desperate.

'Do you think its necessary now, the séance I mean?' I asked. 'I really feel fine.'

Yorke was seated, drumming his fingers on the table top.

'You've had one sleep, granted. It's interesting, I admit, but it doesn't give us the cause of your nightmares. I think you ought to see De Paolo, now more than before.'

'Very well,' I agreed, more out of deference to the support he had given me than agreement with his views.

While I tucked into the food, feeling relaxed for the first time in days, Yorke merely picked at his, a faraway look in his eyes. Suddenly he banged the table with his fist, making all the crockery jump and rattle.

'I have it!' He banged his fist again. 'You have only suffered these nightmares while you have been sleeping in your own rooms, haven't you?'

I shrugged.

'You mean I have taken some allergy to my rooms at Mrs Dobson's place?'

'No; the nightmares only started the night, the very same night, that you bought the statuette. Isn't that so?'

I nodded agreement.

'And that statuette is a vivid part of your dreams?'

'Yes, but don't forget the girl - the girl I saw in the Strand last night.'

Yorke made a dismissive gesture with his hand.

'Yes, yes. What I am getting at is this. Today you slept well and hearty in these rooms of mine. Before you bought the statuette you used to sleep well in your own rooms, isn't that so? After you bought the statuette...'

He clicked his fingers.

Seeing my blank expression he sighed.

'You slept here but the statuette is not here, it is in your rooms. *And so,*' he emphasised, 'you slept well.'

I looked at his triumphant face and frowned.

'Don't you see, man,' he urged. 'The statuette is some sort of medium in itself - the statuette is emanating the nightmares which keep you awake!'

'Oh come now,' I said slowly, 'that's ridiculous. You've been reading those rather sordid stories by that American - what's his name - Poe. Edgar Allen Poe. The statuette is a medium!'

But Yorke's face was serious.

'You know me, Welsford. We've known each other for a long time. You came to me because you knew I was the only person who could help you, that my knowledge would help you where others with conventional ways had failed. Believe me, the unknown always passes for the marvellous, the impossible, until someone explains and it becomes commonplace. We maintain our ignorance of the unknown, the world beyond our feeble realities, because this condition is the indispensable condition, the *sine qua non*, of our existence. Just as ice cannot know fire except by melting and vanishing, we cannot grasp that which is beyond our mortal boundaries except by the destruction of our mortality. But the reality of the unknown is a reality nevertheless.'

I smiled a little.

'Steady,' I urged. 'Pretty soon you will be quoting Shakespeare: "There are more things in heaven and earth, Horatio, than are dreamt of in our philosphy".'

Yorke took my sneer well.

'Perhaps you would do well to consider that, Welsford,' he said quietly.

We sat in silence for a little while.

'I'm sorry, Yorke, old man,' I said, regretting my cynicism. After all, he was doing his best to help me.

Yorke grimaced.

'I believe it is important that you come tonight - and bring the statuette with you. There is something strange happening to you, old man, and you need all the help you can get. Believe me.'

'Alright, Yorke. I trust you. I'll come.'

Yorke smiled and extended his hand.

'I don't think you'll regret it in the long run,' he said.

It was something I shall regret all my life.

CHAPTER EIGHT

Having picked up the dragon statuette from my rooms, we hailed a Hansom and Yorke gave an address off the Commercial Road, Whitechapel. The cabby shot us a curious glance, for few gentlemen are seen in that particular area of London. I must confess that I was more than a little excited by the adventure, even to the extent of momentarily forgetting the reason behind it. The East End of London is like venturing into another country which is dirty, squalid and over populated.

Whitechapel lies immediately contiguous to the old City and was once the centre of a thriving weaving industry at the turn of the 19th Century which attracted many foreign workers to settle there. It is an area of narrow, disreputable lanes, lined on both sides with cheap lodging houses and dirty little shops filled with children by day and with brawling men and women by night.

Commercial Road, lying to the south of Whitechapel High Street, is a wide and well-kept thoroughfare. When the cabby halted at Yorke's instructions, the street was crowded with people. Paying off the cabby, Yorke took me by the arm and led me down a narrow intersecting side street which ran south towards the River Thames and the dock area.

Women and men, half drunk, mauled each other in vile caresses while others argued with such degrading blasphemies that I turned physically sick in my stomach at the sound. All were bold. Many of the women accosted us, pressing against us with thick painted lips, foul-smelling clothes, and stale alcohol perfuming their breath.

Grimly Yorke pressed through them all and I followed in his wake.

Loathsome vapours rose from the sewer-like gutters which spilled over the pavements, under doors, spreading a murky torrent of offal, animal and vegetable, in every state of putrefaction. The alley was undrained and reeked like nothing I had smelt before.

A thought struck me accusingly: England was the very heart of the world, extending her empire to every known corner of the globe, an empire on which the sun would never set - yet here, in the heart of England's very capital, was to be found such squalor, such poverty, such human suffering that I am sure would never be found elsewhere in the world. It seemed strange to me and very wrong.

Yorke paused before a tall tenement house which stood in darkness at the far end of the alley. It stood a little apart from the other houses, fronted by tall iron fencing in which was a gate. A bell chain hung outside, and this Yorke pulled twice. A light glanced from a window from which a blind had been swiftly drawn back. Then darkness again. But a moment later there came the sound of a bolt being withdrawn and an old woman opened the door and then unlocked the iron gate, standing aside to let us enter.

Yorke had obviously been to the place before because, without hesitation, he led the way through a small dingy hallway and up some creaking wooden stairs to a room on the first floor.

The room, which was a large one, was filled with people. During the meeting I actually counted twenty of them. They seemed a cross-section of people, mainly from the tradesmen classes. The room was lit by two lamps, one standing on each side of a slightly raised platform on which had been placed a comfortable chair. A silver-haired man, in a rough homespun suit which immediately labelled him as a countryman, looked round from this platform and then pulled out a large silver watch.

He sighed heavily.

'Right, ladies and gentlemen', he said with a soft burr to his voice that I associated with people from the West Country. 'Take your seats, please.'

There was a scramble for seats and Yorke and I found ourselves sitting towards the back of the room with a clear view of the platform.

The silver-haired man in homespuns gazed down on us for a moment. I saw that all the faces in the room were upturned expectantly towards his. Most of them, I observed, were women, women worn with household cares, without legions of servants to pander to their needs.

'My friends,' began the man, 'my friends. Welcome. I would like to commence the evening by singing the hymn 'O God, our help in ages past.'

There was a weird ring of exultation in the voices which took up the refrain led by the elderly master of ceremonies. I was surprised to see that Yorke, too, joined in with a lusty voice.

'And now, my friends, a short prayer - a short invocation to help us this night.'

I did not know whether to smile at these earnest but deluded people, or to feel a great pity for them. Did they really believe that they were able to communicate with the dead, defying the laws of science and religion?

'And now, my friends, I want to introduce our guest for the evening - a very famous clairvoyant from Italy who is renowned throughout Europe, Professor De Paolo.'

There was a murmur of appreciation as a curtain behind the platform was swept aside and a tall, dark-haired man emerged. He bore a striking resemblance to Benjamin Disraeli, the politician, whom I had encountered several times in my work at the Foreign Office. The nose was large, almost hooked, the hair thick, black and curly, the eyes kindly.

'Buona sera... good evening, ladies and gentlemen,' he spoke with a pronounced accent.

The gentleman in homespuns shook his hand, then turned back to the audience and held up a hand for silence.

'Professor De Paolo,' he began, pronouncing the name 'dee-pay-oh-lo', but was interrupted by the smiling professor who corrected it to 'di pow-*lo*'.

'Quite so,' said the gentleman hastily. 'The professor is one of our most successful mediums. He works by clairaudient... that is... '

The professor coughed loudly and pointedly.

'Er, yes. Quite so,' went on the gentleman. 'Quite so. We hope the professor will be able to commune tonight but, as you know, these events depend on laws beyond our control - a sympathetic atmosphere is most essential to good results. And now, the professor.'

The gentleman in homespuns sat down promptly.

The professor smiled down on us.

'Ladies and gentleman ... you must do your best to get me the good vibrations, is it not so?'

He sounded so like a stage Italian that I almost laughed, for he seemed to put an extra vowel sound on the end of each word.

'Helpful vibrations, no?'

He stood swaying on the platform a moment, his eyes closed.

'It would help, perhaps, if you all sung a verse of a hymn.'

The audience roared forth another chorus of 'O God, our help in ages past ...' by which time Professor De Paolo had opened his mouth and started a peculiar gabble. I looked at Yorke in amazement, thinking the man was quite mad. Yorke whispered: 'He's seeking vibrations, trying to get onto the spirit plane.'

Suddenly De Paolo straightened himself and looked towards the audience.

'I have a message... for you, signora.'

He pointed dramatically at a woman in the second row who smothered a little scream.

'A spirit is building up behind your seat...'

She half turned.

'Yes, yes... it is a man. A man, a short man, short and slightly stocky... a black moustache... do you recognise him?'

'Oh me gawd!' moaned the woman. 'It's me 'ubby... 'E... 'e passed over last year.'

'He has a message for you,' went on De Paolo. 'He says... says, do not worry. He is alright. He sends his love and blessings.'

'O me gawd!' exclaimed the woman.

Suddenly I felt De Paolo's eyes on me, then he glanced at Yorke.

'There is someone here who wishes to ask me something...yes, I feel definite vibrations... someone wants to ask me about something which is worrying them, causing them a lack of sleep. It is something about an animal .... no, no, a statue of an animal.'

I turned to Yorke, my mouth opened in amazement.

Unperturbed, Yorke stood up and took from my hands the bag in which I had brought the statuette of Draco.

'Yes, sir,' he said. 'I would like to ask you about this.'

De Paolo looked at him and then back at me.

'Yet you are not the one who would seek to know the answer; you are not the one who is affected by this statuette?'

Yorke inclined his head.

'Yet I seek the information on behalf of a friend.'

'Very well. Bring it here. Take it from the bag and place it on the table.'

Yorke did as he was told, placing the green-black dragon on the small table on the platform.

'Now return to your seat.'

We watched as De Paolo went and stood before the statuette, gazing down at it as if deep in thought.

Suddenly he shuddered violently.

'Dio mio! Cattivo... evil... malvagio!'

He was standing facing us; the table on which the statuette stood was in front of him. He was standing looking at the dragon without touching it. I could see beads of sweat suddenly standing out on his brow and his face became a mass of twitching muscles.

'Malvagio,' he whispered again.

The man in homespuns put on a stage whisper: 'Try to keep in English, professor.'

De Paolo did not seem to hear.

'It is old, ancient almost beyond time,' he whispered, his eyes still on the statuette. 'It emanates great evil... such evil as I have never known before... it burns with evil. Get rid of it, get rid of it if you value your immortal soul...'

Suddenly he was looking up and his eyes were boring into mine.

Icy hands caught at my chest as I knew he was speaking directly to me.

'Get rid of it or you will never know peace in this life or that which is beyond. Be rid of it, my friend. Destroy it, throw it away. But be rid of it... above all beware of a journey... beware of the land beyond the forest. Does it mean anything to you? Beware of the land beyond the forest!'

His voice had the quality of hysteria to it.

The audience looked upon him in surprised satisfaction. Had they come for a show, they were certainly receiving their money's worth.

'What else can you tell us about it, sir?' cried Yorke.

'There is nothing else!' snapped the professor, starting back as if from the statuette.

'We must know', insisted Yorke.

I reached up and tugged at his sleeve.

'No, Yorke. It is alright. We know enough.'

Yorke, an excited look in his eyes, shook his hand free.

'Professor, there must be something more.'

I looked at the professor and was puzzled by the sight of him pushing backwards with his body and yet, at the same time, reaching his hands, seemingly unwillingly, towards the jade dragon.

'No, no! Non posso, non posso!' he cried, yet all the while his hands seemed to be closing towards the object.

It was as if he were engaged in physical combat with some unseen force which was trying to make him pick up the statuette against his will.

Even as we looked his hands closed about the jade creature and he clasped it to his bosom with a sudden scream.

'Are you alright, professor?' asked the man in homespuns.

The professor stood, a tall quivering frame. Eyes closed, face twitching.

'Bruciatore, bruciatore, bruciatore...'

His voice became a solemn chant.

'What is burning professor?' demanded Yorke, who knew some Italian.

The professor did not answer.

Abruptly his eyes opened.

I gasped, for they were no longer the kindly twinkling eyes of a few moments ago.

They were large, black and shone with a curious malignancy.

Even his face seemed to change, it seemed to elongate, become more pointed, the cheeks more pale, almost white, the eyebrows drew more closely across the bridge of the nose, the lips became redder and thinner and through their slightly parted smile, the teeth seemed oddly longer than a moment before and shone with a peculiar whiteness.

My heart pounded within me as those awful black orbs searched me out and held my gaze as if in a vice.

'You will come to me.' Even the voice was changed. It was harsher and contained a curious accent which was certainly not Italian.

The silver-haired gentleman raised an excited voice.

'A trance manifestation,' he chortled. 'A trance manifestation. I did not know the professor was able to ...'

Realising he was ruining the vibrations, he stopped.

I stirred uncomfortably, unable to release my eyes from the black night eyes which gazed into mine.

'You will come to me, do you hear me... come across the seas, over the mountains to my home beyond the forests. You will come to me, do you hear me? You will come to me,' the voice had a soft, almost soporific effect, slow, mesmerising.

'I am the master, the master who will give you eternal life and blessings. You will come to me when I call you. You will come to me and bring the god Draco. You will come to me. Do you hear me? Do you hear now? I am the master... across the seas, over the mountains, to the land beyond the forests. I shall be waiting... soon... soon...'

Suddenly there was a great cry of pain, of soul-searing agony.

The professor threw up his arms, the statuette of the dragon was flung across the room and crashed against the wall near me.

The professor himself seemed to be slammed backwards against the platform and crashed to the floor in a mass of splintering woodwork as it disintegrated under the weight of his impact.

Many of the audience had leapt to their feet and a babble of voices rose in surprise and horror. ·

I sat, staring numbly in front of me.

Yorke hauled me to my feet, giving me a shake to awake my senses, and retrieved the statuette.

'It's not damaged,' he said, replacing it in the bag and then jostling forward to the group who were standing around the prostrate form of the professor.

'Stand back!'

'Give him air!'

'Has he fainted?'

'Is he alright?'

'*Please*, stand back now.'

I moved forward in a daze, and joined Yorke in trying to peer over the tops of the heads and look down on the prone man.

The homespun man was leaning over him, his face working. He

felt for the pulse, then the heart, tried to pour a drink down the man's throat, felt for the heart again and then turned a horrified face towards the surrounding audience. His mouth opened and closed without saying anything. Then he managed to blurt out: 'My God! He's dead! Dead!'

In the screams and babble that followed I was dimly aware that Yorke had gripped me by the sleeve and hauled me from the room, down the stairs and back out along the putrid alleyway, back to the bright lights of the Commercial Road.

'Come on, old man, pull yourself together now,' he whispered, pushing me forward.

'But, Yorke,' I gasped, 'he died... that man died...! Was, was I to blame?'

Yorke said nothing but turned and spent his best endeavours in trying to hail a cab. Cabs were few and far between along the Commercial Road and it was some minutes before he found one depositing a fare and promptly hired the man to return us to the Strand.

I was speechless with the shock of what I had witnessed.

Yorke hauled me out at a little tavern, the George Inn, I think it was, and propelled me into a quiet booth where he ordered whisky for the both of us.

'Of course we are not to blame for the man's death,' he said, after a while.

'Then why did we run away?' I demanded.

Yorke shrugged his shoulders expressively.

'There will be police, enquiries, you know the sort of thing... it won't look good if we are reported to have been in that sort of area. What would Lord Molesworth say, eh? A personal secretary at the Foreign Office mixed up with spiritualists in Whitechapel... what would the newspapers say, eh?'

I thought it over.

'I suppose you are right, Yorke,' I said after a pause.

'Of course I am.'

'But Yorke,' I persisted, 'what killed him?'

Yorke pursed his lips.

'Who knows? A heart condition, some other illness... who knows?'

'I find it frightening.'

'Well, old boy, I'll tell you one thing - the thing you should take deadly serious about the whole business.'

'What's that?' I asked.

'You must not accompany Lord Molesworth to Romania next month.'

CHAPTER NINE

The nightmare came to me again that night. But this time it was slightly different.

Again I walked through the exotic night garden; again my stomach heaved at the oppressive sickly-sweet smell of jasmine.

The same monotonous chanting began.

All the while my mind was still conscious that this was some illusion; I knew, behind it all, that I was still lying in my bed in my rooms at Charing Cross. Yet the scene was still vivid to my senses.

Through the velvet blackness of that night garden, towards that white-pillared fantasy of a temple and the evil grinning edifice of the dragon god, my unwilling footsteps were led once more.

But instead of the girl waiting for me in the white moonlight there stood a man.

From head to toe he was draped in black. He bore a strange resemblance to the dead medium... Professor De Paolo. Yet I knew that it was not the same man.

He was a tall man, elderly it seemed, for a long white moustache drooped over his otherwise clean-shaven face. Even in the uncertain drifting of my dream I could see his face was strong - extremely strong - aquiline with a high-bridged, thin nose and peculiarly arched nostrils. His forehead was loftily domed and the hair grew scantily round the temples but profusely elsewhere. The eyebrows were massive, nearly meeting across the bridge of the nose.

But above all it was the mouth that captured my eyes. That mouth set in that long pale face: fixed and cruel looking, with teeth that protruded over remarkably ruddy lips which had the effect of highlighting his white skin and giving the impression of extraordinary pallor. The strange thing was, where the teeth protruded over the lips, they seemed peculiarly sharp and white.

The eyes suddenly caught and held mine.

They were large and shone with a curious red malignancy.

'You will come to me,' he said slowly, a smile curving his lips - those, oh, so thin, red lips.

The voice was mesmeric, a strange voice, rich in tone and full of alien accents.

'You will come to me, do you hear me... come across the seas over the mountains, to my home beyond the forests. You will come to me, do you hear me? You will come to me.'

I was aware that I stood before this dark, forbidding shape like a rabbit before a fox; my eyes wanting to close, to sleep, letting the drone of his voice lull me...

'I am the master, the master who will give you eternal life and blessings. You will come to me when I call you. You will come to me and bring the god Draco, you will come to me. Do you hear me? Do you hear now? I am the master... across the seas, over the mountains, to the land beyond the forests. I shall be waiting... soon... soon...'

Suddenly the figure was gone, dissolving before my eyes into elemental dust which suddenly shot like a beam of silver along the pale rays of the moon.

My senses reeled.

Then the dream took on its old form. From nowhere the girl appeared with her accursed sacrificial knife - for such I now knew that weapon to be.

Again the ritual; again the incantation.

Again the knife rose...

Something sounded in my ears: a bang, a bump, I am not sure. The next thing I knew was that I sat bolt upright in my bed, my eyes and ears straining in the darkness of my room.

Fully awake, I was aware of the rapidity of my own breathing, sounding deafening in the stillness of the night.

A creak from a loose floorboard in my sitting-room caused my heart to beat in a wild tattoo.

There was someone in the next room!

For a moment I let my imagination loose in strange fantasies but then I pulled myself together. I was letting my nightmares and Yorke's strange behaviour colour my fertile imagination. Who could it be but some common thief? And if it was, I was twenty-six years old and strongly muscled, for I believed in keeping healthy and attended regularly at a school of fencing, a sport designed to keep anyone in excellent physical condition. In a position such as mine, which keeps one seated before a desk most of the day, it is so easy to become lazy and slack, to let the body become little more than useless.

Cautiously, I drew back the coverlets and climbed out of bed.

If it was a common burglar, with an envious eye on my collection of *objets d'art*, he would pay dearly for his insolence.

I walked carefully to my bedroom door and slowly, cautiously, turned the handle, prising the door open a few inches.

My sitting-room was in total darkness, the drawn curtains allowing no light from the lamp-lit street. I opened the door a little wider and slipped swiftly into the room.

The paler shades from my bedroom infiltrated the sitting-room so that, after a while, the darkness was not as pitch-black as it had been before. I stood very still, peering forward to examine each corner of the room.

Then in a corner I saw it!

A small dark shadow.

With a bark of triumph I flung myself across the room and snatched at the figure.

It was far smaller that I was, a good head shorter, and seemed light and lithe. But as my hands closed around the small arms they swung up to repel me and such was the incredible strength they seemed to have that I was propelled backwards for several feet and only my colliding with a sideboard stopped this backward propulsion. For a moment I stood leaning against the sideboard, stunned; not stunned by the actual push that I had received, but by the fact that such a small person could be possessed of such strength.

The figure had flown to the door. Recovering myself, I hurled myself after it. The impact of my attack pushed the figure heavily against the door. For a few moments I was able to bring my arms around those of my assailant. Then that incredible strength re-asserted itself and I was flung off as if I had been a mere child attacking a fully grown man.

The figure was fumbling with the door handle.

64

I recovered myself a second time and tackled the legs of the person.

The impact of my third attack sent the figure hurtling backwards, an object which had been held in one hand went flying across the room with a resounding crash. The figure went over, with me on top of it. I struggled to my knees to meet the counter-attack which I assumed would follow, but the figure lay supine on the floor of my room.

Breathless following my exertions, I rose to my feet and looked down. In the darkness I could make out little except that I could hear stertorous breathing and presumed I had knocked out the would-be burglar. I walked to the table, fumbled for matches and lit the lamp.

'Mr Welsford!' There was a sudden thumping at my door. I groaned inwardly as I recognised the imperious tones of Mrs. Dobson. Well, at least I had a good enough excuse for disturbing the tenants of her rooming house this time.

'One moment!' I cried and turned, raising high the lamp to observe my thief.

The blood rushed dizzily about my head, singing in my ears, as I peered down aghast at the beautiful girl who lay on the floor. That face, which I had seen so often, now lay in calm repose. Only the mouth, slightly parted, was twisted unnaturally and issued the sound of uncomfortable breathing. It was the same girl from my nightmares, the same girl that I had seen by gaslight in the Strand a few nights before.

'Mr Welsford!'

Mrs Dobson's knocking sounded once more.

I stirred myself with difficulty.

What was I to do? Firstly, I had to get to the bottom of this amazing situation.

'Mr Welsford!'

The voice of the landlady was high and angry.

Reluctantly I went to the door and opened it.

Mrs Dobson stood in her dressing gown. She was red-faced, blotched in anger. She stood with her massive hands placed on her hips.

'Now then, Mr Welsford, I have warned you before about these

65

noises. I told you they must stop. I won't say it again. You are disturbing my tenants. If you can't stop this noise I must ask you to leave. Do you hear me?'

'Yes, Mrs. Dobson,' I replied meekly, not wishing to do battle with this reincarnation of Antiope, Queen of the Amazons.

'Well, Mr. Welsford?'

She fixed me with her gimlet eyes.

'Mrs. Dobson?'

'What's the meaning of this noise?'

My mind raced rapidly.

'Why... I stupidly left my window open last night and a cat must have made its way in over the roofs. I just had a devil of a time chasing it out. I'm sorry I disturbed you.'

'A cat?' There was a heavy suspicion in her voice.

'Yes, Mrs. Dobson.'

'Well, I shan't warn you again, Mr. Welsford. I keep a respectable house here, and I'm the one who has to receive all the complaints. Never heard anything like it, a cat, indeed! Opening windows in December!'

With a scowl and a snort of indignation, Mrs. Dobson turned on her slippered heel and disappeared down the stairs.

With a sigh of relief I closed my door and put my lamp back on the table.

The girl was still lying on the floor, her breathing slow and erratic. I bent over her and felt for her pulse. It matched her breathing.

I picked her up in my arms, registering how light she was and frowning in disbelief as I remembered the strength she had displayed a moment or so ago. I took her into my bedroom and laid her carefully on my bed. The fire was still crackling in the hearth and I quickly built it up into a blaze and turned on the gas lamps.

A careful examination of the girl's head, to see how she had rendered herself unconscious, showed no lumps or bruising. Yet she was clearly not in a natural state; it was as if she were in some sort of stupor.

I tried to awaken her from it by chaffing her hands and wrists and applying a cold, wet flannel to her forehead.

There was no reaction.

Wondering what to do, I placed a kettle on the hearth, thinking that maybe I could force her to take a hot drink, for it did not enter my church-raised mind to offer alcohol to a lady.

It was then I suddenly recalled that as she fell something had flown from her hands - released by impact - and thudded across the room. I went into the sitting-room and picked up the lamp to search the floor.

I had no difficulty in finding what it was.

There in the corner, where it had fallen, was the small jade statuette of the god Draco.

In bewilderment I picked it up and replaced it where I usually kept it on my sideboard.

It grinned evilly at my puzzled gaze.

What could it mean? The strangeness of the events was now so confusing, so perplexing, that for the first time in my life I was really apprehensive as to my sanity. I suddenly realised that for all his esoteric ways and his mysticism, perhaps Yorke was truly the only person who could help me solve this mystery - Yorke and, of course, the girl who now lay unconscious on my bed.

I returned to the bedroom.

She lay, pale and beautiful in repose. How can I describe her? She was in her early twenties, perhaps not more than twenty-one or twenty-two. The face was heart-shaped, the eyes were wide-set, the lids lined with curling, graceful lashes. I knew that beneath those lids there lay deep-green eyes that must have been the sort of eyes that Helen used to ensnare Paris of Troy and his brother Deiphobus, and Theseus and Menelaus before them. The pale face, with its delicate rose red lips, was surrounded by a tumble of raven coloured hair. She had an exotic, remarkably foreign look about her. And her figure, ah, it was injustice to say it was well shaped; it was a figure that Aphrodite might have been jealous of.

It was while I stood thus, breathing in the essence of her beauty that I suddenly became aware of a fact which had not struck me before. The girl was wearing no outer garments, no coat nor hat, but simply wore a tightly buttoned costume with a white blouse pinned high at the throat by a single cameo broach. Yet the night outside was chilly and cold. I would not venture far without a heavy overcoat and muffler.

Had she come far?

Another thought struck me, and I leant over her and unloosened some of her garments to make her more comfortable, blushing even while she lay in her unconscious state. But her health was to be put before gentlemanly breeding and I fumbled at the unfamiliar buttons of her costume coat, carefully unfixing the cameo brooch and loosening the top of her blouse and then the tight waistband of her skirt.

Her skin was white and cold to the touch.

I wondered whether I should leave her and go in search of a doctor but I knew not where to find one at this time of night. I glanced at the clock and saw that it was actually morning, nearly six o'clock. I resolved that if I were unable to rouse her by seven o'clock I would set off to Soho to bring the doctor I had consulted there.

I made some tea and tried to administer a few mouthfuls to the girl in an effort to revive her. While she seemed to swallow automatically, it created little change in her condition.

I drank a cup of tea myself and then paced up and down trying to make sense of the events of the past few days, trying to link them together in some sort of pattern. But the task was too much for my racing brain to cope with.

At last, I pulled up the blinds to watch the grey fingers of dawn creeping up the Thames from the direction of Saint Paul's Cathedral.

The girl's breathing now seemed slightly more regular, more normal, even her pulse more even.

I sat in a chair by the bed, trying to focus on the forthcoming day, but my eyelids grew heavy and, against my will, I fell into a dreamless but uncomfortable sleep.

CHAPTER TEN

A sobbing caused my eyes to start open.

The winter sun was shining full into the room. I blinked and my next reaction was to peer at the clock which now registered nine-thirty. I was about to rise from the chair when another loud sob arrested me and my eyes were drawn to the lithe figure on my bed and the events of the night flooded into my mind with alarming clarity.

The girl was awake, at least her eyes were open, and staring wildly about her.

'Hello,' I smiled, not knowing what else to say.

She stared hard at me and then raised a pale hand to dash away the tears that lay upon her cheeks.

'Wh... where am I?' she asked in a tremulous voice.

'You are safe,' I replied, 'don't worry. But... are you feeling alright now? You had me worried.'

A frown of puzzlement crossed her face as she stared up at me.

'I... I seem to know you and yet, yet...'

She bit her lip as if trying to dredge up some long lost memory.

Suddenly it must have occured to her that she was in a strange man's room, lying on his bed, her clothes in an unloosed fashion.

She gasped and tried to sit up but appeared a little weak from the effort.

'Don't move,' I admonished. 'You are a little weak after your adventure. I'll make some tea. That should make you feel better.'

Her eyes darted about in alarm.

'Where am I?' she demanded.

'You don't remember?' I asked.

'I remember nothing. I went to bed in my room last night as usual. Then...' she frowned and passed a hand across her brow. 'I seemed to have a strange dream. I can't recall... I've been having so many peculiar dreams of late. I just can't recall.... But where am I? How did I get here? And who are you? Have we met before?'

I held up my hands to still the questions that came tumbling from her lips.

'One question at a time,' I implored. 'Firstly, my name is Upton Welsford and these are my rooms. We are near Charing Cross. Now who are you?'

I could see my name meant nothing to her.

'I am Clara Clarke. My father is Colonel George St. John Clarke of the Egyptian Rifle Brigade,' she added, as if it were some formula which might protect her. 'What am I doing here?'

I poured out a cup of tea and handed it to her. She sipped at it slowly, leaning back against the pillows.

It was all so strange that I scarcely knew how much to tell her.

I decided to be scrupulously honest and her eyes grew wide in disbelief and then horror as I recounted my experiences, describing in detail what had happened the previous night.

'I don't believe it,' she gasped at the end of my account. 'But... but it seems to fit in with those awful, ghastly dreams...'

She peered hard at me and I turned a trifle pink beneath her scrutiny.

'Who are you?' she asked again, 'and why is it that I seem to know you? I am sure I have seen you before.'

I sighed.

'I do not wish to complicate matters Miss Clarke,' I said, 'but I, too, seem to have met you before last night.' It was then I told her the exact nature of my dreams. I recounted everything that occurred and as my narrative proceeded, the girl grew pale and once or twice pressed a hand to her cheeks.

'This can't be true... this can't be happening,' she gasped.

I thought she was about to faint and sprang from my chair in alarm.

'Miss Clarke,' I cried in agitation, 'it is not my wish to distress you further but we have been the objects of such mysterious events that I feel we must be totally honest with each other.'

She nodded slowly.

'Indeed, you are right, Mr. Welsford,' she answered gravely, having recovered her composure. 'Although your tale is most

70

horrific and leaves me in apprehensive bewilderment, I must tell you that, in a peculiar way, it gives me comfort, for during the past week I have found myself similarly circumstanced and so terrifying have been my dreams that I thought that I was going insane.'

She paused and shuddered as she seemed to recall unpleasant memories.

'If you would pour me another cup of tea, Mr Welsford.' she gave me a weak but brave smile, 'I shall tell you my story.'

It was a story which was, in every detail, as perplexing and as terrifying as mine.

Her father, as she had mentioned before, was a serving officer in an infantry regiment stationed near Cairo in Egypt. Some twenty-one years previously, which confirmed my estimation of her age, he had met and married her mother, an Egyptian princess, and married her although such a liason was greeted with disapproval by both the British authorities and by the princess's family. After Clara had been born, Colonel Clarke and his wife had sent her to England for her education. She had lived with a matronly aunt in Sussex, returning to Egypt for holidays with her parents. Three years previously, her mother, Princess Yasmini, had died from some fever and Clara had gone to Egypt to take on the duties of looking after her father's house.

A month ago her father had been ordered south, into the Sudan, to command a punitive expedition against rebellious tribesmen. Clara had returned to England to visit her aunt.

Her boat had docked at Wapping five days ago and it was from that very date that she had started to fall prey to strange nightmares. The nightmares concerned her home in Egypt and were then mixed with weird images of ancient temples, of her own mother in ancient costumes, of blood sacrifices in which she - Clara - seemed about to plunge a knife into a young man who stood helpless before her.

As she told me this, she suddenly started and peered closely at me.

'Why... it is you. You are the man in the dream - but that is impossible, surely?'

Her voice had an unmistakable pleading quality to it.

I shrugged my shoulders.

'If I can dream of you, and my dreams began several days before

71

your boat docked - so it would be impossible to claim that I had seen you before and subconsciously imagined you in my dreams - then it is equally possible that you have dreamed of me. I do not understand it; I cannot explain it; but the facts remain.'

She shuddered.

Continuing her narrative, she told me that the dominating feature of her dreams had been of a vast image of some wild beast - a serpent-like beast.

'A dragon?' I interposed.

She nodded eagerly.

'A black dragon, that's it. I am always standing before it in my dream. Could it be the same beast that you said appears in your dream?'

I said nothing and she continued that two days previously her dreams altered a little. She began to hear a voice calling to her, telling her to take the dragon and bring it to... to somewhere, to someone, but she could not remember who or where. It was terribly confused.

I went into the next room and returned with that accursed statuette.

'Is this the dragon statue in your dreams?' I asked, thrusting the jade forward.

She gave a tiny scream, suppressing it with the back of her hand.

'That's it... why, what does it mean?'

'When you came here last night, you were trying to make off with it,' I said, grimly. 'You must have been answering the call of the ... the someone in your dream.'

She shook her head from side to side helplessly.

'I must be going mad, none of this makes sense to me.'

'Nor me,' I agreed. 'Yet there must be a sense to it somewhere. Somehow there is logic to all this madness. There is a link, that is certain. But what it is, I have absolutely no idea. People do not dream of people they have not met, and yet who exist, without a reason.'

'Perhaps we are insane?' the girl whispered. 'It is too fantastic, too unreal to make sense.'

An idea was already forming in my mind.

I reached forward and, with a sudden boldness, took her hand in mine.

'Miss Clarke,' I said. 'I am determined to get to the bottom of this mystery; and get to the bottom of it I shall before I depart for... for abroad.'

She raised her grey-green eyes to mine and nodded.

'What do you plan to do?' she asked.

'I have a friend, Dennis Yorke, who is something of an expert in matters of mysteries and dreams. He already knows that I have been suffering from such maladies but I think it would put a new perspective on matters were he to know that you exist in reality and to hear your own story.'

'I will do anything to get rid of these terrifying nightmares,' she agreed eagerly.

'Very well. If you are well enough, perhaps we can go to his rooms right away. There is no time like the present for dealing with the matter.'

She gave me a wan smile.

'I am feeling better.'

'But wait.' another thought struck me. 'Is there not someone who will be looking for you?'

She shook her head.

'No. I am staying alone at a small hotel near here and I have not yet let my aunt know that I am coming.'

'Have you no companion, no servant, who accompanied you?' I asked, puzzled.

'No,' she replied. Seeing my look of amazement she laughed. 'Colonial women don't need the pampering afforded by English society. And now... if you have somewhere that I could bathe my face...?'

Excusing myself for my inconsiderateness, I pointed to a small closet which adjoined my bedroom and while she was at her toilet I dressed and prepared a modest breakfast.

It was nearly twelve noon before I hailed a hackney and gave the driver Yorke's address.

CHAPTER ELEVEN

Yorke raised his grave face and stared solemnly at Miss Clarke and then at me.

Miss Clarke had just finished her narrative, substantially as she had told it to me that morning, and now we waited expectantly for Yorke to make some pronouncement.

He said nothing for a while to alleviate our suspense, but rose to his feet and took down an old briar pipe from his mantleshelf, filled it from an ageing leather pouch and lit it with a taper held in his fire. He drew several breaths of the perfumed smoke and then sighed.

'My friends, we have a profound mystery here. You, Miss Clarke, and you, Welsford, are both the subjects of some force which is trying to communicate with you both, for what purpose I cannot yet say. But,' he raised a warning finger, 'this I know, and I do not wish to sound melodramatic nor frighten you in any way, that force is evil. Of that I am sure.'

I sighed impatiently for I had expected something more from Yorke, some explanation, some rationale.

'Come, Yorke,' I said, 'we need help, not warnings.'

He turned his serious eyes upon me.

'Sometimes a warning is helpful when heeded.'

The girl looked apprehensive.

'Mister Yorke,' she said softly, 'what are you trying to tell us? That we are in some danger from... what? Something or someone?'

Yorke nodded over his pipe.

'Just so, Miss Clarke. Let us say it is something.'

'But from *what?*' she appealed

Yorke frowned.

'I only wish I knew, Miss Clarke. For many years, as Welsford will tell you, I have been a student of the occult. I have dabbled in natural sciences and in spite of the years I have studied, my sum total of knowledge is infinitesimal. But I do know that the occult is not something to be laughed at. There is a real and powerful force at work here.'

'Look, Yorke,' I interposed, 'a week ago I would have laughed at you. This past week I have seen a few things which have raised my curiosity and, quite frankly, have frightened me. I am certainly inclined to be a little more open-minded on the subject of the occult, and I agree that there is a very real and powerful force affecting us. But I want to know more.'

The girl interrupted me.

'Mister Yorke, as you know I have lived many years in Egypt and my mother is of Egyptian blood. I know enough of some of the ancient mysteries that are even today practised among the ordinary folk of that country. That knowledge makes me accept many strange things as natural and I realise that there are many unknown forces still unaccountable to our modern sciences. So my mind is open to your suggestions. But what *are* your suggestions?'

Yorke seated himself before the fire.

'I believe that in some way, Miss Clarke, you and Welsford are mediums - unwilling mediums, perhaps - and that some unknown force, spirit or what you will is trying to communicate either to you or through you. The link seems to be the jade statuette of Draco.'

'Draco?'

The girl's voice was startled.

Yorke nodded.

'I have given some thought to what you have said and my own observations of Welsford have made me come to the conclusion that the force, or whatever you like to name it, uses, or emanates from, the statuette.'

I looked at him in surprise.

'How do you make that out, Yorke?' I demanded.

'Simply this: you say that you started to get your nightmares on the very day you bought the statuette?'

I nodded.

'You could not sleep for days - and every time you dreamt you dreamt in the vicinity of the statuette?'

'That is so.'

'Then you came exhausted to my rooms yesterday and slept peacefully all day, without dreaming, having left the statuette in your rooms.'

'You propounded this theory to me yesterday.' I reminded him.

'I say it again now.' Yorke said emphatically. 'Did you notice how the medium, De Paolo, went into some sort of trance when the statuette was placed before him and how, when he placed his hands upon it, he became another entity entirely? The shock of mediumship killed him.'

'But what of me?' asked the girl. 'I started to dream before I even set eyes on the jade statuette.'

'Indeed.' said Yorke. 'And yet all your dreams were aimed towards the jade; in your dream state you were directed to Welsford's rooms where the statuette was and he caught you in the act of removing it. It was as if you were mesmerised into searching out the statuette.'

She bit her lip thoughtfully.

'So you think the jade is what links Mr. Welsford and myself?'

Yorke nodded.

'That is my theory. What the force is, what it seeks, I do not know. There is something malignant, something evil about it, though. And something which links the forbidden cult of ancient Egypt with modern Transylvania.'

'Why Transylvania?' asked the girl, puzzled. 'And where is Transylvania?'

Yorke threw me a look.

'You have not told Miss Clarke?' he accused.

'Not everything, Yorke. I am a government official and my business in Romania is secret.'

'Some secrets are beyond governmental boundaries, Welsford. You can trust Miss Clarke in this matter.'

The girl turned her luminous green eyes upon me and laid a soft hand on my arm.

'Your secret is safe with me, Mister Welsford.' she said imploringly.

I mellowed in her gaze.

'I quite believe it, Miss Clarke. I really do...'

'Good,' said Yorke, a little sharply. 'Transylvania is a principality which lies next to Hungary and is currently part of the Austro-Hungarian Empire. It straddles the Carpathian Mountains.'

The girl was puzzled.

'And what has this to do with this... this business?'

'Quite a lot, or so I deduce.' went on Yorke.

Without giving away too many details of the Foreign Office connection, he told the girl of my forthcoming visit to the new state of Romania and the possibility of a visit to the neighbouring principality of Transylvania. Then he told her how he had taken me to the two mediums and how both had warned me against going to Transylvania. He described in detail the metamorphosis of De Paolo during the séance.

I echoed the story by adding how I had dreamt of a tall man in black repeating the exact same message De Paolo had given me.

Yorke banged his hand on the rest of his chair in triumphant agitation.

'There, by Jove! That proves it. There is a connection.'

'But what connection could there be between Egypt and Transylvania... and with this ancient dragon cult of which you speak, the worship of Draco?' asked the girl.

Yorke shrugged.

'I do not know... yet.'

'But how can we find out?' I asked.

Yorke leaned forward, an eager expression on his sensitive face.

'An experiment.' he said. 'An experiment under carefully observed conditions.'

'How do you mean?' asked the girl.

'What I propose may not be pleasant for either of you...'

'But what do you propose, Yorke?' I insisted.

He looked from the one to the other of us for a moment.

'I propose that you, Miss Clarke, and you, Welsford, spend the night here - with the statuette. I shall be here also to observe what happens. I have various instruments which will help me study the psychic phenomena and through clinical observation we may be able to ascertain what this force is and what it is seeking.'

He sat back.

'Well, what do you say?'

I looked doubtfully at Miss Clarke.

'If you think that there is a possibility of putting an end to this nightmare then I am quite willing to undertake this experiment.'

Yorke looked at me.

I nodded slowly.

'If Miss Clarke is prepared then so am I.'

Yorke rose and clapped me on the back.

'Excellent, excellent! I am sure we can get to the bottom of this mystery. And now,' he pulled out his silver hunter watch and glanced at it, 'now I want some time to prepare. Perhaps, Welsford, you would care to take Miss Clarke to luncheon, then pick up the statuette and return here - but return before nightfall.'

He laid a heavy emphasis on the last words.

Yorke ushered us out and already I could see that his mind was miles away, locked in his strange world.

I helped Miss Clarke into a carriage and ordered it to Charing Cross. A thought struck me and caused me to bang my hand in agitation.

'Miss Clarke, what a confoundedly selfish ass I am.' I spluttered.

She turned mildly amused eyes on me.

'I should take you to wherever you're staying. I haven't even asked. You will obviously want a change of clothes and... and...'

She gave a low chuckle.

'Dear me, in the excitement I forgot all about such things. I am staying at the Nelson Hotel, just behind the hospital at Charing Cross. I certainly would like to change my clothes and pick up a few things for tonight.'

I passed the address to the cabman.

'After I came ashore from my ship,' explained the girl, 'I registered at the Nelson expecting to stay only a night or two before taking the train from Charing Cross station down to Sussex where I was going to stay with my aunt. But those dreams have made me so exhausted during the past few days that I haven't been able to face the journey and,' she lowered her voice confidingly, 'one needs stamina to stay with my aunt.'

Her chuckle was musical and caused my pulse to beat more rapidly. I believe it was about that time that I knew that I had fallen in love with this exquisite creature. I do not know what chemistry it is that works to bind men to women in only a moment's acquaintanceship. We are told such things only happen in works of fiction and are scorned by philosophers and men of sobriety. But this I know, the fabled 'love at first sight' is a fact of life, for I was deeply, irrevocably and almost idolatrously in love with Clara Clarke.

'Won't your aunt be worried by your non-arrival?' I asked.

The girl shook her head.

'I told you before that she doesn't even know that I am in England. My departure from Cairo was sudden, on an impulse, and in the rush of leaving I quite forgot to send her a letter. Even if I had, by the time she received it I would already have arrived.'

'In that case,' I ventured, stumbling a little over my words, 'perhaps, after tonight, you could stay a little in London and I could escort you to a theatre or a vaudeville show or... or... something before you go down to Sussex.'

She smiled gravely.

'I would like that, Mister Welsford. It seems rather ridiculous to spend two nights with a man,' she gave a mischievous grin, 'and then refuse his invitation to the theatre.'

I blushed furiously.

She leant forward and placed her hand on mine.

'I'm sorry,' she said, with more than a hint of amusement in her voice. 'We colony-raised young ladies are quite shameless and ill-mannered.'

I protested hotly that she made the ladies of England as pale as a winter's moonlight.

She laughed at my lyrical protestations, but not mockingly.

Then a serious look caught her eyes.

'When is it that you leave on your mission?'

'The first week in the New Year.'

'And do you realise what day it is tomorrow?'

I shook my head.

'The day before Christmas Eve.'

I gave a low whistle of amazement. The mysteries of the past week or so, together with my researches on Romania, had so ensnared me in a world where time was of no importance, that I had not noticed its passing.

'I can stay only one more day in London,' she said with what I felt was a genuine regret. 'I really must go to my aunt's for the Christmas festivities. However, if I came up to London for a few days afterwards... before you leave...?'

I could not suppress the joyous grin that spread over my features.

'That would be wonderful indeed,' I said.

The cabman halted his horse before the Nelson Hotel. I dismissed him and accompanied her into the foyer.

An elderly bespectacled man, obviously the hall porter, shuffled forward and handed her a key, giving me a look of deep suspicion.

'Afternoon, miss,' he said. 'We began to wonder where you were...'

She merely thanked him for the key.

'Will you wait down here for me. I have to change. I shall not be long.'

I sat fretfully for a good half hour trying to read *The Times*. Then she returned, dressed in a neat cobalt-blue costume and a matching coat and hat.

Together, arm in arm, we walked to my rooms, overcame the glowering resentment of Mrs. Dobson, who was overseeing the removal of another unwelcome guest and his luggage, and collected that hideous, green-black statuette.

We had a late luncheon, for it was fully three-thirty when we sat down at the Connaught Rooms and even before the main course arrived we had dropped the 'Mister Welsford' and 'Miss Clarke' and had become plain 'Upton' and 'Clara'.

I have never spent a happier day; yes, in spite of the grim realities that hung like a dark cloud over the two of us, the terrifying, unfathomable mysteries, we rejoiced in each other's company and for that all too brief span of time we were happy together.

Finally, noticing the pressing gloom of the early winter evening, I ushered Clara to a Hansom and together, clutching that infernal object between us, we made our way to Dennis Yorke's rooms in Bloomsbury.

CHAPTER TWELVE

Yorke greeted us with a wan smile.

In his sitting-room he had placed a green baize covered table in a central position. On opposite sides of the table he had positioned two comfortable armchairs while, a little behind and to one side, a third chair had been placed. Beside this chair was a pile of old books and a few odd looking gadgets.

We divested ourselves of our outdoor clothing and warmed ourselves before the roaring log fire which Yorke had built up in his hearth. Yorke had taken the statuette of the dragon in his hands and had placed it carefully in the centre of the table. He then took one of his strange gadgets, which had some sort of meter attached to it, and ran it over the jade object.

'What are you doing, Yorke?' I queried.

'Testing for any peculiar currents emanating from the dragon,' he replied without looking up from his task.

Clara frowned.

'How can you do that, Mister Yorke?'

'I admit this is a very crude method,' replied Yorke, gesturing at his apparatus. 'I am not even certain that this is a sure method of testing. This is a galvanometer, for which we have to thank Luigi Galvani of Bologna.'

'I am no nearer understanding,' I said a trifle impatiently.

'The air about us is filled with unseen electrical currents, even our bodies contain electricity. A few years ago electricity was thought to be the source of life. Run a comb through your hair and place it on a piece of tissue paper and you will find yourself able to pick it up as if you were holding a magnet and the paper were iron. The galvanometer measures these electrical currents. And my theory is that this force which communicates itself to you should create a positive electrical disturbance and can therefore be scientifically

81

demonstrated.'

Clara suppressed a shiver of apprehension.

'Is there any electrical disturbance now?' she asked.

Yorke shook his head.

'Nothing. But I shall attach the galvanometer to the statuette by these wires and bring them across to where I shall be sitting; away from the table and able to observe you both.'

He busied himself for some time fixing up his apparatus.

'Right,' he said finally, 'that's it.'

I pointed to the pile of books.

'Have you been able to find out any connection between ancient Egypt and Transylvania?'

He shook his head regretfully.

'No, I have been able to find several references to the cult of Draco, though. But there is nothing to connect it with Transylvania. Certainly dragon worship was not known there, although dragons, or *balaur* as some Romanians call them, have long been connected with witches and evil events. Strangely enough there was one Romanian prince who lived in the Fifteenth Century who was called 'the Son of the Dragon' or Dracula. But he ruled in Wallachia and not in Transylvania. Although he seems to have gathered an evil reputation among the Saxons and Turks, because of his habit of impaling them on wooden stakes, among Romanians he seems to be regarded as something of a national hero because he drove the Turks out of Wallachia. The Saxons reckoned he was so blood-thirsty that they openly called him a vampire. But there seems no connection between Dracula and Draco.'

'There's a similarity of name,' I pointed out. 'Are there descendants of Dracula living today?'

'Linguistic similarities are often misleading,' Yorke admonished.

'From the Egyptian *Draco*, the Greek *drakon*, the Latin *Draco* and so forth, we all seem to have similar words for the dragon. No, my friends, I can see no easy connection. We still have to solve the mystery.'

He looked at his watch.

'And now, my friends, I think we should begin.'

Clara cast a worried glance at me.

'Begin?'

Yorke gave one of his reassuring smiles.

'You and Welsford will have to make yourselves comfortable in the chairs before the table. We will stand Draco in the middle. You will merely compose yourselves as if for an ordinary night's sleep. I will stand by to measure any electrical currents in the room so that we can observe whether this force may be gauged. I will also be able to witness anything else that transpires. First we must see what the nature of this beast is.'

Under his gentle reassurances we seated ourselves in the comfortable armchairs. For some hours - certainly, the last time I looked at the clock, it was striking midnight - we could not sleep but sat tensely in our chairs, our eyes on that hideous green-black monster between us.

Even now I cannot recall exactly how I fell asleep.

All I know was that there came to my nostrils that tremendously sickening sweet smell of jasmine, choking and burning at my throat so that I started to cough. I raised my head to warn Clara and Yorke that something was happening.

But when I looked up I was not in Yorke's room at all!

I tried to raise myself from the chair but found some invisible bonds kept me fast.

The dragon, the green baize covered table, Clara, Yorke, the room, had all vanished.

I tried to call out but found such a constriction in my throat due to the sickly odours that the feat was impossible.

I calmed myself, my brain reasoning that I was still in Yorke's room and that this was a mere hallucination. I must observe clinically, as Yorke would do. I must take in every detail so that I could report fully to Yorke what I had seen.

I was in a high-roofed room, so high that the roof above me vanished in the gloom. Firebrand torches rested in metal fastenings along the walls, illuminating strange murals in blue, red and ochre. They seemed familiar to me and I realised, with quickening apprehension, that I had seen such murals in the Egyptian Rooms of the British Museum. There were a few benches around the walls and I sat on such a bench in one corner. The bonds that held me were shackles of metal.

As if appearing from a swirling mist, Clara stood before me clad in white robes, a tiny golden circlet on her head and a silver chain around her neck from which hung the image of a dragon. She looked down at me and there was sorrow in her eyes.

'So, Ki, Kherheb of the false god Ammon, are you prepared to renounce?'

She spoke in some weird tongue, an ancient tongue, and yet I seemed to understand it perfectly.

'Never, Sebek-nefer-Ra!' I heard myself reply, a harshness in my voice.

Her eyes grew rounder and sadder.

'Will not even your love for me force you to reject Ammon?' Her voice was tremulous.

'No, I cannot be false to the god of peace and plenty even for love of you, Sebek-nefer-Ra... great though that love may be; timeless though that love must be. I shall not desert my god to follow yours'.

The girl before me stifled a sob.

'Then there is nothing I can do to save you, Ki. Already the people are gathered for the sacrifice. They call for the blood of all followers of the false god Ammon, especially for the blood of his priests. You are Kherheb of the Ammon, High Priest of the two kingdoms of Egypt. Yet if you renounce and follow the true god Draco, I can still spare you, and you will be allowed to live as a great example to the people.'

'Oh princess and new made queen of the two kingdoms,' I heard myself say, 'turn aside from this heretical folly. Do not resurrect a god of hate and evil. We who have loved each other know well that this will plunge the kingdoms down into the abyss of ignorance from which there is no return.'

'I have sworn an oath to Draco,' cried the girl, drawing herself up. 'Immortality must be mine! I will not grow old and wither as others have... I am Sebek-nefer-Ra, queen of Egypt, and I shall live for ever!'

She stamped her foot.

'I shall sweep away the old gods, the gods who promise nothing in this life. My god promises everything in this life and that it will last forever. Now, Ki the Kherheb, do you recant your god, will you join me - sit at my side - as the convert priest of Draco?'

'Never!'

'Then so be it.'

She turned and was gone from the room.

My mind raced, the reasoning part, saying that this could not be happening and yet, at the same time, it was all so familiar as if I had lived the experience before.

Then came the part of the dream I knew so well.

I was walking through the garden, through the smell of jasmine. This time I knew that there were two strangely-clad soldiers at my side and that my hands were bound.

There was the tall marble edifice, its pillars disappearing into the heavens. There was that accursed statue, grinning evilly down on me, the eyes wide and staring, the mouth twisted, showing its evil canine teeth and its obscenely protruding forked tongue.

In the background came the monotonous chanting of unseen people, filling me with fear and foreboding.

Before me, back turned towards me, stood Clara's boyish figure. Two arms were raised in supplication towards the brooding statue of the dragon, two pale white hands, palm outwards, paying homage to the beast.

Her voice, as in my previous dreams, came like the tinkling of crystal, unreal, ethereal.

'I come from the Isle of Fire, having filled my body with the blood of Ur-Hekau, Mighty One of the Enchantments. I come before thee, Draco, I worship thee, Draco, Fire-breather from the Great Deep. You are my lord and I am of thy blood!'

The chanting died away.

Her voice continued:

'The time is come when the world must be filled with that which it has not yet known. The time is come when you must take your rightful place in the world and fill it with your abundance. Take then this offering which we, the followers of our lord Draco, give you freely... the blood of an unbeliever, the blood of a priest of the accursed false god Ammon. For blood is life and here is blood of our blood, life of our life!'

And now she turned, slowly turned towards me, arm raised once more aloft with the knife flashing in the flickering torches.

Then, as it started to descend, the girl vanished.

Before me, seemingly surrounded in a mist which billowed and swirled around him, stood a man clad all in black. The same pale-faced man with the drooping, long white moustache, the cruel red mouth and the eyes - those malevolent eyes - glaring balefully down on me.

'You will come to me, do you hear me... come across the seas over the mountains, to my home beyond the forests. You will come to me, do you hear me? You will come to me.'

It was the same, slow mesmeric incantation as before.

'I am the master, the master who will give you eternal life and blessings. You will come to me when I call you. You will come to me and bring the god, Draco, you will come to me. Do you hear me? Do you hear now? I am the master... across the seas, over the mountains, to the land beyond the forest. I shall be waiting... soon... soon.'

I raised a hand, or tried to do so, tried to call out, to demand, to reason, to implore... then a sudden giddy sickness seized me. I felt myself pitching forward, forward, forward and down, down, down into a blackness to which there seemed no end.

I was aware of something cold and wet on my face.

I pushed up my hands and struggled.

'Steady, steady old fellow.'

The concerned face of Yorke came into focus, peering down at me, while over his shoulder another face hovered - pale and out of focus. I blinked my eyes and stared hard. Clara, a frightened expression on her features, was peering over Yorke's shoulder.

I lay on the floor of Yorke's sitting room.

I struggled up into a sitting position, my head feeling that it was exploding into a thousand pieces.

I groaned.

A glass of brandy was thrust into my hands by Yorke and gradually I was helped back into my chair.

The first thing I registered was that it was nearly three o'clock in the morning. The room was the same. There was the table and the green jade statuette upon it.

'What... what happened?' I mumbled. Then, as a thought struck me, 'Are you alright, Clara?'

The girl smiled and reached out her hand to grip mine.

'I'm fine, really I am.'

Yorke nodded.

'You are the one who has given us cause for concern,' he said gravely. 'For the past fifteen minutes you have been shouting and rolling over the floor.'

'Did nothing else happen?' I asked.

I could not conceal the disappointment in my voice, for I had expected Yorke to recount some terrible manifestation.

Yorke shrugged.

'Nothing spectacular happened but I presume we shall know more after we have compared notes of our individual experiences and sought a common denominator.'

He rebuilt the fire and prepared a hot drink for us all while we digested inwardly our thoughts and feelings.

'Let me begin,' he said, as we sat before the fire, sipping the strong hot coffee. 'Just after midnight it seemed as if a gust of cold air blew into the room. I looked up, fully expecting to see a window had blown open. But they were all closed and the curtains were still in place. Then I looked at my galvanometer and the needle was dancing wildly about. All of a sudden, the apparatus burst...'

He showed us the meter: the needle was indeed bent and the glass splintered into fragments.

Yorke continued:

'I felt a momentary excitement. I think I even called to you to tell you what had happened. Then I noticed that you were both asleep - but your breathing was stertorous, laboured as if you were unconscious rather than in a natural sleep. I tried to get up from my chair but suddenly felt very tired. So tired that I too fell asleep. I awoke from a doze to find you, Welsford, crashing to the floor, screaming. Miss Clarke was already out of her chair...'

He paused and cast a searching look at Clara.

'I've just remembered. You seemed about to pick up the statuette.'

There was a note of accusation in his voice.

Clara nodded unhappily.

'I don't know when I fell asleep but I do recall dreaming... I seemed to be in some black room, a cold, dank-smelling place... almost a crypt. At one end of the room there stood a very tall man. There was not much light in the place but he seemed elderly in spite of his tallness, with a pale face and long white moustache...'

I started.

'Did he have blood red lips, thin and cruel, and protruding teeth?' I demanded.

She turned to me in amazement.

'That would be how I would describe him,' she agreed.

'What happened then?' intervened Yorke.

'He told me to come to him; to take the statuette and come to him..."over the seas, beyond the mountains, to the land beyond the forest"... those were his words.'

Yorke and I exchanged glances.

'Incredible,' breathed Yorke. 'Then what, Miss Clarke?'

The girl shrugged.

'I do not know. I know that I wanted to obey him. The impulse to obey was stronger than anything I have ever felt before, even though it was against all my rational and moral instincts.'

'And?'

'I suppose I was trying to obey him when you woke up; you saw me reaching for the dragon...?'

Yorke made an affirmative gesture.

'And Welsford's cries probably brought you to your senses.'

The girl leaned forward and laid her hand on my arm.

'It seems, Upton,' she said quietly, 'you have suffered more distress than any of us.'

It was then that I recounted my vivid dreams and told them the parts which I had dreamt before. They sat listening to me with incredulous expressions on their faces.

As I finished Yorke stood up and paced the room. His eyes held that faraway expression which characterised the man when his mind was wrestling with a weighty matter.

We watched him in grave silence.

After a while he turned and looked thoughtfully at me.

'I think I begin to see... Welsford, Miss Clarke - I implore you to beware; it is as I suspected, you two are mediums, receiving thoughts and orders that are being transmitted by some unknown force which requires this object, this statuette, for some important purpose.'

I looked at him incredulously.

'But what force? For what purpose?' demanded Clara.

'As yet, I do not know for what purpose,' replied Yorke solemnly. 'Nor do I yet know the precise nature of the force... a person with immense powers of telepathy, perhaps? But this I am sure of, that force, whatever or whoever it is, represents evil and that evil lies somewhere in Transylvania.'

CHAPTER THIRTEEN

'What shall we do?'

It was Clara who agitatedly voiced my thoughts.

Yorke considered.

'I believe that while you are the receivers of this telepathic communication, the actual means of contact is this infernal idol. I propose that I be allowed to keep the statuette for a while to see whether you are troubled further.'

I agreed at once.

'Something has to be done,' I said. 'Your suggestion seems alright to me.'

'But there are several mysteries which remain to be cleared up,' declared Clara. 'If, as you say, Mister Yorke, some unknown force or person is seeking telepathic communication with us - and I will admit my ignorance on this subject - the purpose seems to be to entice one of us to take this statuette to this country called Transylvania, which I have never heard of before. But why does Mr. Welsford dream so vividly of ancient Egypt as I have done on occasion?'

As Yorke opened his mouth she stayed him with a motion.

'Oh, I know that the statuette originated from there and it features in these dreams. But why does Mister Welsford dream of me as Sebek-nefer-Ra and himself as...'

'Ki, a priest of Ammon,' I supplied as she hesitated.

She nodded and turned back to Yorke.

'Why do we dream these things?'

Yorke reflectively stroked the side of his nose.

'Do you believe in reincarnation?' he asked abruptly.

'I have lived in Egypt,' said Clara simply. 'Reincarnation is an accepted fact of life. Although it seems opposed to western orthodox Christianity, I am inclined to believe in it.'

90

I looked at her in surprise. My Anglican Church background rejected the idea.

'And you, Welsford?' asked Yorke.

'What *would* the son of an Anglican minister be likely to believe in?' I asked. 'However, had I not experienced the events of the past few days I would have said we are all mad anyway. So what is your theory?'

Yorke gave me an almost paternal smile.

'You may be surprised to know that reincarnation was once part of early Christian doctrine.'

I sighed.

'Nothing will surprise me, Yorke. But say on, why do you think reincarnation has anything to do with our dreams?'

'This,' Yorke jabbed his forefinger at me, 'I believe you and Miss Clarke are reincarnations of two Egyptians involved with the flowering of the Draconian cult. That Miss Clarke was once Sebek-nefer-Ra and you, Welsford, were once Ki, Kherheb of Ammon. In your dreams, triggered by the vibrations of the statuette which played an important part in your former life, you have relived a dramatic part of that life. The force which is seeking contact with you picked up the vibrations that emanated when you first made contact with the statuette and is now using the power of those vibrations to call you to it.'

'You mean,' Clara was gasping, 'that I was really Sebek-nefer-Ra and that, thousands of years ago I killed Upton?'

'Five thousand years ago, to be precise, Miss Clarke,' agreed Yorke. 'Yes, five thousand years ago Sebek-nefer-Ra became queen of Egypt. She led the overthrow of the more liberal gods, including Ammon, who had replaced the older cult of Draco. Draco was then re-established not only in Egypt but throughout the known world.'

'And what of Ki?' I asked.

'Obviously Ki was the High Priest or Kherheb of Ammon. From your dream it seemed he loved Sebek-nefer-Ra when she was a young princess but when she came to power and led the overthrow of Ammon he refused to desert his god. The people demanded sacrifice. She tried to save Ki by asking him to recant and when he refused she was forced to perform the sacrificial ceremony herself.'

'How awful!' shuddered Clara. 'Poor soul.'

Yorke nodded thoughtfully.

'A poor soul, indeed, Miss Clarke. And it seems that finally, after all these years, the soul of Sebek was reborn in you and the soul of Ki was reborn in Welsford... strange indeed.'

'But why the mystery concerning Transylvania?' I cried, feeling the frustration well up within me.

Yorke shrugged.

'I have told you: as yet I do not know. But we will learn in time.'

'And in the meantime?' I demanded.

'I am sure that the statuette is the key and while it is safe with me, safe under lock and key, and with you both out of its vicinity between the hours of sundown and sunrise, at which times this telepathic link seems to have its strongest effect, then I think you will have no more nightmares. In the meantime I will do my best to wrest its mystery from it.'

Clara was clearly worried.

'Is there no danger to yourself?'

'I think not,' returned Yorke. 'I have dabbled in this sort of thing long enough to know how to take elementary precautions.'

A thought occured to me.

'And what of my trip to Romania? Do I refuse to go?'

Yorke massaged his temples with the tips of his lean fingers.

'I think I can answer that nearer to the time you are due to leave. By then I should have reached some conclusion in my researches. I would say, initially, that so long as the statuette remains in London this force has no way of contacting you.'

Clara shuddered and I automatically drew an arm around her shoulders. She made no objection to my boldness.

'Is there any other way we should protect ourselves?' she asked.

'Any symbol of goodness as opposed to evil will more often than not provide the right - how shall I describe it - vibrations to combat the evil. For example,' he rose and went to a drawer in his desk and drew out a small box, 'these things will afford you a degree of protection and I will give you them to wear as an added precaution over the next few days.'

He drew out two tiny silver-white crucifixes of delicate workmanship hanging from thread-fine silver chains. As *objets d'art* they really were exquisite pieces of craftsmanship.

'How beautiful!' ejaculated Clara.

'Take them and wear them at all times,' admonished Yorke, handing one to each of us.

'They are beautiful pieces,' breathed Clara again, fastening hers around her shapely neck.

'They have been blessed by the Pope and thereby have been doubly sanctified,' explained Yorke. 'Do not let that prejudice your Anglican mind,' he added as I looked dubiously at the ornament.

Clara smiled.

'But what use is Christian symbolism in combating an ancient Egyptian evil?' she suddenly asked. 'Christianity was not born until three thousand years after this cult of Draco died out, so how can one combat the other?'

'It is the symbolism that matters, Miss Clarke,' declared Yorke, earnestly. 'Symbols of good against symbols of evil. Today, in our western society, it is the crucifix that symbolises goodness, peace and all that is worthy in our moral life. Yet two thousand years ago that very crucifix symbolised an ignoble death, degradation, the symbol of the Roman master race throughout its empire. Equally you could wear any other symbol of religion which preached goodness and light... yes, Welsford,' he gave a half-scornful glance towards me, 'in spite of your 19th Century Anglican morality, there are other religions, even non-Christian ones, which have the same moral code as your own.'

I shrugged. I had long passed the stage of argument. But sometimes I think Yorke despised my unquestioning Anglican faith instilled in me by my father, a most god-fearing man.

Yorke was continuing his illustration.

'You could wear a sprig of mistletoe, symbolic of the ancient Druidic religion of the Celts. That was the first European religion to teach the immortality of the soul. A religion of goodness and light. The ancient Greeks, such as Aristotle, claimed to have picked up much of their own philosophy on immortality from the Celtic peoples.... the ancestors of the now despised Irish, Welsh and Scots.'

He paused as he warmed to his subject.

'You could,' he told Clara, 'equally wear a swastika*...'

'A what?'

Yorke reached into his drawer and came out with another tiny gold charm hanging on a fine chain. The little object was a cross but with arms bent at right angles running clockwise.

'It's lovely,' said Clara, 'but what is it?'

'This,' said Yorke, holding it up, 'is one of the most ancient and worldwide symbols of goodness. It is emblematic of the sun. It is called a swastika from the ancient Sanskrit word svastika - *sú*, meaning well, and *asti*, being. In fact, I tend to wear it when I need such symbolism for it is far older and thereby more powerful a symbol of good than the cross.'

He grinned at me.

'You had better not repeat my heresy to your father.'

'So any symbol of good, not necessarily Christian, can combat evil?' I asked, ignoring his jibe.

'Yes; even the looped cross of ancient Egypt or any other such symbols from religions where light overpowers darkness.'

'And you think it is alright for us to continue our lives as before?' I pressed. 'From now on these terrible dreams will end?'

Yorke nodded.

'Although I am not absolutely certain, I would say that all the probabilities are in your favour.'

'And how will you be able to find out more of the statuette?'

'Leave that part to me. What I suggest is that you both go and enjoy your Christmas holidays and when you return to London next week, contact me. Hopefully I will have a report to make. If you feel any ill effects cable me directly. Above all, wear those crucifixes and never leave them off for one moment. I do not think anything will happen to you, but one must guard against all contingencies.'

'Look!' ejected Clara. 'Why, it doesn't seem possible...look!'

Those who have early Macmillan editions of the works of Rudyard Kipling will see that emblem carried on these books. Similarly, with 1920s George Newnes paperbacks, the emblem was also used as decoration. The symbol was unfortunately adopted by the German Nazi Party and, and through it, became debased into an anti-Semitic racist symbol. **Tremayne.**

She pointed to the curtains where a beam of grey light was filtering in.

The clock chimed the hour of eight.

'Another day,' observed Yorke. 'We'd best all have breakfast and then you had better go and get some rest.'

'Tomorrow is Christmas Eve,' I reflected. 'I have quite a bit of work to catch up on at my office.'

'I shall travel down to my aunt's home later today,' said Clara. 'I'll come back to London next Friday,' she added, catching my anxious gaze. 'You can escort me to a theatre or two before you depart on your mysterious journey.'

I sighed.

'I wish I didn't have to go but...'

'But you have your career to think of Upton,' she replied.

It was true; I knew it. Even now I was worried at what Lord Molesworth was going to say about my protracted absences from the office and my lack of results concerning my work.

We breakfasted together, Yorke, Clara and I, and the mood was light and bantering. I suppose we were filled with a great relief by Yorke's explanation, although I was haunted by nagging doubts, being unable to accept such theories as reincarnation, mediumship, and evil forces without some degree of self-questioning.

After breakfast I took Clara to her hotel and waited while she packed a suitcase and reserved her room for the following weekend, and then I accompanied her to the railway terminus at Charing Cross. I saw her seated on the train to Horsham, a little town in West Sussex, and made sure she was well provided with magazines and chocolates for the journey. Then I waited until the train began to pull out of the station. As it did so she suddenly leant forward from the carriage window and planted a soft kiss on my cheek. 'I am *so* glad I've met you Upton,' I heard her whisper before the hiss and whistle of the steam engine drowned any further conversation. She waved until the creaking line of carriages was hauled out of sight round a bend in the track.

I was soon in my office in Whitehall, bending my head to my tabulations of papers on Romania.

It was just before midday when the doors opened and my chief entered. My apprehension died away as he turned a smiling face to

95

mine.

'Good show, Welsford. I need you today. I'm meeting with the PM at one o'clock.'

'With Lord Palmerston, sir?' I asked.

'Indeed, m'boy. Indeed.'

He glanced at the papers on my desk.

'Nearing completion with the background information, are we?'

I put on an air of confidence and nodded.

'Good, good. Will you have them ready first thing after Christmas?'

I swallowed.

'I'll do my best, sir.'

He pulled out some papers and put them on my desk.

'Fine. We shall be a party of ten going to Romania. That's not including all the official representatives from the royal family and others who will represent Queen Victoria at the celebrations for this Prince Cuza chappie.'

I ventured to correct him.

'Prince Alexandru, sir.'

'What?' he snapped.

'Cuza is his surname, sir,' I explained. 'His title will be Prince Alexandru.'

Molesworth guffawed.

'So 'tis, so 'tis. 'S what comes of making an ordinary fellah into a Prince. Nevertheless, glad you're with me to remind me of protocol and all that rubbish, eh?'

I examined the list of ten names that comprised our Foreign Office delegation. Viscount Molesworth headed the list and my name followed immediately as official delegation secretary. A further party, comprising members of the royal family and military and naval observers, was to travel separately to take part in the ceremonials and the state opening of the Romanian parliament.

'When are we to go, my lord?' I asked Molesworth.

'When? Dear me,' he fumbled with his diary for a moment. 'Ah yes, just over a week, young feller. Gives you time to have a decent Christmas and then January the Second... that's when we'll set off for this Romania place, eh?'

CHAPTER FOURTEEN

I shall not recount the boredom of that Christmas. I sent a cable to my father at Gisleham, doubtless upsetting him, and informing him that I could not join him for the festive season as work at the Foreign Office had to be my primary consideration. I then locked myself in my room - venturing out only to partake of a second-rate Christmas dinner in a nearby hostelry. All through the Christmas I bent my head over the papers which I had neglected and by the following Thursday I, at last, had everything in order for my superior to check before we embarked.

One thing needs to be said: Yorke was totally correct in his prognosis. No dreams came to me, no fantastic nightmares, no summonses from across the water, no ceremonial sacrifices in ancient Egypt - just deep, dreamless, refreshing sleep. I slept the sleep of the just, never waking from the time I placed my head on my pillow until the time I stirred with the morning sunlight on my face. Yet, just in case, I always made sure that I wore Yorke's little silver crucifix.

The journey to Romania was going to take several weeks and would depend on the winds and the tides. At the most, the journey could last four weeks, and, at the least, it could be as little as two weeks. The idea was to embark on the *Agrinion* out of Tilbury and bound for Gibraltar. There, as a British diplomatic mission, we would change ships for a fast naval frigate which would take us through the Mediterranean, the Aegean, entering the Sea of Marmara, protected by the fact that Britain was still legally an ally of Turkey, and then turn into the Black Sea for disembarkation at the port of Constanta, which was the largest seaport possessed by the new Romanian state. From Constanta we would journey by coach or train to the capital at Bucharest.

It was quite an exciting prospect, this journey to a strange new country, for a young man embarking on his career. But the prospect paled as I thought of Clara and I grew panic-stricken as I thought of being absent from England for one long, long year.

I could scarcely conceal my impatience that Friday morning as Lord Molesworth's voice droned on and on explaining the arrangements for our journey. But suddenly the clock was striking one and Molesworth, remembering he had a luncheon engagement with Lord Clarendon, left in a flurry of hurried instructions. No sooner was he gone through the door than I, too, departed and managed to arrive at Charing Cross just as the one-thirty train from Horsham was approaching the platform. My heart was bumping wildly within me as I stood watching its slow approach.

Many people spilled along the platform but I had eyes for only one - the girl with the pale heart-shaped face and the tumble of raven black hair.

Her face, anxious, saw me and the anxiety was driven away by her smile like snow before the sun. She waved and called to me, and I laughed at the startled disapproval of her fellow passengers edging their way towards the ticket barrier.

'Upton! I'm so pleased you are here.'

We stood awkwardly for a moment, looking at each other and smiling, saying nothing, expressing everything; then a porter snorted in my ear and muttered about people who have nothing to do but block platforms. Red-faced, I seized her baggage and ushered her to a cab.

'The Nelson?' I asked.

'Please, Upton,' she replied. 'I want to dump my baggage and then you can take me to luncheon. I am really starving... you haven't eaten, have you?' she asked anxiously.

'No,' I assured her. 'I thought I would wait for you. How was your Christmas?'

'Terribly boring,' she confessed, 'but I suppose that is just as well. No dreams, no visions, just good peaceful sleep. And you?'

'The same.'

'After I had been in Horsham a day I almost began to regret not having a dream,' she went on. 'My aunt, who is elderly and matronly, has not altered with the years. She still disapproves of me and everything about me. I nearly came back to London immediately.'

'I wish you had,' I said ferverently.

She laughed delightedly.

'How scandalous it would have been. London society would have crumbled and the Empire too, no doubt. Your father would have had the hounds out to hunt you down.'

I grinned.

'But are you sure you had no dreams?' Her face suddenly grew serious.

'No,' I replied. 'I never slept better in my life. Mind you, I wore Yorke's crucifix constantly.'

'And I,' she confessed. 'It seems rather ridiculous now.'

She paused, a hand coming up to absently finger the little cross at her throat.

'Have you seen your friend, Mister Yorke, recently?' she asked.

'Not since before Christmas.'

The cab pulled up outside the hotel.

'Maybe we had better call to see him after luncheon,' she said, alighting.

I waited while she registered and had her luggage taken upstairs to her room and then we went to the Strand and had a magnificent luncheon.

It was a gorgeous day for late December. After luncheon we even walked by the river; yes, even the muddy, brown-coloured Thames could not daunt the happiness of spirit which possessed us that afternoon.

We talked of many things, things I cannot even recall now - of our childhood, our prejudices, things we enjoyed and things we disliked. It was not until six o'clock that we guiltily recalled our resolve to visit Yorke and see how he was progressing in his investigations. We strolled arm in arm across the city to Bloomsbury and were soon knocking on Yorke's door.

He opened it and stood for a moment staring at us in some surprise. He was puffing his usual foul-smelling briar and wore a red smoking jacket that I recalled from our Oxford days.

We accepted sherry and told him how things went with us.

'Me?' he responded to our queries. 'Yes, I have been working hard. But I feel unable to make any pronouncement as yet. The fact that you have suffered no further unpleasant experiences makes me sure that we have this force, whatever it is, under control now. I suggest that you both carry on as you have been doing. Now, let me see... Welsford, you leave on the second of the month, don't you?'

I nodded, a melancholy feeling catching at my breast.

I saw Clara bite her lip.

'Well,' continued Yorke, obliviously, 'the day before you sail I want you and Clara to join me for dinner. I shall have some news by then... and I think I can assure you that it will be interesting. Very interesting.'

Then before we knew it, Yorke had dismissed us and we were standing outside his rooms.

As if by some unspoken agreement we turned and walked down to the Strand.

I must confess that my thoughts were not on Yorke, nor on the terrible experiences to which he was engaged in seeking a meaning. My thoughts were of my departure, of my losing Clara when I had only just found her.

Her hand found mine and squeezed it. It was as if she knew and understood my thoughts.

'Will you be away long?'

'Probably the best part of a year,' I replied morosely.

I heard her slow intake of breath.

'It is too long,' she said simply.

'I know,' I replied, almost harsh in my fervour.

'Perhaps, after you have gone out there and discovered what it is like, and if you think the country is suitable, perhaps...'

'Yes?' I encouraged eagerly.

She gave a little laugh of embarrassment.

'It's just that I am used to travelling.'

I stopped and pulled her close to me.

'Upton!' she rebuked. 'We are in a public street. Everyone will see!'

'Let them!' I said savagely, lowering my lips to hers. With a sigh her arms came up to encircle my neck and she responded with a soft lingering kiss. I felt myself go weak at the sensation of those two soft lips on mine and that curious, gentle, darting tongue. Then I felt her pulling away, casting a nervous glance around and straightening her hat.

'Goodness me, Upton,' she rebuked. 'I swear you'll have to make an honest woman of me now.'

I laughed joyously.

'Anything you want, my dear.'

She gazed at me coquettishly.

'Anything?'

'Anything at all,' I affirmed.

'Then I want... the best meal in London followed by a vaudeville or music hall!'

Laughing gaily, much to the horror of the passers-by, we linked arms and set out to find a cab.

The evening passed in a dream, a wonderful never-ending dream. If you were to ask me what I ate or, indeed, what music hall we went to see, I could not tell you. The time passed in a wonderful carousel of sounds, tastes and laughter.

When we came out of the theatre I hailed a cab and helped Clara into it. 'The Nelson Hotel,' I ordered but, to my amazement, Clara, though blushing furiously, told the driver to go to my address.

'You see, my love,' she whispered as she nestled close to me in the leather upholstery of the Hansom, 'you are going soon and who knows how long it will be before I see you again. I... I want to remain with you as long as I can. Is that so wicked?'

I kissed her gently on the forehead.

'I love you, Clara,' I declared.

She sighed and closed her eyes.

It was late when the Hansom deposited us before Mrs Dobson's rooming house. I paid off the cab and we entered stealthily and did not dare to draw breath until we were in the privacy of my own rooms. It took a while to raise a blaze in the hearth of my bedroom and Clara asked if she could freshen her face. While she was at her toilet I went into my sitting-room and selected a bottle of malt whisky from my cabinet, placed it on a tray and, polishing two glasses, set the tray ready. I mused that if my father could see me he would have taken his horse-whip as an aid to teaching me morals.

I suddenly realised that Clara had been a long time.

'Clara?' I called softly through the door of the bedroom, 'Are you alright?'

There was no reply; but I heard a gentle rustling sound like the movement of starched cloth.

'Clara?'

A little alarmed, I pushed into the bedroom.

The first thing that caught my eye was Clara's coat and hat strewn across a chair. The second thing was the dress which she had been wearing and which now lay in a pile on the floor alongside some garments which, frankly, I could not describe.

I must have stood looking at them in perplexity for some moments for there suddenly came a low rich chuckle from the bed.

There, between my sheets, with only her head showing and her black hair tumbling across the whiteness of my pillows, was Clara.

My throat went dry and the blood sang in my ears.

She gazed at me with a smile of amusement on her face.

'It's cold, Upton,' she whispered, but there was an edge to her voice, a tone which I could not place. 'It's cold. Come to bed.'

Like one in a dream, I turned down the lamp so that the room was lit only by the flickering fire from the hearth. My hands trembled, not from fear but from a strange desire which had seized my whole body, as I carefully unbuttoned my clothes and, finally, naked as I was born, climbed in beside her.

For a second she drew away, but only for a second, before she nestled close to me.

I leant on one arm looking down at her exquisite face which gazed up, childlike and trusting, wanton and yet innocent.

'Be gentle with me, Upton,' she whispered, 'it is... I have not... it is my first time.'

Could I tell her that I, too, had yet to know the opposite sex?

I bent down and kissed her softly on the mouth. Our lips parted and it was as if a charge of electricity passed between us. Suddenly we were gasping, snatching, hungry and demanding, feeding from each other. When we paused for breath I let my hand stroke the soft coldness of her well-rounded shoulder, then slip down to her firm breasts whose nipples were raised hard with desire. Then my hand went further, across the cold flatness of her stomach, feeling the tautness of anticipation in the hardening muscles as my hand slid further to that mysterious cavern between her thighs.

She groaned, a sound hard and unreal.

Then she suddenly pulled me to her.

Never in all my experience was there such enjoyment, such pleasure, such feelings of love which through that act linked two people. This, surely, was the pinnacle of all human experience.

After it was over, we lay against each other, our bodies still fiercely intertwined, and fell into a gentle sleep.

All the feelings of guilt associated with such an act which had been impregnated on my young mind, with the morals and religious teaching of my youth, fell away; I realised how evil were the people who would try to make us feel ashamed at such a thing. This was natural, this was Nature herself, and they were debasing Nature, debasing mankind's creativity, by their narrow prudery. They were debasing God Himself.

I lay back feeling, for the first time in my life, complete.

The next day passed in a dream; what we did I have little remembrance of except that we made love, went for a meal, returned and made love again with the passion and enthusiasm of thirsty wayfarers in a desert who, coming upon an oasis, drink from the well as if it were the first and the last water that they would ever taste in their lives.

On Sunday evening Clara had to return to her hotel. Our plan, concocted in our starry bliss, was that Clara should accompany me to Romania as my wife. My sailing date was Tuesday and I reasoned that I could obtain a special licence and be married on the Monday. If that plan failed, I determined that Clara would accompany me anyway and we would get the captain of the ship to marry us once it was standing out to sea.

We moved in a delirium of happiness.

Having made our plans that Sunday evening, Clara said she would return to the Hotel Nelson, pack her luggage and return to my rooms in preparation. She laughed outright at my suggestion that it would create a scandal if Mrs Dobson saw her return with luggage.. 'How so,' she demanded, 'when we shall be man and wife tomorrow?' I realised that there were some aspects of my narrow moral upbringing which would take some time to replace.

I started to get ready to accompany Clara, but she said that she would collect her bags by herself. After all, the hotel was not far away and she had only two cases with her. I could utilise the time by getting started on my neglected packing.

We kissed fondly and she left to accomplish her task.

In a rapturous dream I mooned about my rooms, trying to concentrate on filling my suitcases with the items I would need for my journey. It was done with much contemplation, sighing and dreaming, for I am of a romantic turn of mind.

It was while I was searching the bedroom for a lost cravat that my eye was attracted to a tiny flash of silver from the bedsheets. I bent down and discovered, with a degree of surprise, one of Yorke's tiny crucifixes. My hand went automatically to my throat and felt my own little cross still in its place. It must have been Clara's, I realised, and - ridiculously - I kissed the blessed thing for her sake. With an inward blush I realised that the cross must have come loose in the excesses of our lovemaking. Well, there was no need for charms now. The nightmares had long stopped. I scooped up the silver object and placed it in my pocket.

An hour later I began to expect the return of Clara.

Two hours saw me pacing the room in nervousness, eyes upon the clock to assure myself of the passing of time.

When three hours had passed I was sick with anxiety and my hands fluttered with agitation, for I could not keep them still.

On the striking of that third hour I grabbed my hat and coat and went down the stairs to the street. It was about nine o'clock in the evening and the streets were fairly deserted. I set off at a brisk pace towards the Nelson Hotel and was soon standing in its dimly-lit foyer, agitatedly ringing the bell on the reception desk.

A prim-faced woman of fifty came through a curtained doorway and stood regarding me with hostile eyes glinting from behind rimless spectacles.

'I wish to see Miss Clarke.' I said

I could scarcely keep the impatience from my voice and the woman looked at me with deep suspicion.

'Miss Clarke?' There was a nasal drawl to her voice.

'Yes, yes. Miss Clara Clarke. Which room?'

The woman shook her head.

'I am afraid Miss Clarke left this hotel two hours ago.'

I staggered back as if I had been hit. Two hours! Plenty of time to return to my rooms. There must be some mistake.

'She... she's gone?' I asked incredulously.

'That is what I said, sir,' said the woman, stonily.

'When will she be back?' I pressed, not understanding.

'Miss Clarke vacated her room in this hotel,' said the woman heavily, as if talking to a child.

'Well, where has she gone?' I almost shouted.

'The lady would not be likely to confide in the staff of this hotel as to her movements,' was the unhelpful reply.

I backed out into the street in a daze. My world was suddenly shattered.

How could she have left without saying a word to me? And where would she have gone to? I suppose, ridiculous as it was, my first thoughts were to the effect that I was an injured lover - deserted by my love, that Clara must have been using me to some purpose. No sooner had the angry thought flashed into my burning head than I rebuked myself strongly for giving even momentary credence to such an uncharitable thought. I stood on the pavement, outside the hotel, trying to decide where she had gone.

A cab came idling by. I hailed it and directed it back to my rooms. Asking the man to wait, I raced up the stairs to my apartment, but they were still desolate. I scribbled a hasty note to Clara, lest she should return from some perfectly innocent mission in my absence, and pinned it to the door. Then I hastened back down the stairs to the waiting cabman and gave him Yorke's address.

I do not know what moved the feeling within me but, as we trotted through Bloomsbury Square and turned up the small thoroughfare in which Yorke had his rooms, I had a strong feeling of disquiet. On reflection I think it was sparked off when my hand strayed to my pocket and started to nervously finger an object there. It was some moments before I realised what it was - Clara's silver crucifix.

Then, as I alighted and told the cabby to wait once again, I heard a terrified feminine scream from the house in which Yorke's rooms were situated. I wheeled abruptly towards the door, and finding it open, I pushed my way into the building. I took several stairs at a time and reached Yorke's landing in a moment.

Outside his door was a dowdy little woman whom I recognised as the housekeeper.

'Oh sir, oh sir,' she sobbed as she caught sight of me.

'What is it?' I snapped.

'It's Mister Yorke, sir,' and she began to sob in a frightful manner.

'What's wrong?' I almost shouted.

'He's groaning in there something awful, sir. I heard it not long after the young lady left...'

'Young lady?' I cried, seizing her by the shoulders. 'What young lady?'

She backed away from me looking frightened.

'I don't know, sir. I came up here but the door was locked and so I went away again. That was an hour ago. But a short while since I heard a banging on my ceiling, my rooms being immediately under Mister Yorke's, and I came up here to find out what the matter was. A few minutes ago he gave such a terrible groan... oh sir, something is awfully wrong.'

My blood running cold, I tried the door. It was locked.

'Do you have a master key?' I asked.

She shook her head.

'Mister Yorke is very particular about who has his keys, sir.'

'Then there is only one thing for it,' I told her. 'I must break down the door.'

Without waiting to hear her protests, illogical protests in view of the situation, I put my shoulder to the door. It was heavy and would not budge. The noise, by now, had attracted a police constable who, ascertaining the position, and finding it to be somewhat dire, leant back and used his heavy boot against the door. Three kicks had the lock snapping and the door swinging open.

'Seeing you're a friend, sir, you'd best go in first,' advised the constable.

I entered and stood appalled.

To say that the room was in disarray would be an understatement.

It looked as if a whirlwind had struck it. China and ornaments lay in smashed profusion; furniture was broken and splintered wood was littered everywhere.

A heart-rending groan brought me to the figure of a man lying face-down on the littered floor.

My first reaction was one of relief.

It could not be Yorke because the figure had a mane of white hair.

I bent over the man and slowly turned him on his back.

It was then that my world started to spin rapidly. Behind me the housekeeper let out a squawk of horror and fainted dead away for I heard her body slump heavily to the floor.

I reached out a hand to grasp a support.

The face of the man before me was old... lines cracked across a bloodless, white parchment skin. The mouth was twisted back as if in terror, the eyes were wide and staring, the shock of white hair was like snow... but it was the face of my friend Yorke.

CHAPTER FIFTEEN

'My God!' I exclaimed aghast.

The policeman looked from the prostrate housekeeper to my ashen face in bewilderment.

'Your friend, sir?' he asked quietly.

I nodded, unable to speak. I breathed deeply several times to recover control of my senses and then advised the constable: 'You had best call a doctor... oh, and take the lady downstairs.'

'Right, sir.'

The constable lifted the unconscious woman from the floor and went out.

I bent and felt for Yorke's heart and, incredibly, I felt a faint flutter.

'Yorke, old fellow. It's me, Welsford. Can you hear me?'

The terrified eyes tried to focus.

That ghastly twisted mouth moved. I heard a faint breath and bent my ear to his lips.

'Welsford...'

It seemed a great effort for him to speak.

'Yes, old friend. It's me,' I replied encouragingly.

'Failed, Welsford... underestimated the power...'

He paused gasping for breath.

'Don't worry, old man. A doctor will be along shortly.'

He moaned and shook his head.

'No... no good. Too late.'

'Can you tell me what happened?' I urged as gently as I could.

'Power made contact... she... she came... unprotected... power made contact...'

My heart lurched.

'She? Clara?' I fought hard to keep the agitation out of my voice.

'Yes... unprotected... power, underestimated power. She

obeyed... statuette... taking it to... land beyond the forest...
controlled by power...'

He was racked by a rasping cough.

'Tried to stop it... power rebounded on me... power through
Draco... through statuette...'

I felt myself growing cold with horror.

'Clara came here?' I pressed him. 'Clara came here and the power
which you say emanates from the statuette took control of her
mind? She is taking it to Transylvania?'

He nodded weakly.

'Yes, yes... tried to stop her... power rebounded on me. Done
for.'

Suddenly he grasped my wrist in an almost superhuman grip.

'You must stop her, Welsford. The statuette is the key.... destroy
it. If you fail... evil will spread into the world like waters bursting
through a dam...' His voice was strong now and a fierce light burned
in his eyes. 'Welsford, do not underestimate the power as I did...
remember to protect yourself with the symbols of goodness and
light.'

'Yes, I understand, Yorke,' I gulped. 'Try not to talk anymore.
The doctor...'

He gave an abrupt rasping cough and fell back.

I did not need to be told from his glazed, staring eyes that Yorke
was dead.

A moment later the constable re-entered.

'A doctor is on his way, sir,' he said.

'Too late,' I sighed, getting up from the floor. 'He's dead.'

The constable let out a long, low whistle.

He looked around the room with a professional eye.

'Looks like a burglary, sir. Was he attacked or was it his heart,
sir?'

I hestiated.

'I don't know,' I said heavily. 'He didn't say anything.'

The constable regarded me thoughtfully for a moment.

'Thought I heard you talking to him a moment ago, sir?'

I shook my head.

'I tried to rouse him but he didn't respond,' I lied, realising that if
I told the truth he would think me as insane as I nearly believed

myself to be.

'Look here, sir,' the constable had found a new interest, 'this tin box... do you know what he kept in it?'

It was the box in which I had seen Yorke place the jade dragon.

'Some valuables, I believe,' I hedged.

The policeman gave a snort of triumph.

'Nothing in it now.' He held it towards me. 'Look at the way it is dented and look at the black burn marks on it... it's as if someone used some explosive to open it, or as if it was struck by a bolt of lightning. Curious, eh?'

He placed the box aside and took out a notebook.

'Now, sir, I'd better get some details before my sergeant arrives.'

It was nearly two hours later before I returned to my rooms. My heart was cold within me and I was gripped by a terrifying apprehension.

The police had regarded the matter as one of simple burglary with Yorke suffering from some form of heart attack at the shock of it. I did not amplify on his ghastly change in physical appearance and I understood the housekeeper was in a state of shock and would not be able to be questioned for several days... by which time, I reasoned, I would be on the high seas and therefore unable to answer the obvious questions which would arise.

I must have sat through the night locked deep in thought, for it seemed but a few moments before the sun was sending brilliant cascades of light through my window.

I stirred myself and tried to finalise my thoughts.

Firstly, I had to find out if Clara was still in London. Yorke had said that she was under control of the strange power emanating from the jade dragon and that she was taking it to Transylvania - 'the land beyond the forest'. I had no reason now to disagree with Yorke's explanation that some mysterious force was calling her, controlling her and forcing her to take the ancient statuette of the dragon god.

No one could surely scoff at the idea after witnessing the scenes that I had seen.

There was no doubt in my mind that I, Upton Welsford, was Clara's only salvation in this weird nightmare. I must track her down and destroy the dragon god before it destroyed her. It was as simple as that.

Having made that resolve, I felt better and the adrenalin began to flow once more in my veins.

I ate a meagre breakfast and went immediately to Lloyd's Register of Shipping to make enquiries about vessels sailing directly for the Black Sea ports. The clerk looked through his ledgers.

'There is one vessel, sir. In fact it is the only vessel that will make the direct voyage for a fortnight. But,' he gazed at the clock, 'I don't think you will make it, for it is due to sail on the morning tide from Tower Wharf.'

A surge of excitement went through me.

'The name of the ship?' I demanded.

'The *Psyche* out of Liverpool, sir.'

I had no complaints about the way the cabby thrashed his horses through the narrow streets towards London Bridge and then along the north bank through Billingsgate Fish Market to the Tower of London. He did not draw rein until we had raced through the dockyard and onto the Tower Wharf itself.

My heart sank within me.

The wharf was deserted.

An old man in a sailor's grubby jersey and cap sat on a bollard whittling at a piece of stick with an old clasp knife.

'Has the *Psyche* sailed already?' I demanded.

The old man gave a toothless grin.

'Reckon so, mister,' he said and jabbed his stick towards the empty wharf.

'Has she just gone?'

'Nope,' he said, intent on his whittling again.

'Here,' I said, pressing a shilling into his hand. 'Tell me, what time did she sail?'

He pocketed the coin and gazed at me reflectively.

'Happen about midnight. 'Gainst regulations, too, but her captain is a greedy man, so he just slipped her cables on the night tide.'

I frowned.

'What do you mean by that?'

'Happen like this: I'm in the Black Anchor over there, see? I'm having a drink with a friend o' mine, Chalky White, when old Ben comes across and says the *Psyche* has upped and slipped her cables. Old Ben works on these docks, you see. He says about an hour towards midnight a cab drives up with a woman - a pretty young woman at that, says Ben - she's all alone with only a couple of pieces of baggage with her. Old Ben hears her book a passage on the *Psyche* then she tells the captain that there is a nice bonus in it for him if he slips his cables there and then.'

'Where did she book to?'

'You interested in the *Psyche* or in the girl, mister?' asked the old sailor, a flicker of amusement in his eyes. 'If 'tis the girl then I can't help you. Old Ben didn't hear. If 'tis the *Psyche* then she's bound for the port o' Varna carrying a cargo of corn seed.'

'Varna?' I gasped. 'That's near Constanta on the Black Sea.'

'Aye, that it be. I sailed into Varna and Constanta many a time in my day. Turkish ports they be, though not in Turkey-land proper.'

'How long do you estimate it will take for the *Psyche* to get to Varna?' I asked.

'Oh, two weeks mayhap. More likely three weeks because she's a slow enough vessel even in calm seas. She carries too much weight on her beams.'

My mind raced. There was still time then. If, as scheduled, we - Lord Molesworth and the Forein Office party - sailed tomorrow and made the transfer to the British naval frigate quickly at Gibraltar, then the frigate might have us at the Black Sea ports before the *Psyche*.

I thanked the old sailor with another shilling, climbed into the cab and returned home.

It was a chance, but it was my only chance.

CHAPTER SIXTEEN

The *Agrinion* sailed from Tilbury on the morning tide the day after my futile attempt to follow Clara aboard the *Psyche*. On board were Lord Molesworth, myself, and the entire British Foreign Office delegation to Romania. Of the journey to Gibraltar there is little to recount except that during our stormy crossing of the Bay of Biscay Lord Molesworth took me aside in his stateroom and, without preamble, demanded:

'What the devil is the matter with you Welsford?'

'Matter, sir?' I feinted.

'Matter,' he echoed. 'You have worked for me for some years now and I have never seen you in this state before. You are nervous, even fretful... if you continue this way, Welsford, you will be worse than useless to me when we reach Bucharest.'

How could I tell him what my situation was?

It was while I fumbled for my response that I decided to tell him a half-truth.

'Well, sir,' I began, my mind rapidly forming my story, 'I became engaged to be married at the weekend.'

Molesworth looked startled.

'The deuce, you say!' he exclaimed.

'I do say, sir.'

'And who is the... the young lady in question?'

'Miss Clara Clarke, sir, the daughter of Colonel George Clarke.'

One of Molesworth's gifts was an incredibly retentive memory for certain types of information such as people in the British service, serving abroad.

'Clarke, eh? On the Egyptian staff? Good man. Congratulations, Welsford. But how does that fact explain your attitude?'

'I discovered that Miss Clarke, my fiancée, thinking no doubt to surprise me, sailed for Varna on a ship called the *Psyche* yesterday.

I am naturally fearful for her safety.'

Molesworth chuckled.

'Damn me, she sounds a spirited girl, Welsford. Headstrong family, the Clarkes, you know. Must take after her father. Held back a whole tribe of Afridis single-handed during the war in... well, never mind. Any girl who will do that for a man is not to be treated lightly.'

He clasped my shoulder.

'Don't worry, Welsford. She'll be alright. We'll soon find her, don't worry. Get it out of your mind. Now, how about a little snorter to celebrate the betrothal, eh?'

I felt pleased because, when we reached Constanta, I would at least have an excuse to leave the delegation to go in search of Clara at Varna.

The rest of our passage to Gibraltar passed uneventfully enough, apart from the continuing high winds and seas which seem to be a feature of the coast of Biscay. It was calm enough when we reached Gibraltar but we did not go ashore, for which - in my fretful state - I was thankful. Instead we transferred to a naval ship, which turned out to be a sloop not a frigate, although I am not sure what the difference is exactly. It was a sleek black and white coloured vessel named *Centurion*.

The captain was a ruddy-faced, youthful lieutenant-commander who had spent most of his life sailing in the waters of the Near East and had many a tale to tell about slave trafficking between Africa and Arabia. In other circumstances I would have been a fascinated audience. But I had no cause to complain about delay, for the *Centurion* was a fast enough craft which, with the trade winds behind her, cut through the water like a knife. The navy had orders to put the delegation ashore in Romania in time for the state ceremonials at the end of the month and the captain was determined to carry out the orders to the letter. The first officer, an even younger looking man than his captain, a Lieutenant Brown, took a pride in praising sail over the 'new-fangled steam', as he called it.

'Mark me, Mister Welsford,' he would say, thumping his hand on the taffrail, where we were standing, 'steam will never replace a good set of sail in the Royal Navy. A good set of sail handled by experts will run rings round steam and ironclads any day.'

114

It was common talk that new steam ships were being built on the Mersey for the young Confederate States of America and designed for use in their war of secession against the Union. These ships were equipped with heavy iron armour plating. The navies of the world were witnessing a revolution on the sea. In fact, it is worth noting that, within a few months of our conversation, on March 8, 1862, the first great naval engagement between ironclads was fought between the American Confederate ship *Merrimac* and the Union American ship *Monitor* which was to mark the greatest change in sea fighting since a cannon fired by gunpowder was mounted on ships four hundred years ago.

Such conversations helped to pass the hours as the *Centurion* sped through the calm blue waters of the Mediterranean.

We made fast time from Gibraltar and passed the Balearic Isles to the north, passed the southern coast of the island of Sicily and were bearing south of the Ionian Sea when there was a yell from the lookout at the foremast top.

'Sail ho! Bearing off the larboard bow!'

I was on the quarterdeck at the time, trying to find shelter from the hot rays of the sun and unable to bear the stuffy close-quarters of my cabin. The cluster of officers raised their glasses towards the black pinprick which was some miles in front of us.

'Lugger, sir,' sang out one man. 'She's weathering all her canvas. Must be in a devil of a hurry.'

The captain nodded curtly.

In the monotonous life at sea, a passing ship was at least something to look at and converse about and Lord Molesworth joined me at the taffrail watching the black speck grow larger and slowly take on the aspect of a low-bowed ship under full sail.

During the late afternoon the first officer made another examination of the ship, which we were fast overhauling. His remark set my pulses throbbing.

'I recognise her, captain. It's the old *Psyche* out of Liverpool. She often trades in these waters.'

'The *Psyche*?' I gasped. 'May I borrow your glass?'

With amused surprise at my eagerness, the lieutenant handed me his telescope.

The *Psyche* must have been two miles away, still bearing in front

115

of us under full sail. I could make out only her silhouette and see some tiny black figures moving on her decks.

'We're overhauling her sure enough,' said the lieutenant over my shoulder. 'Another two hours should see us abeam of her.'

I swallowed hard. An idea flashed into my mind.

'Do you think it possible to lay alongside her?' I asked.

'Alongside?' There was amazement in the first officer's voice.

'Do you think it possible that you could put me aboard her?' I persisted.

'Good Lord! Put you aboard the *Psyche*, Mister Welsford?'

The captain, overhearing my remarks, joined in the conversation.

'It is imperative I go aboard her,' I said somewhat lamely.

It was Molesworth who drew the naval officers aside and told them, I suppose, the story that I had told him. They turned back with sympathetic grins.

'Tell you what, Mister Welsford,' said the captain with a smile, 'if the weather holds, I can put a skiff across... maybe you would like to bring your fiancée back aboard and continue the voyage with us?'

I grasped his hand and blurted out my thanks.

'Think nothing of it, Mister Welsford,' said the naval officer with a ghost of a wink. '*Cherchez la femme* and all that, eh?'

In agony I stood by the rail watching the *Psyche* looming closer and larger, trying to hide my impatience at the slowness of the process.

Abruptly, the blue-blackness of the velvet Mediterranean night started to sweep across the horizon, like the sudden rolling down of a blind.

'Break out the skiff,' called the captain who turned to me and added, 'We have time to put a boat across before it becomes too dark to see.'

I echoed my gratitude once again.

The skiff was lowered into the water and four burly seamen and the first officer clambered down into it. I was given a hand down and sat in the stern of the little craft, next to the first officer, as it started to gather speed over the still black waters, propelled by the firm strokes of the sailors at their oars.

The *Psyche* seemed to be standing almost motionless a hundred yards or so to our larboard side. The wind had died down and although she still had on every stitch of canvas there was not a sufficient breeze to fill them.

As we started away from the side of the naval sloop, the captain leaned across the rail with a megaphone in his hand and hailed the *Psyche*.

'*Psyche* ahoy! This is Her Majesty's Sloop o' War *Centurion*. We are sending a boarding party across.'

There was no reply from the now dimly-seen shape of the lugger, standing hove-to in the twilight.

I cannot quite recall what happened next.

One minute we were rowing swiftly across the calm sea, through the twilight but still with an excellent degree of visibility of both our own ship and the *Psyche*, then the next minute we were surrounded by a mist, almost a fog of some obnoxious green-brown substance. I swear it had some sickly sweet smell to it, which for the moment, I could not place.

'Avast pulling!' snapped the lieutenant.

The sailors rested on their oars and looked round in bewilderment.

'Where did this stuff come from, sir?' asked one.

'Jesus, it don't 'alf smell putrid,' commented another.

'Silence!' ordered the first officer.

The silence surrounded us as completely as the mist or fog. There was no sound except for the gentle slapping of the sea along the bottom of the boat.

'Is it usual to encounter such mists in the Mediterranean?' I whispered.

The first Lieutenant shook his head.

'It doesn't seem to be passing, whatever it is, he said.

He sat back in his seat and cupped his hands to his mouth.

'Ahoy! Ahoy there!'

We listened.

The voice seemed to be lost in the thickness of the mist.

'*Psyche* ahoy!'

There was no answer.

The lieutenant turned in the direction we had come from.

'*Centurion* ahoy!'

117

There was no sound but the slap, slap, slap of the waves on our keel.

'Blamed me if I sees anything like it,' swore the sailor.

'Shall us row back, sir?' enquired another.

The lieutenant plucked at his lower lip.

'No, we might have swung right round in the fog and then where would we be?'

I could see the logic of this.

'What shall we do if it doesn't clear,' I asked

'Of course it has to clear,' retorted the officer but I could see worry etching his face.

We sat for a while in complete silence: it was so uncanny, that silence, the slapping of the water and no other sound except the occasional cough as the putrid green-black mist swirled into our lungs.

The faces of the sailors gradually formed expressions of annoyance and then apprehension.

'Rooney,' the lieutenant finally said, 'You'll find a storm lantern in the bow locker behind you. Better light it, it might be seen by the *Centurion*.'

The seaman nodded and executed the order.

The storm lantern was a futile gesture; even from our position in the stern we could barely make out its flame in the bow which was only twelve feet away.

The first oficer was perplexed.

A chilling feeling began to grow within me. I could hear Yorke's agonized voice: 'I underestimated the power!' Could the power, whatever it was, of the force that held Clara an unwilling servant be so strong as to be able to create such conditions? A shudder of horror ran through my frame.

Lieutenant Brown, observing my shudder, attributed it to the wrong cause and clapped my shoulder reassuringly.

'Don't worry, Mister Welsford. We'll soon be out of this mess.'

His bonhomie sounded strangely false.

'Hold hard, sir!' snapped a sailor. 'I think we are nearing a ship... listen there!'

We all strained our ears.

There was a slight difference in the sounds of the sea. I was too much a landlubber to pick them out but I understand that a trained ear can make out the hollow smack of the waves against a big ship's hull, the running water from the cable lines and other queerly distinctive sounds that can only be associated with a larger vessel.

For a moment there seemed a break in the mist and the lieutenant gave a cry of exultation.

'Over there!' he pointed. 'Pull you swabs. It must be the *Psyche* for she's a large vessel squarely rigged fore and aft.' He raised his cupped hands again. 'Ahoy! *Psyche* ahoy!'

The silence was still unbroken by a reply.

'Curse them all for deaf idiots,' swore the lieutenant.

The sailors strained fiercely at their oars and brought our skiff nearer to the great silent vessel.

My apprehension of a moment before returned like a deep gnawing pain in my stomach.

'Do you smell anything, lieutenant?' I whispered anxiously.

He sniffed cautiously.

'Great guns! It smells like dead fish and decaying seaweed. Ugh! What can they have aboard?'

Abruptly, without warning, our skiff bumped into the solid black side of the ship.

One of the sailors put out a hand to steady the skiff and drew it back uttering a cry of disgust.

'Slime, sir,' he said, holding out his hand in the light of the storm lantern. 'Bloody slime! The sides of the ship can't have been swabbed down for ages.'

'Ahoy!' The lieutenant raised his voice once again, standing up in our small craft and peering towards the deck.

There was no answer.

'I don't like the look of it,' muttered one of the seaman.

The lieutenant sat down in the stern again, a worried expression on his face.

'I can't make this out, Mister Welsford. The ship seems deserted.'

The four seamen started to mutter among themselves.

'Avast!' snapped the lieutenant. 'Quit your blubbering and take the oars..'

'What are you going to do?' I queried.

'We shall row round the vessel and see if we can raise anyone; if

119

not, I propose to board her. We can then wait until the mists clear, make contact with the *Centurion* and claim prize money... remember that, you fellows,' he admonished the seamen.

Bemused I asked: 'What prize money?'

The lieutenant jerked a thumb towards the black hulk towering up beside us.

'If she's deserted then we are entitled to salvage.'

Under his guidance, the skiff was rowed alongside the vessel, which stank in a terrible fashion. There was no light on the ship at all and it soon became obvious that the ship must be a derelict. We passed round her stern but could see no name plate at all. One thing was certain, this was not the *Psyche* which we had been rowing for. But where had this strange vessel appeared from? There had been no sight of it before we set out for the *Psyche*.

As we rowed up the other side of the vessel we came to a rope ladder hanging from an open gangway.

'Make fast,' ordered the first officer.

The skiff secured alongside, the lieutenant grasped the rope ladder and started to draw himself up.

'Careful as you come,' he called over his shoulder, 'the ladder is wet and rotten.'

A sailor, who I noticed had stuck a belaying pin into his waistband, followed the officer up to the deck. I was next. The deck was shrouded in gloom and even when the sailor, Rooney, followed us with the storm lantern, it cast little light on the ship. The deck was wet and slippery beneath our feet and the whole superstructure seemed to be covered with a slime such as usually appends itself to breakwaters and suchlike which are almost permanently under water.

'Well, one thing is certain,' said the lieutenant, 'this is a derelict and by the look of her condition she must have been drifting for years.'

'But what's become of the *Psyche*?' I demanded. 'There was certainly no other vessel near us when we left for her.'

The officer shrugged.

'Devil I know, Mister Welsford. But there's not much we can do for the time being, we'll just have to wait until the mist clears or the sun comes up.'

120

'Guess we'll have to spend a hungry night, sir,' observed a broad-faced, well-muscled seaman - the one who had been wise enough to arm himself with the belaying pin.

'Right enough, Hampden,' replied the lieutenant. 'Still, now we are here, we might as well explore the vessel. We can at least find out who she is and what happened to her.'

There was a murmur of reluctant assent.

'Hampden, you take two men and search for'ard. I'll take Rooney and Mister Welsford and search the stern.'

Hampden knuckled his forehead.

'What about the lantern, sir.'

The officer swore.

'As you were. We'd best see if we can find any other means of lighting.'

In a body we moved towards the stern and entered what must have been the chart room and captain's day cabin. It was fairly dry inside and there were several storm lanterns on a shelf. Hampden seized a couple and checked them for fuel. He made a taper out of a piece of crumbling chart and lit them.

'We'll go for'ard and check things out, sir.'

The lieutenant, the seaman Rooney and myself were left to explore the papers in the cabin.

'Well, I'll be...' the lieutenant suddenly gave a whistle. 'This is the old *Ceres*, a Russian ship out of Varna. She's been missing for five years or more. The crew were saved, abandoned her during a storm off Crete... they were a bit mad, complained of peculiar happenings on board, you know what foreign sailors are like.'

His voice was tinged with all the superiority that a British Royal Navy Officer has towards a foreign seaman.

'Well, well. I'll bet we're in for a tidy penny in salvage. The crew thought the *Ceres* had foundered off Kásos. I wonder if her manifest is still...'

Just then a terrified scream echoed from the forward part of the ship.

CHAPTER SEVENTEEN

We turned with startled glances.

The lieutenant was the first to recover his composure and grabbed at a rusty sword which hung in a rack in the cabin. Then, followed by Rooney and myself, he pushed his way out onto the slippery deck.

The three seamen, led by Hampden, were slipping and falling along the deck towards us.

'Jehosephat!' swore the lieutenant. 'What on earth is going on?'

Hampden collided heavily with the officer, unable to stop himself on the slippery planking. The lieutenant grasped at the rail and managed to retain his balance, thus preventing them both from falling.

'There's something back there, sir. Hoskins saw it.'

The seaman named Hoskins turned a white fear-ridden face towards us.

'Saw it? I'll say I did. The eyes, sir, oh my Gawd, those eyes.. red, 'orrible, they was!'

The lieutenant snorted.

'For heaven's sake control yourself man! Eyes indeed! What eyes? Whose eyes?'

'The very devil himself, sir!' swore the seaman with some vehemence. 'Tiny red eyes, sir, red and small, staring unwinkingly at me sir.'

The lieutenant, much to our surprise, suddenly threw back his head and bellowed with laughter.

'Hoskins, Hoskins,' he laughed helplessly. 'Have you never seen ship's rats before this? Tiny red eyes, indeed! This ship has been adrift for five years, it's the old *Ceres*, and it must be acrawl with rats.'

Hampden turned on Hoskins with anger replacing a momentary

look of sheepishness.

'You blamed fool, Hoskins!' he snarled.

'Enough of that, Hampden,' admonished the lieutenant. 'Rats can be dangerous too, especially on a derelict. They might have been without food for a long time, so don't dismiss them too lightly.'

Hampden lapsed into silence.

'You'd better continue to search for'ard but keep a careful watch.'

The sailors returned to the forward part of the vessel while the lieutenant, Rooney and myself went back to the chart room.

I watched while the officer sorted through a pile of papers which had been scattered about: they were wet and soggy and had been partly eaten, obviously by rats in search of food.

'Nothing here of interest,' he pronounced after a while.

For my part, I was still pondering on the mystery of the fog and the *Psyche*.

'It seems strange,' I said once again, 'that we did not see this vessel before the fog closed down on us.'

Lieutenant Brown nodded.

'Strange things do happen at sea, Mister Welsford,' he said, a trifle too glibly. His smile indicated that he was probably thinking of the salvage money which would be due to him come the morning when the *Centurion* could take us in tow.

'Isn't this ship too rotten to salvage?' I wondered.

'Probably it is too rotten to refit, but salvage is salvage,' replied the officer.

We walked out onto the deck and stood peering around in the mist-shrouded gloom.

'The smell is really vile, commented Lieutenant Brown.

'Ay,' mumbled the usually silent Rooney. 'It's as if the ship has been dragged up from the bottom of the ocean after lying there for who knows how long.'

I agreed with Roony's description.

Hampden and the others rejoined us and admitted to seeing nothing of interest apart from the odd glimpse of baleful red eyes staring at them in the darkness.

'Must be thousands of the bloody little creatures below decks, sir,' observed Hoskins with a shudder.

'So long as they stay there,' replied the lieutenant lightly.

It was then that the gloomy silence around us was split with a long mournful howl. It froze us like stone statues, so unexpected was the sound. It was the mournful howl of a hound hunting its quarry.

But here? Here on an old derelict, five years adrift in the ocean?

'Christ! Look, sir, Look there!'

Hoskin's finger was raised and trembling towards the quarter-deck.

Standing on the raised deck, seeming to tower high above us, stood the grotesque black shape of a dog. But it was a dog so large that it dwarfed even an Irish wolfhound, the biggest of the species. It was gazing at us with large luminous eyes. It was something I had never seen before and a sight that I never want to see again. Even as we watched it, it threw back its muzzle and howled again... long, drawn-out... echoing like a thousand banshees in the gloomy mist.

It was the lieutenant who was the first to recover his power of movement.

He brandished the rusty sword in front of him.

'Careful, men,' he whispered softly, 'draw back for'ard, a step at a time now and slowly does it. Don't frighten the beast now.'

'Frighten it? Me frighten it?' croaked Hoskins. 'Lawd! What d'you think it's doing to me?'

'Shut up and move back there!'

We started to edge back along the deck. Our three lamps were held high. We had not gone back many paces when the huge brute suddenly leapt from the quarter deck and landed on the main deck not ten yards from our group. I registered unconscious surprise at the agility of the great beast which must have sprung a distance of twenty feet, landing in the thick slimy wetness of the deck without one slip or falter in its step.

With the lanterns held high, the light from them spilled across the ghastly vision as it glared malevolently at us from those vicious red eyes. It was a hound. No! It was more a grotesque parody of such an animal, large as a lion and as black as jet. Its eyes gleamed with an unholy aura like glowing red coals. Its great white fangs were bared and its muzzle and dewlap were dripping with saliva and tinged with blood.

We had barely gone back a dozen more paces when the creature began to gather up his hind legs beneath the sleek black body and I knew that the beast was about to spring.

In desperation my hands clenched in my pockets.

My hand closed on the tiny silver crucifix which had reposed in my coat pocket since that frightful evening when I found it after Clara had left me. Dimly I seemed to hear Yorke's rasping breath: '... remember to protect yourself with the symbols of goodness and light.'

With a terrifying howl, the great beast sprang forward.

Two things happened. Rooney suddenly hurled his lantern full at the creature at precisely the same moment as I flung the tiny crucifix into its gigantic maw.

I know not which was the cause of what followed, nor do I precisely know exactly what happened.

There was a terrific flash of blinding light and even as I averted my eyes the great beast seemed to dissolve into thin air. Yes, one moment it was there and the next it had vanished. And a strange thing seemed to happen - even now I am not sure whether it was a strange trick of the gloomy light - the great black shadow of the hound seemed to dissolve in flames, dissolve and then twist itself into a tiny winged creature - the shape of a small black bat - and flit upwards into the blackness, uttering strange human-like cries, as if of rage.

At that instant the derelict gave a lurch and a strange creaking seemed to echo from all sides.

The lieutenant gave a warning cry.

'My God! She's breaking up! Back to the skiff!'

The sailors needed no second urging for, above the creaking of the spars and deck planking, and the strange lurching of the doomed vessel, we could hear the high pitched and terrified squeals of hundreds of thousands of rats. And even as I hesitated in following the seamen towards the gangway, below which the skiff was fastened, the rats started to erupt onto the slime-covered deck. I paused appalled by the sight of the countless black creatures with their red darting eyes, spilling through doors, portholes, hold covers, even through gaps in the planking itself.

'For God's sake, Mister Welsford,' screamed a seaman.

But I stood rooted in horror.

Someone - I think it was Hampden - grabbed me by the collar and bodily heaved me over the side into the skiff. Rooney was already untying it and, as soon as Hampden flung himself aboard, the rest of the men were working the oars and sending the craft shooting away from the doomed derelict; away from the frightful noise of the squealing of the drowning rats which rang in our ears so loudly that I thought my very brain was on fire.

Even so, so desperate were some of those terrible creatures that many of them leapt from the deck and several even fell into the skiff.

Disgust governing all reason, the lieutenant and I seized belaying pins and laid about us with a will, smashing viciously at the animals before they could recover from the impact of landing.

It seemed that the entire ocean heaved and boiled around us as countless rats leapt into the water and swam for their lives, seizing upon any floatable objects they could find, fighting each other for the possession of the smallest oar or plank of wood.

There was a great gurgling sound and the sea seemed to open up and swallow the dark shape that had once been the *Ceres*.

We rowed into quieter water and, examining the waters around us and observing no wreckage nor any sign of the rats, the sailors rested on their oars while the lieutenant and I bowed our heads in a silent prayer of thankfulness.

'Look, sir!'

It was Hoskins.

We looked up.

As if by some miracle the green mist had completely evaporated. The white moon shone with a pale brilliance down out of a rich blue Mediterranean night sky which was littered with a myriad of white pin pricks where stars shone. The sea was perfectly calm and clear and a mile away we could make out the lights of a ship and even its dark silhouette against the lighter blue-black of the night.

Of the wreck of the *Ceres* there was no sign at all.

The lieutenant wiped his mouth with the back of his hand. I could see a faint tremble in it and saw the sweat standing out on his brow.

We had all been through a lot that night.

'Stand out for that ship,' ordered the lieutenant. 'Put your backs into it now.'

126

The sea was peaceful and the skiff made rapid progress across the intervening distance.

As we approached, Hampden swore.

'Bless me, sir, ain't that the old *Centurion*?'

Hardly had he spoken when a voice hailed us.

'Skiff ahoy!'

We could make out some of the crew hanging over the rails. It was the *Centurion* right enough. Willing hands pulled us aboard. The lieutenant made his report but his precise naval manner conveyed none of the terrors of that strange ship.

We were soon taken below for a hot toddy.

Molesworth was there, clapping me on the back and smiling.

'Thought we'd lost you, dear fellow,' he murmured.

The captain looked thoughtful: 'Damned strange thing,' he remarked. 'There was the *Psyche* and ourselves in sight when that beastly mist came down. Then, when it lifted, there was no sign of anything. Thought you'd vanished or at least made it aboard the *Psyche*. Then you suddenly appear out of the night, so to speak. Damned strange.'

There seemed no answer.

'Well, we'd best get under way...' the captain turned reluctantly out of the cabin. 'Don't forget to write a report for the log entry, mister,' he told the lieutenant who, like me, was tucking into a hot stew in some effort, I should imagine, to re-identify with reality.

The captain paused at the cabin door and looked back at us with a worried expression.

'Damned strange,' was his parting remark.

CHAPTER EIGHTEEN

The rest of the passage passed uneventfully. I had a lot of time in which to examine the strange affair from the very beginning. I had now come to terms with what I was doing. I was facing some terrifying occult power which was so colossal that it could control mists and mirages. I was now firmly convinced that it was the throwing of Clara's crucifix into the maw of the hell-hound which had destroyed it. Rooney swore that the lantern he had thrown had smashed against the beast, soaking it in petrol and incinerating it. And the lieutenant had rationalised that the hound was nothing more than a ship's dog, left behind when the crew of the *Ceres* abandoned ship. The beast had then grown wild and primitive in its instincts during the five years of drifting, probably prolonging its existence by eating the rats that populated the ship.

It seemed that only I had seen the swiftly-flitting shape of the bat spring from the flames and flap its way into the gloom of the night.

I shuddered. If I had rationalised this way a few weeks ago I would have had myself committed to some asylum. I fingered the remaining silver crucifix which never left my throat and pondered a long time on what Yorke had told me. The evil power which had ensnared my beloved Clara had to be tracked down and destroyed. But how? And was I strong enough to accomplish the task?

The captain, ironically enough, apologised to me for missing the *Psyche* in the mist. He seemed a trifle puzzled as to how he had come to miss the ship and I did not venture any explanations.

It was his guess that the *Psyche* was now way behind us and that it would be ruinous to the success of the British delegation's mission should we attempt to circle back to try to sight her. I was inclined to agree. If the *Psyche* was, indeed, a slow ship, then the sooner we made for Constanta the sooner I could arrange to have the ship met at Varna. In this the captain was quite helpful and - after the proposition had been placed before Molesworth and met with his approval - it was suggested that I should be put ashore at Varna which is, in fact, a little south of Constanta and therefore would be passed by the *Centurion* on its way to the Romanian port. Molesworth agreed, stressing that I must press on from Varna as soon as the *Psyche* docked and join the delegation in Bucharest at the earliest opportunity.

The journey was now given up to relaxing and trying to revitalise my anxiety-torn mind and body. From Cape Matapan, the most southerly point of the Morea Peninsula in Greece, the voyage was somewhat idyllic and I began to relax a little. I found time to speculate that I could appreciate how Odysseus must have felt on his return to Ithaca after his voyages in the balmy Aegean seas. No wonder he stayed away so long in such waters, dreamy, blue and restful. I had always suspected that Penelope must have been a rather boring person; any woman who waits twenty years in chastity for a man who might never return, all the while sewing some ridiculous tapestry to keep prospective lovers at bay, must have little love of life. Perhaps Odysseus was in no hurry to return?

Through the Aegean, which the sailors called the Archipelago, we crossed into a small channel named the Dardanelles which cuts through the Turkish territory into the Sea of Marmara. Some Turkish naval craft stopped and boarded us in spite of the Union flag at the jackstaff and the ensigns of the Royal Navy fluttering from our mastheads. We were not held up long and soon entered the hot Marmaric sea. Here we were somewhat slowed by lack of wind and twice the captain, in order to make time, had the ship's boats hoisted out and the sloop towed for a few miles before the wind came up again.

At the eastern end of the Marmaric sea we could see the great city which the Turks now call Istanbul. It had once been Constantino-polis, capital of the Byzantine Empire and chief city of the Greco-Roman world. In other circumstances I would have given anything to have been allowed to wander ashore, to walk through its fascinating streets, see its fantastic mosques, its colourful Orthodox churches and its other historical monuments.

Soon we found ourselves once more in a tempestuous sea - the great Black Sea across which so many of our brave lads recently travelled to their deaths in the Crimean Peninsula. Once into its choppy waters we turned northwards across this huge inland sea and stood out for Varna. Two weeks and five days after leaving Tilbury in London, I stood by the rail of the *Centurion* looking on the exotic eastern seaport.

I was rowed ashore at Varna and stood at the quayside of this strangely Mediterranean-looking seaport, watching the skiff speed back to the *Centurion* which was already hoisting its sail for Constanta. My arrival did not seem to excite much curiosity, for the port was apparently a busy one. Standing off its harbour waters I could make out a menacing squadron of Russian warships, sleek and deadly, for these ships of Tsar Alexander dominated all the Black Sea trading routes. There were merchantmen of all types in the port, loading and unloading. Large, cumbersome vessels from the Ukrainian seaport of Odessa, trading cargoes of iron ore from Krivoi Rog; there were sleek and exotic looking vessels from Georgia, weather-beaten ships from the Crimea, oddly alien looking vessels from the north Turkish coast and many others. The quayside was filled with all manner of men in many varied costumes and the variety of languages would have done justice to a visualisation of the Tower of Babel.

I became aware of a small, sallow-skinned man with a long drooping black moustache. He stood before me waving some sort of a ledger and speaking with a raised voice. He was flamboyantly dressed, wore a fez, a red brimless conical cap of wool from which a black tassel leapt in time to the jerking of his head. Over a white shirt hung an embroidered waistcoat and once-white pantaloons were tucked into black shiny boots. A long, curved sword hung at his waist. Incongruously, he wore a small pair of rimless spectacles perched on the end of a large, bulbous nose. The whole effect was comical but I am glad that I had the sense not to laugh.

Behind him stood two bored-looking men in a sombre type of uniform which pronounced them to be soldiers of some description.

The man, or so I presumed, was some official... perhaps the customs officer of the port. I asked him if he spoke any English at which, to my amazement, he spat on the ground and set off in a tirade of what I judged to be Turkish. I then addressed him in French and, when this failed, I spoke in German. By this time he had gone red in the face and the two soldiers were grinning at his anger.

I was wondering whether I was going to be hauled off to some police station when a ship's officer came across and addressed me in German.

'You are English?'

I admitted that I was.

'Permit me, Graff Von Hubeck, kapitan-leutnant of the *Otto Klaus* of Bremen,' he waved his hand towards one of the vessels in the harbour. 'I understand you have trouble in interpretation, is it not so? I will interpret.'

He was a clean-shaven, red faced man of thirty-five, or so I guessed, meticulously dressed and obviously used to giving orders.

He snapped a series of sharp questions at the Turkish official who seemed to deflate before him. The Turk's replies were offered in an apologetic manner.

'This man,' said Von Hubeck, nodding towards the Turk, 'is the customs officer of the port. All foreign travellers entering here must show their passports.'

I smiled.

'Ah, I guessed as much but could not seem to find a common language as a means of communication.'

'Ach,' grunted Von Hubeck, 'usually in these parts you can get by with German. From ancient times Saxon merchants and traders have travelled and settled extensively in the area. You won't have much trouble once you travel among the ordinary people, the Bulgars or the Wallachians, or go north into Transylvania. The Turks are the exceptions - they never seem to learn any language but their own. Your German is excellent,' he added as an afterthought.

I bowed.

I suddenly noticed the Turkish official waiting somewhat impatiently and I drew out my passport.

'Will you tell him that I am travelling on a British diplomatic passport... that I am one of an official British delegation enroute for Bucharest? I am in Varna for only a few days, waiting to meet someone from a British ship, the *Psyche* out of Liverpool, which should be calling in here shortly.'

The German Count, for such is the meaning of the title Graf, repeated this in his excellent Turkish.

The Turkish official grunted, examined my passport, drew some sort of rubber stamping device from his pocket, spat on it, and pressed it firmly on the visa section. He handed it back to me and said something in Turkish.

'He says,' interpreted the German, 'that the Government of the Emir Abdul Mejid welcomes the representative of the British Government to Varna and trusts your stay will be fruitful.'

I bowed towards the Turk, who elaborately, returned it.

'He also says that if you require any assistance, he will be honoured to receive you at the harbour entrance where his office is situated.'

The Turk and his bodyguard hurried away and I was left to thank the German for his aid. He saluted and extended an invitation for me to take wine aboard his ship at any time I felt like paying him a visit.

Taking my single bag, which I had brought ashore with me, I made my way through the busy harbour environs into the town, up the sunbaked streets in search of a hotel. I decided that I had two priorities; firstly, to find myself a room and secondly, to find myself somebody who would act in the function of guide, interpreter and servant.

The problem of a hotel was almost immediately solved. Walking up a wide thoroughfare, I came across a building on which large lettering proclaimed it to be a hotel. Attached to this sign was an intriguing postscript: 'Inglez speaken' which I interpreted as being 'English spoken'. Indeed, as I found out on entering and making my wants known 'Inglez' was certainly 'speaken'.

A fat little man, bald but with a full black beard and a permanent smile distorting his formidable features, bustled about me.

'Inglez? I spoke fine no? You a Jollee Jik?'

I frowned and then enlightenment dawned.

'Oh, you mean a Jolly Jack Tar - a sailor? No, I'm merely a traveller.'

He led me to a plain room which had a commanding view of the harbour.

'You stay in Varna... wait for ship?'

His pronunciation was actually '*Yo wet fi sheep?*' but, after a while, I grew accustomed to the meaning of his strange diction.

'I wait to meet someone from a ship,' I replied. 'Then I go on to Bucharest.'

'Bucharesti, no?' he nodded enthusiastically. 'Is good. New capital. Brother lives there.'

I finally escaped a long lecture on his brother's noble character and the fact that his brother owned a grand café in Bucharest. My problem now was to find an interpreter and then wait patiently for the arrival of the *Psyche*. I was in Varna for two days without discovering a suitable person.

After a light luncheon on the second day I decided to explore a part of the town I had never been to before: a dingy little district which fronted onto the wharves and was clearly the slum area. I had traversed several streets when I realised I had made a mistake: it was not the sort of area for a well-dressed foreigner. I started to walk quickly along a side street, hoping to break out into a main thoroughfare when I found my way blocked by three vicious - looking brutes, one of whom held a cudgel in front of him and muttered in a menacing way.

I turned rapidly back the way I had come but another man appeared at the other end of the street and started to walk slowly towards me.

I halted and decided to try to bluff it out. I ordered them to desist in every language I knew, none of which was Turkish or Bulgar, the local languages. Suddenly I heard a street door open and, idiotically, I cried aloud for help in English.

A young man of perhaps twenty-two years was coming out of a house further up the street. He paused and turned at my voice and then, seeing what my situation was, his hand suddenly slipped into the pocket of the coat he was wearing and came up with a small pistol. He walked swiftly along the street, levelling it at my would-be assailants and called to them in a loud, commanding voice.

All four paused, open-mouthed, and then turned tail and ran off.

I mopped my brow and, feeling a litle weak about the knees, turned to thank my rescuer.

He was a pleasant-faced man, with the high Slavic cheekbones, twinkling greeny-blue eyes and a mop of touselled black hair.

'That's okay, sir,' he silenced my stumbling thanks with a soft Transatlantic drawl. 'You should never be out in these parts without a pistol handy, though.'

He thrust his weapon back into his coat pocket.

'I guess you could do with a shot of liquor.'

He pointed back down the street.

'I have a room there and, if the animals haven't raided it already, I guess I still have the best part of a quart of malt liquor there.'

I followed him into a decidedly derelict looking building.

'You're an American?' I asked.

To my surprise he shook his head violently.

'No sir, don't let my English fool you none. I'm a Romanian from Buzau.'

He pushed open a rotting wooden door and led the way up a rickety stairway to a room that was appalling in its dankness and squalor.

He ushered me in and then dropped to his knees by the bed. After a moment's frantic search he finally pulled out a bottle of amber-coloured liquid and gave a sigh of satisfaction. He poured two generous glasses and handed me one.

'Scotch!' I exclaimed, tasting it.

'No sir!' he ejaculated. 'That there is pure American.'

'Whisky, anyway,' I smiled.

'Mebbe, mebbe. But there are whiskies and whiskies.'

'How does it happen that you are a Romanian from Buzau and yet speak like an American?' I asked.

'Both my parents were killed in the insurrection in 1848. My uncle decided to go to the States and take me with him. I was nine years old at the time and so I've gotten most of my education in Richmond, Virginia. Two years back, when there was this talk about finally setting up a Romanian state, I decided to come back to my homeland. I still consider myself to be a Romanian, still talk the language as well as a smattering of Turkish, Bulgar and German. Another shot?'

Without waiting for an answer he refilled my glass.

'So I came back. My uncle, he stayed on. Said at least he had peace and security in America. Then he goes and gets himself killed last July fighting under Colonel Pergam at Rich Mountain down in West Virginia, trying to defend his new homeland. Ironic, aint it?'

He sighed.

I was looking round his squalid room and he noticed my gaze.

'Yeah, you might say I've fallen on hard times,' he said as I flushed with embarrassment. 'Fact is, I *have* fallen on hard times. I've been working up at Bucharest as an interpreter and odd job man for the past two years. Then I undertook to take a party from Bucharest down here and see them safely on a ship. So here I am. Been here ever since, trying to pick up something.'

It was too good an opportunity to miss, even though I acted on the spur of the moment.

'You've worked as an interpreter?'

He nodded.

'You know the country between here and Bucharest?'

'Sure I do. Why?'

'How would you like to work for me? I need an interpreter, a sort of guide, translater and odd job man. How about it?'

He grinned.

'Now that depends on what you're paying.'

'Can you afford to be that fussy?' I asked, unused to financial frankness.

'I can always afford to be *that* fussy,' he smiled.

It demonstrated something of his character and I took a sudden liking to the man. Soon a bargain was agreed and I learnt that his name was Avram Murgu. I told him a sketchy version of my story confining myself, more or less, to what I had told Lord Molesworth - that I had to meet my fiancée off the *Psyche*. We agreed that he should come and take a room, at my expense, in the hotel where I was staying and, the following day, start to earn his keep by making enquiries for a coach and horses to transport us northward to Bucharest.

It was the morning of the third day after our meeting when my general factotum, for I know not how else to call him, shook me awake.

'Up you get, Upton,' there was no distinction of man and master, or creed, class or nationality in Avram's upbringing. 'Up you get. It's the *Psyche*. She put into harbour during the night.'

That brought me leaping from my bed and hastily throwing on my clothes. I did not even pause to breakfast but rushed down to the harbour with Avram trailing in my wake.

The *Psyche* was easy to find, tied up alongside the quay.

I went up the gangplank and was met by a surly-faced man at the rail.

.I wish to see Miss Clara Clarke,' I announced.

To my surprise, the man almost winced.

'That 'un! Bad cess to 'er!'

I felt the hot blood course through my cheeks as he turned and spat over the side of the ship.

'Mind your manners, fellow,' I admonished.

The man glowered at me.

'I 'appen ter be the master o' this 'ere ship, matey. Captain Raikes. An' I tell ye, bad cess to that woman, if woman she be. Two men dead, the rest o' the crew a feared o' their own shadders. Two spars lost. Stranded in a weird fog. Me cargo 'alf eaten by rats. Never 'ad a worse trip and why? Never take a lone female on board ship... it aint natural. We've 'ad the luck o' the very devil. All hell's to pay on this trip.'

My fears were mounting at his recital.

'Where is Miss Clarke?' I demanded, a catch in my throat. 'Is she safe?'

The man laughed, a snarl of a laugh.

'Safe? I guess she is. Thanks to my stupidity. I should 'ave throwed her overboard in Biscay. 'Stead of that I stand to lose me boat.'

'Where is she then?' I persisted.

'Gone.'

He drew out a plug of vile looking tobacco and bit off a chew.

'Gone?' I repeated stupidly as if not understanding.

'Ay, can't 'ee talk plain English, mister? Gone, I say, and curse her too.'

I fought to control my rising temper.

'Gone where?'

'Who cares?' snarled the surly master.

I reached forward and grabbed him by the collar.

He gave a yelp which ended in a fit of coughing as he swallowed

136

his chewing tobacco.

'If you value your life,' I hissed at him, 'as well as you value your ship, you'll tell me where she's gone.'

'I don't know mister, and that's God's truth. 'Swelp me! We docked afore midnight and not long after a carriage arrives on the quayside. Next thing I know she - Miss Clarke - is climbing into it with never a please nor thank you, captain, for the voyage. Lucky she paid her passage money in advance, though small good that will do me.'

I let him wriggle free from my nerveless hands.

'Gone,' I whispered incredulously.

Avram, who had been watching my exchange with bewilderment, caught me by the arm.

'Perhaps we can find out where she went from the harbour master?' he suggested.

In a daze, I followed Avram to a building where the same Turkish official, who had greeted me on my arrival, stood - the epitome of politeness itself.

No, he replied to Avram's question, he had not been on duty the previous night. A Bulgar had been in charge and, by coincidence, the man arrived at that precise moment. He was a stocky, pleasant-faced man. I was surprised to see that his face paled at Avram's questions. Yes, he had seen a coach. It was about one o'clock, or near enough. A black coach and four had entered the harbour and gone straight across the quayside where the *Psyche* from England had just tied up. Intrigued by the late arrival, he had watched and seen a young lady come from the ship and climb aboard. Yes, she did carry some luggage. The coach then left and, against all regulations, had refused to stop to let the lady's passport be checked and registered. He had written his report in his record book. What direction had the coach taken? Why, it had turned along the road which led to the main Bucharest highway. Could the English gentleman hazard any guess as to why the young lady had refused to stop in compliance with passport regulations?

Avram said something which appeased the officials, I am not sure what, and led me white and trembling back to the hotel where he forced me to eat a hot breakfast.

'Seems as if you have a mystery on your hands, Upton,' he

drawled. 'Guess the lady thinks she is meeting you in Bucharest. What do you say?'

I tried to pull myself together.

For a moment I wondered whether I should confide the whole of my story to him but then I realised how ridiculous such a tale would seem, told in the pure light of day to someone as earthy and stolid as Avram. Even as I thought about it Clara's beautiful face flitted before my eyes and I could hear Yorke's dying breath as he urged me to rescue her and destroy the dragon god.

I forced myself to smile.

'That must be it, Avram,' I said. 'She has gone to Bucharest, thinking to meet me there. Perhaps, if we set off immediately, we could overtake her? Can you cancel the arrangements for a coach and get two good horses here within the half hour?'

I pretended not to see the look of deep suspicion which Avram gave me as he left the room to attend to our needs.

CHAPTER NINETEEN

By midday Avram and I were cantering our horses at an easy pace along the highway which led to Bucharest. The day was fine and the way fairly easy, the road for the first leg of the journey followed the course of a large river from Varna. Several times along the route Avram stopped and made enquiries concerning the passage of the black coach. More often than not his enquiries were met with sullen looks and the shaking of heads. One old woman gave a cry and made the sign of the cross before slamming her door in our faces. But several times we encountered peasants who were courteous and helpful, assuring us that a black coach and four had passed on the road not more than twelve hours before.

We spent the first night in a sleepy hamlet called Sumla and the next morning turned north for Bucharest. We were annoyed to learn that the coach had halted at a village called Isiklar for the day. Instead of stopping the night at Sumla, had we ridden for another six hours we would have overtaken the coach because it did not set out from Isiklar until midnight.

'It seems odd,' commented Avram suddenly, 'that this coachman prefers to travel by night and rest by day.'

I nodded without speaking. It was some moments before the fact suddenly struck me with some significance. Was there a limitation to this strange power which, Yorke said, was based in Transylvania? Could it be that the power, whatever it was, was weakened by day and could only exercise its strength at night? Surely a telepathic power as incredible and as strong as I had witnessed it to be, would not suffer such limitations. But the coach was laying up by day and travelling at night. And, thinking more closely on the subject, all the manifestations which I had witnessed had occurred *after* sunset.

'Tonight, Avram,' I announced, 'we'll continue to ride until we overtake the coach.'

Avram gave me a puzzled stare.

'You seem certain that what the coachman did last night he will do again tonight?'

There was a question in his statement.

'I think he will,' I replied, refusing to say more in spite of the penetrating look the American-Romanian gave me.

Along the route, through the town of Ruscuk which we reached during the late afternoon, we continued to ask about the coach. From this point onwards the peasants did not seem as forthcoming as before. Many doors were slammed to our enquiries and many men and women crossed themselves, some holding out two fingers towards us which Avram afterwards told me was a sign of protection against the evil eye.

Avram grew more unhappy and puzzled by these reactions and finally he pulled his horse up and looked me firmly in the eye.

'Upton, you must tell me, who is it or *what* is it we are following?'

'Don't be ridiculous, Avram,' I snapped. 'I have told you - we are following my fiancée, Miss Clarke.'

For the rest of the day we rode in silence and when evening came, sending its chill black fingers entwining around the landscape, we stopped for a meal at a small wayside inn. Then, by mutual consent, we rode onward. All through that silent, freezing night we rode, through the long dark hours until the early hours of the morning. Our horses were blowing and clearly reaching the end of their endurance.

Avram cast a worried look at me.

'We cannot continue far in this manner, Upton,' he chided gently.

I admit I was uncaring for the needs of the poor beasts. My one thought was for Clara. In this manner we might overtake her and destroy whatever it was that held her ensnared in its power.

'We must push on,' I said stubbornly, 'at dawn the coach is bound to halt and we will be able to overtake them.'

'But the horses...' insisted Avram. 'It is no use killing the animals under us!'

I was about to damn the horses when we came to a rise. The road suddenly plunged downhill into a valley, twisting and turning around the contours of the hill. It was as we breasted this rise that the full moon shot out from behind a cloud bank and the valley

140

glinted white in its rays. It was almost as clear as a dull, cloudy day.

Involuntarily, a cry was wrested from my lips.

In the distance I could see a black coach drawn by four black horses thundering along the road ahead. The tall figure of the coachman could be clearly discerned, a black cloak billowing around him, flapping like great wings. In one hand he held a whip and I could hear its crack, crack, crack in the night air as he flayed his beasts unmercifully.

'It is them!' I cried to Avram and, without waiting for a reply, I kicked my horse forward down the hill.

Then it was that I made a mistake.

In my triumphant jubilation I gave vent to the childish cry of the hunter who sights the poor fox.

For an instance I saw the coachman turn his head, caught a glimpse of a deathly pale face turned to mine, and then heard the renewed cracking of the whip. For a while we rode grimly on, although I could feel the beast beneath me growing weaker and weaker. I knew that if I did not stop soon the heart of that stout animal would surely burst...but Clara was only a few hundred yards away and surely one can sympathise with my desperate efforts to reach her?

We were passing through a small copse which straddled the roadway. I was aware of a large river to my left, the Arges as I subsequently learnt. The moon had passed back behind the low-hanging, black storm clouds. A rather fierce drizzle started to patter down which I could hear even above the thunder of hooves and the gasping of my horse.

Then, causing all the other sounds to die away, came the long drawn out howl of a dog - hound or wolf, I know not.

My horse suddenly shied, whinnied and reared, pawing frantically at the air. I lost my grip and slid backwards from the saddle. The impact of my hitting the ground stunned me but did not hurt me. Avram had ridden up and dismounted, trying to quieten the horses, both of which were shying and pulling away. He managed to get them fastened to the branch of a tree, to which he tied them in such a fashion that they could not rear, but they continued to buck and kick out with their hind legs in a clear state of terror.

'Are you alright, Upton?' he asked as I struggled to my feet swearing, more at the shock than at the injury.

'Confound that dog!' I snarled. 'Just when we were so near...'

The coach had already disappeared.

Avram said nothing but stood peering about him.

'The horses are too exhausted to continue,' he pointed out. 'You'll kill them if you go on.'

Reluctantly, I nodded.

We stood under the shelter of a large tree, away from the rain.

Avram had bent down and scooped up a handful of some peculiar white flowers which I had not seen before. I wondered what he was doing and was perturbed to see his face was pinched with anxiety.

'Wolfbane,' he whispered.

'What's that?' I asked. 'I have not heard of it.'

'Even he who is pure of heart
And says his prayers at night
May become a wolf when the wolfbane blooms
And the moon is full and bright.'

The ancient rhyme, which Avram recited in a hollow voice, sent a chill through my body.

'Nonsense, Avram,' I scoffed, purely to keep up my own courage for I could believe anything now. 'You don't believe in that sort of thing, do you?'

'Upton,' he said slowly, 'this land is very ancient, here all the beliefs and instincts of primeval man still survive...'

'Well I am a modern Nineteenth Century sophisticated man, so the writ of primeval man does not run with me,' I said, turning towards the horses.

Another long, low howl riveted me to the spot.

A flash of lightning coincided with the ending of the howl and there, standing glowering in the rain on the far side of the clearing, stood the same massive brute that I had seen aboard the ill-fated *Ceres*.

I heard two shots in quick succession. Avram had drawn his revolver and fired at the beast.

The animal did not even flinch. I could see its ghastly luminous eyes fixed upon me.

It moved forward slowly.

142

Avram fired again. He might just as well have thrown flowers at the beast for all the good it did. The bullets seemed to pass right through the creature.

I knew that I was lost. Like Yorke, I had underestimated the strength of the power that I was contesting. Like a fool, I did not even know what that power was.

The eyes of the creature caught and held mine. They seemed almost human, assuming a glare of malevolent satisfaction, of triumph. I could hear the rasping of its fetid breath, see the bloody saliva dripping from its dewlap, see its hackles rise, see its yellowing teeth, sharply pointed, see the ears flatten on its skull and the muscles ripple in its back as it gathered itself for the leap.

I was lost. I had no will of my own. I was a sacrifice. There was nothing to struggle for.

I was aware of Avram yelling something.

Then the beast sprang. Automatically my hands went up in a futile gesture of defence, my eyes closed and I tensed my body for the impact of those tearing jaws.

It never came.

Avram stood before me, in one hand a large crucifix of the Orthodox persuasion and in the other hand an empty phial.

Of the beast there was no sign.

'What...what happened?' I gasped, collapsing against a tree.

'What happened, my friend?' said Avram in a voice which was curiously calm. 'What happened is that you are lucky to have met me and employed me for your guide.'

I looked at him to gauge the deeper meaning behind his words.

'What do you mean?'

'I think we had best begin by getting out of these woods and finding a dry place. Then you had better tell me the real reason why you are in this country and whose carriage we follow.'

I followed him meekly to the horses.

'Tell me one thing, Avram,' I said. 'What was in that phial you flung at that beast?'

'Garlic salt, that is all,' he returned curtly.

The horses were quiet now, standing trembling and blowing, with steam rising from their glossy coats.

'We will have to walk them awhile,' said Avram. 'It will not be

143

far...there is a little inn not far away. I know this part of the road. Bucharest is within an easy ride if we can get fresh horses.'

We walked along the road without speaking. It was three miles before we came to the tiny inn and knocked resolutely at its door.

I could not help but notice that affixed to the inn door was a large iron crucifix and I wondered why a mass of some strange flowers, whose perfume reeked of garlic, were placed in profusion around the windows. Avram confirmed later that these were, in fact, garlic flowers.

A window above us was opened and a harsh voice echoed down to us. Avram answered in the same language. He later told me that the voice had demanded to know who we were and what we wanted. On Avram's reply, the voice then demanded if we acknowledged Jesus Christ as Lord and Saviour. Only on Avram's assurance that we were Christians was the window shut and, after a few moments, a frightened and elderly innkeeper ushered us inside his warm parlour. Soon a fire was roaring in the hearth and a meal and wine were brought to refresh our needs. The man then went to bed down our horses for the night, regretting that he was unable to supply us with new mounts. We would have to wait until morning before we could continue our journey.

It was while the innkeeper was thus engaged that Avram looked at me and said, simply: 'Well, Upton?'

Suddenly I felt the urge to tell him the whole story, to unburden this ghastly nightmare which seemed to have begun oh, so long ago, long ago in that junk shop in London.

Avram sat and listened to me gravely, throughout the whole of my narrative which I recounted up to the time I had fallen in with him in Varna.

Having finished I sat back and eyed him apprehensively.

'Go on,' I prompted, as he sat silently. 'Go on, tell me that I am a madman and should seek the advice of a doctor.'

He smiled gently and shook his head.

'No, my friend. That is not my intention. I believe you.'

I looked at him in surprise.

'You do? And you a hard headed American?'

He snorted with mock indignation.

'Haven't I told you that I am Romanian?' Then, without waiting for further comment, his face and voice grew serious. 'It is the Romanian who now talks to you, friend Upton, and more than a mere Romanian. When I was sixteen I went to New York where the Romanian emigrant priests and monks have a seminary which teaches the Orthodox religion of this country to the emigrant community. I studied for the priesthood there. Does that surprise you? Oh, I admit that the priesthood was not for me. I left without taking my final vows. But the seminary gave me an education and taught me to believe many things that are unbelievable to the finite mind...'

He paused, as if trying to find simple words to explain a complex concept.

'As a Romanian I tell you that this is a country of shadows, where blood is cheap and flows like water and where the mountains and the valleys and the great plains have been drenched in the blood of many nations and many cultures. This, my friend, is the crossroads of the world. Through the Carpathians came many conquering peoples ... Celts, Huns, Goths, Mongols, Vandals.... every nation that ever rose in Europe came out of these mountains of ours. They came from many quarters of the world to this crossroads of civilisation.

'They came, intermixed their blood and learning with the blood of those they found here, and then pressed on to their destiny... the Celtic tribes who were destined to spread Christian civilisation across Europe when civilisation was dying under the yoke of the Germanic conquerors, the Angles, Saxons, Vikings and others who rose to create new empires. If you like, the genesis of Europe was in the Carpathians.

'And although they passed on, always passed on, it is here that were left behind the beliefs and the superstitions of mankind's pre-history. Here you will find beliefs in religions that were centuries dead before Christ, before Buddha found enlightenment and before Mohammed came into the world as the Prophet of Allah. And who knows how powerful are those creeds of primitive man... and who are we to call them primitive?

'What we know is that there are some beliefs which are morally right and some beliefs which are morally wrong. There is always the struggle of good over evil. The Roman creed of Mythras, god of

145

lightness banishing darkness and evil, was a righteous creed compared with the sacrificial beliefs of Jupiter. Whatever the belief, if it is morally good and beneficial to man and to human progress, then it represents the force of light as opposed to those creeds which keep mankind in subservient ignorance and fear. No one religion has a monopoly of good.'

'But what of this power which has ensnared Clara?' I demanded, interrupting his philosophising.

Avram shook his head.

'I don't know the cause of it, my friend, but I share with you the belief that it is evil and deadly and must therefore be destroyed. We, you and I together, will join forces and I will supplement your strength of purpose with the knowledge I gained as a postulant in the priesthood.'

He reached his hand across the table and gripped mine in a firm, warm grasp.

We called for another bottle of wine and silently toasted our venture...the rescue of Clara and the destruction of the evil power which had her in its thrall.

We had, however, made a bad start to the new venture by losing the coach.

Our exhausted horses enforced our delay at the inn until late the following morning. But I was sure, and Avram grudgingly agreed with me, that the coach seemed to travel only by night. Therefore it was fairly certain that it had not gone far between the time we saw it on the moonlit road and the approach of dawn. Avram seemed certain that the coachman would have been able to make for the shelter of Bucharest itself and, as the new Romanian capital lay so short a distance away, we decided to ride there by lunch time that morning.

We trotted our mounts carefully on the journey for, although they had had several hours rest, the beasts were still fairly weary. But the journey to Bucharest did not take us long and we soon passed over the River Danube, a great river which the natives call Dunarea, and it was not long after that when we found ourselves in the city.

It was a strangely built city to my English eyes; from its architecture one could almost identify the different conquering nations which had passed through its blood-splattered thoroughfares. Here was a mosque, with sullen-faced Turks grouped at its door. Once conquerors, now they were merely immigrants in the new land. There was a simple Catholic church while a street away was a magnificent gold roofed edifice whose flamboyant columns declared it to be of the Orthodox persuasion. Civil buildings, hotels, fountains, markets, all seemed to be as if Rome itself had suddenly been given rebirth in the middle of Istanbul or Damascus.

The city was athrong with soldiers, all armed and imposing as they paraded through the streets and squares. The streets were consistently crowded by carriages and men and women on horseback. Everywhere I saw signs of foreigners - Prussian officers, Turks, Frenchmen, Italians, Russians all attending the birth of the new European nation. At any other time the air of excitement would have seized my imagination for this was history in the making.

The people, for the most part, were good natured and cheerful. Here and there small huddles of them were to be found around the latest news bulletins or proclamations.

The Hotel Concordia was by far the largest edifice in the central part of the city and this was where most of the foreign delegations were staying, including our British delegation. Avram and I made our way there through the excited throng and left our horses at the hotel's stables.

'I'll register at the hotel, Avram,' I said, 'while you start making enquiries to see if the coach has arrived in Bucharest.'

'Hopefully the task won't be difficult,' he said. 'I'll be as quick as I can.'

I watched him hurry away into the crowds and then turned into the magnificent marble portals of the hotel.

CHAPTER TWENTY

As I was being conducted to my room in the hotel the first person I encountered, and whom I had no wish to meet at that time, was Viscount Molesworth. He welcomed me with a hearty bonhomie.

'Welsford! Thought you'd disappeared off the face of the earth. You've missed several important ceremonies, you know. Can't be helped...but where is the lady in question, you young dog? Hiding her somewhere, eh?'

I wondered how I should react to this and, in my embarassment, I asked Molesworth to join me in my room for a drink. There, in order to stop his persistent questions, I told him that somehow I had missed Clara at Varna and learnt that she had come on to Bucharest.

Molesworth snorted.

'Good God! Odd behaviour... what? She hasn't arrived at the Concordia and everybody who is anybody comes here... all the overseas visitors. Even the top men of the Romanian Government are staying here, Welsford. Are you sure she has come to Bucharest?'

I nodded and told him that Avram, who I explained I had hired as a guide and interpreter, was making a search of the town at that moment.

'Well, then, Welsford, you've nothing to worry about. She'll be with you before long, eh?'

I kept my uncertainty to myself.

Oblivious to my anxiety, Molesworth rambled on about the state opening of the new parliament which had taken place on January 22. He told me he had encountered Ion Ghica, the Romanian we had seen in London, who was now a prominent 'progressive' member of the National Assembly.

'Can't say I like the way things are developing,' muttered

Molesworth. 'Been talking the matter over with the French Consul, chap named Béclard, who agrees with my concern. Lot of radicalism here, you know, the spectre of this new fangled communism has got quite a hold.'

I could see that he wanted to talk about the matter and forced myself to concentrate on what he was saying. After all, it was my job which had financed my journey here and, if I did not fulfil my obligations, Molesworth could easily force me back to London on the next ship and God knows what would happen to Clara then.

As if divining my thoughts Molesworth gave me a sympathetic look.

'See here, Welsford,' he said, 'I realise how anxious you are about Miss ... er, whatsis. Tell you what, I'll let you have the next couple of days to yourself to get yourselves settled down, but in three days' time we have an important meeting with the new prime minister of this country, Babu Catargiu, a rather prickly nationalist type. I'll need you for that.'

Molesworth wasn't a bad sort and he had to hold up his hand to stem my gratitude.

'In the meantime,' he continued, 'you'd best know how the situation is shaping up.'

He went on to 'put me in the picture' as he expressed it. The British delegation had arrived in Bucharest to hear Prince Alexandru open the National Assembly, consisting of members of the former assemblies of Wallachia and Moldavia meeting as a single chamber. Prince Alexandru has told the people that the union of the principalities would be 'such as Romania wishes it, such as she feels it should be'. A new age was opening up for the country and 'progressive development of all institutions' was promised.

The majority political group was the National Party, a group of conservatives led by Catargiu who had, on that basis been designated the prime minister of the new state. Catargiu was all in favour of the social *status quo*, of keeping the majority of Romanian peasants in serfdom and of allowing the boyars, or great land owners, who had survived four hundred years of Turkish occupation through wealth and influence, to continue their powerful hold on the country. But there was a strong party of moderate conservatives and liberals in the parliament, led by N. Cretilescu, which favoured moderate reforms to lead the country into a more democratic Western democracy. There were more radical liberals who wished for the emancipation of the peasants and the confiscation of the large estates owned by the Church. Our friend Ion Ghica was among those advocates.

'The most worrying factor,' explained Molesworth, 'is a man called Mircea Malaieru. He is the leader of a peasant movement aimed at radical revolution. Peasants under his command have been put down once after an attempt to overthrow Prince Alexandru and establish some sort of republic... in fact, so far as I understand, the Bucharest regiments put them down with rather an unnecessary amount of bloodshed. The local police chief, a rather nasty piece of work named Bibescu, has simply created martyrs for their cause.

'Unless the situation is handled rather carefully, this country could be split into a rather bloody civil war between peasants and landowners. If so, the Porte and the Turkish Army will simply rush troops into the country on the pretext of keeping the peace and point out that the Romanians aren't ready to govern themselves. After all,' he gave a cynical grin, 'Her Majesty's Government have used that ploy before now. But what will happen to our buffer state in eastern Europe?'

I promised to turn my mind to such matters as soon as I could.

He stood up shaking his head sadly.

'You know, Welsford, it was bad strategy to mix affairs of politics and women at this time. Women and politics simply do not mix.'

'Isn't that a conservative attitude, my lord?' I was stung into replying. Having taken my degree in history I knew that European history was full of instances where women made better politicians than men.

'Nonsense, Welsford,' laughed Molesworth in answer to my rebuke. He poked a playful finger at me. 'At this moment you are prejudiced. But women have no head for politics. That is why they don't have the vote. Indeed, they never will have the vote.'

I decided to say nothing to encourage Molesworth to climb on his favourite hobby horse. But I recalled reading a weighty treatise, published by some Irishman named Thomson in 1825, a contemporary, I believe, of the advocate of the co-operative movement, Robert Owen. As I recall, the book was entitled *An appeal of one half of the human race, women, against the pretensions of the other half, men, to retain them in political and thence in civil and domestic slavery.* 'Shall man be free and woman a slave... never say I!' cried Thomson, advocating female emancipation. I wondered what Thomson would have made of Lord Molesworth and decided to renew the debate at some future date.

'Take my word for it, Welsford,' said Molesworth, pausing at the door, 'women and politics do not mix. But we cannot cry over spilt milk. I hope you are able to get your affairs sorted out quickly because the delegation is in need of your services.'

He took his departure and I groaned a prayer of gratitude. There were more important things to think of than even the political affairs of the new state or the emanicipation of women.

I waited at the hotel until late afternoon, fretful and impatient. I could not sleep or rest. I was just beginning to think about going out to join the search myself when Avram knocked at the door. He carried a small black bag such as doctors are wont to use.

I searched his face intently for signs of news as he came in and poured himself a drink.

'Well?' I finally demanded.

He threw back his head and drained a tumbler of whisky in one gigantic swallow.

'Well indeed, Upton,' he returned. 'I have traced the coach.'

I was halfway to the door.

'Not so fast!' admonished Avram. 'Remember the saying about fools rushing in?'

'But we must rescue her at once!' I cried.

'Wait man!' snapped the American-Romanian. 'First we must review the situation. We must consider exactly what we are up against.'

He poured a second drink and sipped at it gently.

'I questioned some peasants who, just before dawn, saw a black coach and four enter the city. I managed to follow its path, by questioning people who were abroad early this morning, to a small suburb where there are several grand townhouses that belong to rich boyars, or nobles. Men of wealth and power who usually made their way by collaborating with the Turks. Men,' here to my surprise he made a motion of spitting, 'men who are still in power in

151

this land as the so-called native government.'

There was a bitterness in his voice.

'Continue,' I pressed him. 'What of Clara?'

'I'll come to that. The coach was seen entering the grounds of a house belonging to a boyar family whose main estates lie in Transylvania.'

My heart quickened.

'A peasant boy,' continued Avram, 'recalled seeing a pale-faced lady, with black hair, in the coach as it drove into the grounds just about dawn this morning. The boys works as a stable lad in a house opposite and he swears that the coach has not left since sun up.'

'Then we must go there at once... it will be dark soon.'

'Don't worry, my friend,' Avram returned. 'I don't think the power we seek gathers full strength until sometime after sundown.'

There was a tone in his voice that made me look closely at him.

'You sound as if you now know what that power is, Avram? What else have you learnt?'

'I don't know for certain... but I think I know.'

Avram's face was serious.

'Then tell me!' I cried exasperated.

'The house to which the coach was driven has an emblem on its iron gates. I examined the outside of the house very carefully. The emblem was in wrought iron... it was a small grinning dragon.'

I felt suddenly weak and slumped into a chair.

'Draco,' I breathed.

Avram nodded.

'The stable boy who saw the coach enter also told me that the coach carried the same emblem on its doors.... a white dragon which was the only relief to that black vehicle.'

He reached forward, opened his bag and drew forth a sheet of paper. It was a page torn from a book... a book of heraldry.

'I removed this from the local library,' he explained.

My eyes were on the leering head of the white dragon, rampant against a black background.

I gasped. It was the head of my statuette, the head of Draco, the dragon god of ancient Egypt.

Gathering my scattered thoughts, I peered down at the piece of paper.

'It does not say to whom the emblem belongs,' I commented.

'It doesn't need to,' said Avram softly.

'How so?'

'It belongs to a family as old as this land itself, whom everyone in this part of the world has known and feared for centuries. If folk tales and legends are one percent true, then the family represented by the dragon symbol is the source of the evil power which we must fight.'

His voice, tinged with horror, set my flesh acrawl.

'Who is this family?'

'A family that once were princes of this country... and one particular prince who was possessed of an extraordinary power, a man - if you can call him that - whom legend has it has lived more than ten times his normal span of years.'

I suppressed a shiver.

'Nonsense,' I rebuked without conviction in my voice.

'Maybe. Remember I said that it's what legend records,' returned Avram calmly. 'Yet here, among the black shadows of the Carpathians, legend and truth are so intermingled that you can't tell which is which.'

I rose to my feet impatiently.

'You said you knew who this family is?' I said, pointing to the escutcheon.

'I do.'

'Then tell me.'

'The dragon crest is the symbol of the House of Dracula.'

CHAPTER TWENTY-ONE

'The House of Dracula?' I echoed. 'I seem to have heard that name before.'

Even as I spoke I recalled that Yorke had once mentioned the name.

'The Draculas are one of the oldest families in the land, perhaps as old as the Carpathians themselves.' Avram's voice had a strange intensity to it.

'They were the voivodes or ruling princes of Wallachia. The dynasty was actually founded by Mircea the Great who died in 1418 but the family took their name from Vlad III, who was called Vlad the Impaler. He also became known as Vlad Dracula, the son of the Dragon or the Devil. He was also known as the Impaler for, although he drove the Turks out of the country, his very name stank in the nostrils of Christendom because of the unholy and inhuman practices he had of impaling the bodies of his enemies and even his friends on sharp wooden stakes.

'He was vile and bloodthirsty but he was also cunning and brave. He had a mighty brain and iron resolution which went with him to his grave. He died, no one knows how, at the very height of his power in 1476. It was said of him that he had a learning beyond compare, he knew no fear and no remorse and even attended the Scholomance...'

'What is that?' I interrupted.

Even Avram, whom I suspected was something of an atheist, raised a hand and crossed himself.

'The Scholomance, my friend is a school which exists in the heart of the Carpathians where the secrets of nature, the language of animals, and all the knowledge of science is taught by the Devil in person. Only ten scholars are admitted at a time and when the course of learning is ended, nine of the scholars are sent to their

154

homes but the tenth is kept by the Devil as his aide and rides about the mountains mounted on a dragon!'

'The dragon again,' I observed.

'Even so. Dracula was as feared as he was hated throughout the country.'

'And there are Draculas even to this day?' I asked.

'Dracula had a son, Mihail the Bad, who was voivode or prince of Wallachia until 1510. Then his sons Alexandru II and Peter the Lame succeeded him. There was a line of direct male heirs to Dracula until the time an Alexandru, who died in 1632, became prince of both Wallachia and of Moldavia.'

'You know your history well,' I observed.

Avram smiled gently.

'When your country is conquered and your history becomes a forbidden thing, a thing to be belittled and sneered at, then you tend to cherish it all the more. In America I've met countless Irish whose knowledge of their history would put a scholar to shame. It isn't a quality unique to the people of Romania.'

He sighed and then continued: 'The Draculas were never good rulers. The last of them was Mihail Radu. He took the throne of Wallachia on March 5, 1658, and started his reign of terror by murdering thirty of his boyars because of his jealousy of them. In November, or thereabouts, in 1659, there was a great battle at Fratesi and the people overthrew this Dracula and forced him to flee from Wallachia. Mihail was the last Dracula to rule.'

'What happened to him?'

'He fled to Transylvania and settled in some great estate among the Carpathians, somewhere near the Borgo Pass. The descendants of the Dracula family have continued to live there in isolation, shunning the world, since those days. They call themselves 'counts' these days, no longer 'princes'. And I'm told that a Count Dracula still rules these Transylvanian estates. Strange stories have been told about him... stories which even go so far as to say that Dracula himself, the same evil Prince of Wallachia, still lives and rules his family... but that is only a peasant legend.'

'But what could this House of Dracula want with a statuette of an Egyptian god and with Clara?' I demanded. 'And from what source comes this evil power they seem to exercise?'

Avram's face was grave.

'If the evil power we seek comes from the House of Dracula and is what I now suspect it is, then, my friend, we're battling against the curse of the ages... vampirism!'

'Vampirism?' I cried aghast. 'You mean dead men who leave their graves to prey upon the living?'

I looked upon Avram's face to see if this were some ghastly jest, but the deep-etched lines of his face told me he was deadly serious. A few weeks ago I would have laughed outright if a man had told me that he believed in such things but now, now after all that I had witnessed, I merely suppressed a shudder.

'What you say, friend Upton, is a simplified idea of what vampirism is. Going back to ancient Egypt, each nation has its tales of vampires... of corpses that become reanimated by blood from the living, of corpses that cannot lie still in their graves but flit about the world from sunset to sunrise sucking the blood from the living. They live in a state of Undead.

'I have told you that this was the crossroads of the world where blood is a cheap commodity and flows like water from the mountain streams. The fields have been fertilised by the blood of many peoples. Death is no stranger to the people here and, in whatever form it comes, they do not fear it. Look how they fought continually and at great sacrifice against the Turks, shedding rivers of their blood to be free of the curse of foreign domination. But what they do fear is the terrible Undeath, eternal suffering and torture.

'From time immemorial we Romanians have known of those creatures of the night, those who have succumbed to live as immortals in the cursed guise of the Undead.'

'Is it possible that such things exist?' I whispered.

'It is possible and they do. You, yourself, have witnessed many manifestations of their powers. And I believe that the legends about the Dracula family are true... perhaps Prince Dracula did attend the Scholomance and attain such powers as the peasants claim.'

'But,' I cried, 'what has this to do with the statuette? What had the ancient Egyptian god Draco to do with vampires?'

'I've given some thought to the matter,' replied Avram. 'I don't know for certain but I can guess at the answer. Perhaps this cult of

156

vampirism started in those far-off days among the ancient Pharoahs of Egypt. You told me that your friend Yorke said that the followers of the god Draco believed that life after death was a natural fact, that it was possible not only to free the spirit from death but to free the body as well... in other words the ancient Egyptians thought they could make the body immortal.

'The vampire, too, has a mortal body. Didn't your friend say that all those thousands of years ago in Egypt, the Draconians studied ways of releasing themselves from their mortal span? That they experimented with ways of obtaining immortality? Did he, your friend, not say that it was written that the Draconians claimed to be successful in their experiments by which they created what was called - even by the ancients - Undead?'

I nodded slowly, recalling that conversation.

'Then, perhaps,' continued Avram, 'the answer lies in the fact that these followers of Draco created a race of Undead men who needed living blood to prolong their immortality... that five thousand years ago, or more, in ancient Egypt the first vampire was created?'

He paused.

'That could be why they were driven underground by the enlightened religions. And perhaps, seeking refuge, they trudged to the Carpathians, like many before them and many who have followed them. They came here, to the crossroads of the world, and their achievements were spread across the face of the earth like some noxious plague as nations came and went among the mountain passes. That is why every country in the world, from Asia to Ireland, has its tales of the Undead, the vampires. That is why Euripides, Aristophanes and Ovid all knew and wrote of the Undead and why St. Clemens warned the early Christians to beware of them.

'Yes,' he concluded, emphatically, 'the more I think of it, the more I'm convinced that this is the way it happened.'

'And Clara is in the hands of such evil?'

I was sick with apprehension.

Avram laid a hand on my arm.

'Friend Upton, I'd prepare myself for the worst. Maybe we are too late to save her.'

'Too late?' I looked at him in bewilderment. 'But you said that the young boy saw her alive this morning.'

'He saw her, yes.' Avram reached out both hands and held me by the shoulders, looking me squarely in the eyes. 'The Draconians sought immortality for their followers. They created the Undead, the vampires. The vampire is immortal but immortality carries with it a curse: they cannot die but must go on forever multiplying their kind, for all that die from their kisses become as they are - Undead!'

A red fire began to whirl around my brain.

'And Clara... is she in the power of the Undead... will she...?'

Avram nodded solemnly.

The chair seemed to slide away from under me. I seemed to swim down, down, down into a black whirlpool of screaming voices.

I was lying on my back when I opened my eyes. Avram was standing over me with a wet towel which he was applying to my temples.

I tried to start up but he held me down.

'Careful, Upton,' he said gently but firmly. 'You'd best gather your strength for you'll need it.'

'My God,' I cried in anguish. 'Clara... is there no hope?'

'It's possible that the worst hasn't come yet,' said Avram, cautiously.

'Explain yourself,' I demanded.

'The Undead are constrained by bonds of nature. Their power ceases at sunrise; from sunrise to sunset they must return to lie helpless on their native soil, the soil where they were buried. They can't pass over running water except at the slack and flood of the tide. They also hate all symbols of goodness and light, such as the crucifix I see around your neck. They can be easily destroyed by a man of courage, with steady hand and firm eye and a belief in right over evil. They can be destroyed by driving a stake of wood through their hearts, or cutting off their heads and stuffing the mouths with garlic... for garlic is one of the oldest medicinal herbs in the world, used throughout the ages to keep the devil at bay.'

'And why would this make you think that Clara has not become... become...'

'They may need her to do their bidding, to protect them during the hours that they're weakest.'

'But she wouldn't...' I began to protest.

'Not willingly, of course. But she is under their control.'

'Then we must destroy them,' I cried, sitting up.

'But we mustn't rush into the affair without knowing our adversary's power. You've heard his weakness. Now hear his strength. The Undead have the strength of many, can transform their shapes into those of bats, wolves, or can swirl in a mist or come on moonlight rays as elemental dust. They can see in the dark. They cast no shadow nor a reflection in a mirror. They have powers of mesmerisation...'

'And they can control Clara... even sending telepathic commands across thousands of miles from here to London,' I added.

'It's possible,' agreed Avram. 'But they must have some powerful leader to do such things, a leader of astonishing qualities.'

'All the dreams I had, that Clara also had... these emanated from the hypnotic power of these creatures.'

'I'd say that psychic vibrations from the jade statuette also played an important part,' pointed out Avram.

'Then what must we do?' I cried, a surge of anger bursting through my veins. Deep down I knew that my anger was born of the great chill fear that was gripping at my throat. But I kept seeing an image of Clara before my eyes, reinforcing my resolve.

'It's a terrible task, my friend,' said Avram. 'Death isn't the worst thing that can overtake us. And if the curse of the Undead overtakes either one of us, we must resolve to save the soul of the other by driving a stake through his heart. Agreed?'

Silently we shook hands upon that terrible proposal.

Avram picked up his black bag.

'I've purchased a few things that'll arm us against these creatures.'

He drew forth two fairly large crucifixes of the Orthodox Church style and handed me one.

'Keep it in your pocket for protection always.'

He then showed me that in the bag was an abundance of garlic flowers and also a wooden mallet and several heavy wooden tent pegs which, he explained, would serve us as wooden stakes.

'Well now, Upton, my friend, now's the time. Evening is wearing on and we must put our faith in the powers of goodness and light. We must go out to contend with this evil cancer.'

I braced my shoulders.
Without another word we passed out into the darkening evening.

CHAPTER TWENTY-TWO

The house was in an isolated part of the city.

Avram had hired a carriage, which bore a marked resemblance to our own English Hansom cabs, and he directed the driver to a wide, tree-lined avenue along which high walls ran. Behind these high walls I could just make out the tall edifices of gaunt, forbidding buildings which, so Avram informed me, were the town houses of the boyars of the country. Apart from the grim architecture, the prospect was not altogether unlike some avenue in Hampstead.

Evening had descended with its wintery blackness by the time the driver dropped us at the end of the avenue. Avram thought it best not to journey further by the carriage lest our coming rouse suspicion within the household. Instead we walked the last three hundred yards and halted before the great iron gates.

I, too, then saw what Avram had seen. The dragon emblem on those forbidding portals. There was no doubt about it, the image was exactly the same as the jade statuette - the same as Draco, the dragon god.

The house itself stood only twenty yards from the gate and rose perhaps three storeys, which was a remarkable height compared with most of the houses in the outlying areas of Bucharest. There seemed to be no movement within the house. It was dark and, in fact, the overall impression was one of centuries-old decay. All the windows were shuttered but here and there a shutter had rotted away from its hinges and hung flapping gently like some broken bird's wing in the faint evening breeze.

I will not hide the fact that it took courage to follow Avram through the squeaking iron gates. Avram bent his head to mine and whispered: 'You'd best stay here and watch the front of the house. I'll go round to the stables and see if the coach is there.'

I silently envied Avram's courage as he disappeared towards the

161

back of that deserted building. My heart seemed to pound uncomfortably loudly in my ears. The evening air was cold and I gently stamped at the ground, hoping to attract the pumping blood to my feet. There was no moon and everything was shrouded in black gloom, even my breath in the coldness seemed like puffs of dark grey smoke.

An owl hooted on a nearby tree causing me to jump.

It was then I noticed that the door of the house was half open and in the gap stood a small feminine figure.

'Clara?' I gasped, cursing the fact that I had no lantern.

The figure stirred and I fancied I heard a soft laugh.

'Who... who's there?' I demanded, a trifle brusquely in my nervousness.

A sweetly feminine voice answered in what, I presumed, was the local language.

'I do not understand,' I replied.

'Do you speak this language, mein herr?' asked that soft, caressing voice in German.

'I do. Who are you?' I demanded again, resorting to my schoolboy German.

'Do not be alarmed, mein herr. Come in where it is warm.'

The figure opened the door a little further and behind it I could see the hallway was lit by a lantern which silhouetted the figure of the woman, no, no more than a girl whose shape, aye even in silhouette, caused me to catch my breath in admiration. Never have I seen a figure come so close to perfection before. Then I thought of Clara and felt a pin prick of guilt.

'Come in where it is warm, mein herr,' she repeated softly. 'It is cold in the night air.'

I took a hesitant step forward and then my mind remembered our mission to that house and immediately registered alarm.

'Who are you?'

'My name is Malvina, mein herr. I am the *hausmädchen* to the Count and look after the property in his absence.'

My suspicions eased somewhat. At least I did not have to fear this innocent sounding girl. She could only have been eighteen at the most.

'Is the Count at home?' I queried.

162

'Why no, mein herr,' replied the girl. 'He seldom comes here...
but he may be found at his estates at Borgo.'

She shivered suddenly.

'But please come in, mein herr. I am sure you are cold standing
there.'

I hesitated still.

'I am with a friend...' I began.

'Ah yes, mein herr. Do not worry. He has entered the house at
the rear and is upstairs ... going over some papers in the Count's
rooms... he sent me to fetch you.'

'Ah!' I cried. 'Why didn't you tell me this before? I thought... ah
well, never mind. Lead me to him, fräulein.'

She stepped back and I entered the great hall. Apart from the
lamp burning on a side table, the hall was dark and cold. I turned to
the girl to ask why, as *hausmädchen* or housemaid as we would say,
she did not keep a fire burning by which to receive guests. But the
question was not framed. My mouth hung open as I gazed upon the
beautiful young creature before me. My estimation of her age as
eighteen years seemed to be an accurate one. She had a fresh pale
skin with touches of red on her cheeks which were speckled with
tiny freckles so delicate that an artist might have spent hours placing
each freckle to its greatest affect. Her hair was dark and her eyes
blue and wide. She stood there smiling almost coquettishly at me.

'That is better, mein herr, is it not? It is so cold out there... so,'
she paused to find the right word, 'so inhospitable.'

I did not point out that the house inside seemed just as freezing as
the night air outside.

'Where is my friend, fräulein?' I asked.

'Do not be alarmed, mein herr. I shall take to you to him.'

She smiled a smile of such sweetness and innocence that I was
amazed a girl like her could be employed in the services of the
family which Avram had so vividly described to me.

Her face was that of a young innocent, without blemish, without
corruption. Even her coquettishness was without studied affect.

For one wild moment I felt an insane surge of desire which thrust
from me all thoughts of Clara. For a second I fought to control my
wild emotions, closing my eyes and leaning heavily against the wall.
When I opened them I saw her still smiling at me, red lips parted a

163

trifle, showing beautiful milk white teeth over which she momentarily ran the tip of a pink tongue.

'Where is my friend?' I demanded, a harshness in my tone to dispel the wicked desires within me.

'If you will pick up the lantern and follow me, mein herr...?'

She turned and walked swiftly into the gloom of the hall. I hastily took up the lantern and hurried after her, thinking that she must have the eyes of a cat to walk into that darkness with such assuredness. She led the way up a winding flight of stairs and then from the first floor up another stairway. She paused before a door, threw it open and entered.

The room was empty, without fires in the hearth nor light except the rays of the lantern I carried.

I looked around in puzzlement.

'He is not here,' I said, stating the obvious.

The girl, Malvina, smilingly shook her head.

'He will join us, never fear.'

I set down my lantern and peered about. The room lay under a thick covering of dust. Bed, chairs, dressing-table were covered in dirt and, to my horror, several items of furniture were rotting away.

'How long have you been *hausmädchen* here, Malvina?' I asked, amazed that anyone could allow such advanced decay to go unchecked.

'Oh, a long, long time, mein herr.'

'But not long enough to clean the place, eh?' my natural fastidiousness formed the rebuke in my voice.

She pouted, oh so prettily.

'Pah, what is a little dirt? The Count never comes here.'

'You are a poor housemaid, Malvina.'

She gave a low, gurgling laugh.

'Yet I am much better *in other things...*'

The emphasis in her voice left no doubt as to her meaning and it startled me that I should hear this from a child of her innocent mien.

In my embarrassment I turned to the mirror and started to wipe away the dust from its surface, pretending to be interested in its ancient workmanship.

I know the room was dark and the rays from the lantern threw many strange shadows across the room but, as I bent towards the mirror, with Malvina standing smilingly behind me, a cold terror gripped my throat.

I could not see the reflection of Malvina in the mirror!

In growing fear I rubbed harder at its surface, sending cascades of dust this way and that, and when I had cleared a sufficient portion of the surface, I pressed close.

Great gods! I cannot record that terrible feeling as I saw that I stood alone in that room.

I whirled round and saw Malvina standing there, laughing silently as if at some great joke.

Dimly I recalled the words of Avram: 'They cast no shadow nor reflection in a mirror.'

The gentle, innocent face of the girl looked at me in sudden concern.

'Why do you start so, mein herr? Why do you look at me so? I am but a poor girl. Yet why do your eyes stand out in fear? You need have no fear of me.'

Yet, as I stared, her innocence seemed to vanish. Now she seemed so self-assured, so voluptuous. The desire I had but a moment ago vanished in the chill fingers of fear which gripped my heart.

'Who are you?' I breathed.

'I am Malvina, as I have told you. Have no fear of me... rather let your desires suppress your fear.'

She made an obscene, seductive gesture with her body.

'Come, young herr, young, vital herr ... come to me. Let me love you for I worship the warmth of your body, the warmth of your blood, rich young blood... for blood is life... and life is all...come young herr...'

The voice that I had thought so innocent was edged with a grossness, the smile, so beguiling, was now merely lascivious.

Her voice droned on, gently, coaxing, coaxing... I knew I was being mesmerised. I jerked up my head and bit my tongue to let the pain add sharpness to my wits.

'No... in the name of God!'

My hand struggled down to my coat pocket to grab for Avram's crucifix which nestled there.

It froze halfway.

A strange transformation seemed to come over that once lovely creature... aye, lovely - yet spawn of the devil!

Into those softly dreaming blue eyes there sprang the red fires of hell... the eyes seemed to become glowing red coals, blinding me as I stood frozen in time. The lips, now blood-red, obscene things, pulled back from those white, oh so white, teeth. And the teeth themselves seemed to grow longer, sharper, the incisors like flashing knives, and a ghastly red tongue lashed hungrily over them.

A snarl erupted from that once beautiful throat, a snarl that reminded me of the cry of a hunting dog about to spring on its prey.

Hands forward, like grasping claws, the girl moved slowly towards me.

Even as those hands grasped my coat, my fear... pumping adrenalin through my limbs, galvanised me into action. One hand shot out to grasp the soft white throat of the girl, another fumbled in my pocket. But I had not counted on the strength of the creature; she seemed to be possessed of the strength of ten full-grown men.

I crashed backwards against the mirror under the force of her attack.

All the while those eyes - livid hungry coals - burned into my very soul.

I found myself sobbing with fear as I felt her mouth, with those dreadful grinding, snapping teeth, closing towards my neck, felt the awful odour of her fetid breath, whose warmth seemed to burn my skin. Closer, still yet closer, came that obscenely gnashing mouth, that licking tongue, against my neck.

Somehow, just as her lips touched my skin, I managed to swing my left arm around so that, as those terrible teeth closed on my arm, I could feel them, needle sharp, piercing through my skin.

I gave a terrible cry of anguish.

Suddenly the creature pulled back from my body, mouth working, eyes wide in terror.

Avram stood on the threshold of the room, one hand clutching at a crucifix that seemed to mesmerise and terrify the creature.

'Upton... are you alright?' came his anxious voice.

'I think so,' I replied hesitantly.

'Then hold up your crucifix and keep this devil's spawn at bay for a moment.'

I did as I was told.

The creature's terrified eyes turned to the symbol I drew forth and held up. Under Avram's guidance I moved forward until the thing was imprisoned in a corner of the room.

It was like keeping some hissing, snarling beast at bay.

What happened next was my fault. For an instant I turned my gaze to see what Avram was doing and the she-devil was at me, my arm went back and my crucifix, knocked from my hand by the impact, went flying across the room. Then the creature had knocked me to the floor and, in terror, I threw up my hands to protect myself.

Abruptly the creature stiffened and gave a long scream, a howl like the night cry of a wolf.

Her body fell away from mine.

I shall never forget that ghastly scene, lit by the rays of the solitary lantern in that dusty old room.

From the heart of the creature there protruded a wooden tent peg and from it blood pulsated like a terrible geyser. The creature was gnashing its mouth, tearing at its lips until they were red and bloody. It had fallen back on the floor. Avram leant over it and gave the wooden peg a resounding blow with a wooden mallet.

The scream was awful to my ears yet, in fascinated horror, I had to watch.

Avram was mumbling something, which I afterwards understood to be some prayer. Before my horrified gaze the girl... that girl of eighteen years... started to grow old. Yes; incredible as it sounds, her struggles ceased. For a second she seemed young and innocent. Then her skin was wrinkling, aging, the hair growing grey, white and then - horrors - falling from her shrinking skull in great tufts. Then the skin itself became dried and cracked, and withered to dust before my eyes. Even the bones turned brittle and before long there was nothing but a pile of dust upon the floor, indistinguishable from the other dust.

I bent over and vomited.

CHAPTER TWENTY-THREE

The next thing I knew was that Avram was helping me away from that accursed place and soon I was in my hotel room with the American-Romanian bending over me and bandaging my arm.

'Are you feeling better?' he asked anxiously as my swimming eyes finally focused on his anxious gaze.

'I feel terrible,' I confessed, as, groaning, I forced myself into a sitting position.

He handed me a glass of brandy.

'Is it poisonous?' I asked, looking at my bandaged arm.

'I don't think so,' replied Avram. 'I've cleaned it as best I could. The teeth tore the flesh open but didn't strike a vein or artery. In any case, a vampire must drink long and deeply before it has an ill effect.'

I shuddered at the memory.

Then:

'My God! What of Clara!'

She had been the whole purpose of our visit to that monstrous place and I, in my distraction, had forgotten.

'We were too late,' Avram said softly. 'No, no,' he added quickly in answer to my hoarse cry of despair. 'We may still be able to save her. The coach must have left a moment before we arrived. In the stables I found signs of it having been there during the day. But when we arrived it was gone.'

'Gone?' I whispered fearfully. 'Gone where?'

'I'd say that it has left Bucharest, taking Miss Clara with it, and is now heading for the Dracula estate in Transylvania.'

'Then we must follow!' I cried, leaping from my bed.

Avram agreed.

'I've already given the hotel clerk the order to hire us a carriage for it's too far to ride comfortably on horseback. If one of us takes

168

turns to drive, then the other can sleep on the carriage and, that way, we might overtake the coach fairly soon. There are enough post-houses between here and the Transylvanian border to supply us with fresh horses when they're needed.'

As he spoke I flung my belongings into my bag and was soon following Avram to the front of the hotel where the clerk had already obtained a landau drawn by two well-muscled horses.

I did not even spare a thought for Viscount Molesworth or the British delegation, even though it was goodbye to my career with the Foreign Office. Clara, and the fighting of this evil were of greater importance than the machinations of nations playing puny games with each other. But I will say this in passing; later, at the inquiry, Lord Molesworth did speak up on my behalf and tried to get me reinstated in the services of the government, albeit unsuccessfully.

I should also add that Molesworth's political foresight proved correct as regards the new Romanian state. A few months later the conservative prime minister of the new state, Cartargiu, was assassinated outside the Metropolitan Church in Bucharest, soon after leaving the National Assembly. Mircea Malaievu, the head of the radical peasant movement, was blamed. In the turmoil that followed, the Romanian parliament voted by sixty-two votes to thirty-five to grant freedom to all the peasants in the country and free them from the feudal obligations of the landowners. But Prince Alexandru, true to his principles, refused to endorse the law. The birth pangs of the Romanian nation became violent. Alexandru was forced to abdicate and a new 'moderate government' was formed. Unfortunately for the British interests, represented by Molesworth, the throne of Romania was offered in 1886 to Carol of Honhenzollern-Sigmaringen, a relative of the King of Prussia. Our support of the unpopular Alexandru lost us our hold on the country.

By dawn the following day, Avram - taking first shift as coachman - brought our landau and two restless mares to the town of Ploesti within sight of the brooding white peaks of the Carpathian mountains. This particular range, so Avram told me, was the Transylvanian Alps which separated Wallachia from Transylvania. At Ploesti we found a peasant who had been early in the fields and had seen the black coach rumble through the town in the direction

169

of Kronstadt, a town which lay over the Alps, beyond the border. Avram further learned from the man that the Austrians had closed the frontier between Transylvania and Wallachia an hour earlier due to the agitation by some Transylvanians to be allowed to secede from the Austro-Hungarian Empire and join the Romanian union. Even now groups of guerillas fighting for this end were at large in the mountains.

'It'll be difficult to get through to Kronstadt,' said Avram worriedly. 'Still, I think it proves that the coach is heading for the Dracula estates near the Borgo Pass. My guess is that from Kronstadt they will head for Bistritz and then into the Borgo Pass.'

'What shall we do?' I asked. 'How can we follow?'

'To avoid trouble at the frontier, I think our best plan is to keep to this side of the Alps; a few miles east of here the mountains swing northwards. We can follow the eastern spurs of the mountains as far as the town of Piatra on the River Bistrita. There we can cross the border, swing around through the mountains and enter the Borgo Pass from the north-east... in the opposite direction. If we make good time, we can arrive before the coach reaches there and ambush it.'

I looked at him in amazement.

'Ambush it?' I repeated stupidly.

'Exactly, my friend,' he smiled. 'We can abduct Clara from the coach and take her to a place of safety before we're suspected. They'll be thinking that we're following the coach, not sweeping round into a semi-circle to intercept it.'

I realised the strategy of the idea and caught something of Avram's enthusiasm.

Now I took my turn at the reins while Avram dozed in the open carriage. I sent the landau hurtling forward under its new team of horses towards the Piatra road.

Three days of travel, stopping only to change horses and obtain food, saw our landau to the north-east of the Borgo Pass, a flat, desolate expanse which ran through a mountainous crag- and torrent-filled terrain leading down at its south-western extremity to the town of Bistritz. Bistritz was an ancient town, so Avram told me, of some twelve thousand souls. It was surrounded by the ruins of old bastions and towers which, for the most part, had been badly burnt down about five years before. Near the southern entrance of the Pass itself stood a ruined castle which once dominated the entrance and surrounding countryside. According to Avram, only the great Dracula estate still stood to dominate the passage through the Carpathians which led from the main reaches of Transylvania proper up to the small territory of Bukovina where the actual Castle Dracula was situated.

It was the dark side of twilight when we entered the Pass and Avram pointed out a gloom-enshrouded tract of land to the west which disappeared into a valley of its own. That, he told me, was where the Dracula lands lay. It certainly looked a gloomy and forbidding area but we did not halt here. Avram drove on a few miles and, where the road from Bistritz narrowed and rounded a bend with rock walls on either side, we drew up and made preparations for our ambush.

In spite of the length of our journey, I felt strangely refreshed. Perhaps it was the anticipation of the forthcoming encounter. We had carefully worked out the passage of the coach and knew it must arrive sometime during that evening, even allowing for unforseen delays.

Our plan was a simple one. As soon as I, posted on a protuberance of rock, heard the approach of the coach I was to signal Avram who would then drive our landau across the narrow roadway. Having halted the coach we would overpower the driver and then flee in the direction of Bistritz with Clara.

It seemed so simple.

It was ten o'clock when I heard the first rumble of the carriage wheels along the rocky roadway. Then, through the shrouding gloom I could make out a dark shape. There was no mistaking the black coach, for its image had been burnt into my mind ever since our first encounter before Bucharest.

'Now!' I cried, the excitement cracking my voice.

Avram promptly leapt upon the landau's driving seat and guided the horses across the roadway. Then he leapt down and, to my surprise, I saw him grasp his small derringer revolver.

'Just in case,' he whispered.

The black coach was suddenly upon us, thundering at full speed around the narrow bend. At the last minute the black-clad

171

coachman saw our barrier and heaved back on the reins of his four black beasts. From his mouth came a stream of profanities, or so I guessed his invective to be.

The coach wheels locked as he slewed the vehicle round, the brake hard on. The coach itself spun into the rocky walls, snapping the shafts. The horses reared and whinnied and pawed out in a dozen different directions. Then, suddenly, they broke free of their traces and flew off down the road northwards taking, to my horror, our own beasts - trailing our landau - with them.

But there was no time to lament our loss.

The coachman had leapt from his box with a snarl of rage and launched himself at Avram who had no time to use his revolver. The man knocked him back on the ground and I saw the derringer fly off into the night and fall among the rocks. Avram seized the two hairy hands which were gripping his neck and began to prise them apart. Spurred into activity, I rushed up behind the man and kicked him in the lower spine. With a cry of agony he turned from Avram and made a lunge towards me. But Avram, quickly recovering, seized the man from behind.

'Quick, Upton,' he cried. 'Take care of Miss Clara!'

I ran to the splintered carriage and peered inside.

Dear God! Clara was there, just sitting, a faraway look in her eyes and holding that accursed dragon statuette before her.

'Clara, my dear,' I cried, clasping her to me. She was like a marble statue in my arms, cold and immovable.

'Clara, are you alright?' I cried.

But she stared right through me.

I waved my hand before her eyes. There was no reaction. She seemed to be in some strange hypnotic trance. I tore the statuette from her grasp and sent it crashing to the roadway, but with no effect. She sat there, unseeing, unhearing.

'Upton!'

A cry of dismay caused me to look back at Avram. The coachman had seized Avram once more by the throat and was pushing him back against a rock. His hands clawed desperately at his assailant.

Seizing my crucifix, I raced to the man and pushed it into his face, thinking he might be some creature of the night, a pawn of his evil master, as Malvina had been.

To my horror the man leered up at me and then, with one gigantic paw, sent the crucifix hurtling into the night.

The man was human... or enough so as not to be afraid of such symbols.

With one blow of his hand he sent me crashing to the ground and turned back to finish Avram.

'Find my gun, Upton,' cried Avram in despair. 'My gun...'

Panic-stricken, I scrambled over the rocks. It was more by good luck than judgement that I found the cold metal and, clasping it in my hand, I pulled myself up.

How can I forget that sight?

As I pulled myself up and levelled the pistol, the tall coachman had heaved Avram above his head, as if he had been but a child, and then threw him bodily at a sharp, rocky crag. Avram's scream was cut short by the sickening thud of the impact and I saw his inert body slither to the ground. Even in that gloom I could see his head was oddly twisted and the eyes were wide and staring.

A red rage filled me.

I turned to the coachman. He was grinning oddly at me, walking slowly towards me, his arms hanging loosely by his side.

I pulled back the safety catch and fired the gun. The bullet hit him in the chest. He halted in surprise and looked down at the trickle of blood that was spreading over his shirt. A coldness gripped me as he started forward again. With clenched teeth I fired all the remaining chambers of the gun in quick succession. He stood still, and for a horrified moment I thought he was going to come on again, but slowly, ever so slowly, he sank down to the ground and lay there without a sound.

A cold sweat upon my brow, I stood trying to fight the weakness in my legs.

My eyes moved from the still smoking gun to the bloody corpse before me and then travelled to the poor twisted body of my friend Avram.

'Upton...?' Clara's hesitant voice broke the stillness.

I glanced up, startled.

Clara had descended from the coach, her eyes were wide with fear and her clenched fist was stifling the scream in her mouth.

'What has happened? My God, Upton, what has happened?'

173

Her voice was on the verge of hysteria.

'Clara?' I cried, wild with relief, 'Clara? Are you alright?'

She collapsed, sobbing helplessly as I clasped her to my breast.

'... a nightmare... since I left you, Upton... I have been in some terrifying nightmare... oh my God! Is it true? Is it True? Am I... am I one of.... of them?'

'No, Clara, no!'

I tried to comfort her sobbing body.

'You're safe now, everything will be fine. Just fine.'

But fear gnawed my mind.

'We must leave here immediately, Clara. It's a long way to walk but we must try to get to Bistritz.'

'Anything, anything,' she gulped, 'so long as you are with me now.'

I made a hurried search of the wrecked coach but could find no provisions nor anything else to protect us from the perils of the night. There was only Clara's long travelling cloak and this I placed around her trembling shoulders.

I gave her a rather wan smile.

'Come on, dearest, we'll have to step it out... it's a long walk...'

I became aware that her eyes were not focused on mine and were staring wide with fear on something behind my shoulder. I swung round in a defensive attitude and pushed her behind me.

On a little rise, a few yards away, stood an elegant calèche, illuminated by two side lanterns which threw out an eerie red glare. The calèche was black and blended with four great coal-black horses which stood patiently in their traces. But before the little coach stood a man. He stood looking down on us, giving an absurd impression of a great height. He was clad from head to toe in a long black travelling cloak which disguised all his features in black shadows. Only his eyes shone out like two pinpricks of red light, the reflection, I reasoned, of the glare of the calèche's side lights.

'You have had an accident, my friends?'

To my surprise he spoke English, an English strangely accented, his voice deep, almost sonorous.

'You would appear to be in some distress,' he said, when I did not reply. 'My calèche is at your service and my house lies not too far from here. This is a bad place to be during the hours of darkness.

Perhaps the lady and yourself will accompany me so that I may bring you some relief from your plight?'

I recovered my manners and gave a bow.

The man's offer was better than walking to Bistritz through that inhospitable countryside. I stammered out my thanks to the stranger, wondering how I could account to the authorities for this affair, for there was bound to be some enquiry about the shooting of the coachman and the death of poor Avram.

Courteously, the tall man handed Clara up into the calèche and, as I climbed up after her, I heard a sharp intake of breath.

The stranger had bent down and picked up the jade dragon and was holding it up in the light of the calèche's lamps.

'Why, this is a superb piece of workmanship, is it not so? It would be a shame to leave it on the roadway for any scavenger to take.'

Carelessly, he tossed it up on the driver's seat and swung himself after it.

'How far is it to your house, sir?' I called anxiously.

'Not far, my friend, not far,' was the reply.

I heard the crack of the whip and the horses jerked forward.

It was then, just as we were leaving the scene of that terrible encounter, that I heard a terrible howling of wolves seeking their prey. The moon suddenly, for the first time that night, slipped from a cloud and laid a pale white light over the ground. Low black shadows were slinking towards the bodies of the coachman and poor Avram, and I cried out to the tall stranger to stop.

He halted a moment and asked what the matter was.

Leaning out of the coach, I pointed to the snarling creatures who were already beginning to fight over the remains of the coachman.

'We should protect their bodies from those vile beasts, sir,' I began.

To my amazement the man threw back his head and laughed.

'Vile creatures, you say? Poor creatures of the night... and you would deny them their sustenance? They, like man, must live and must kill to live. They have earned their right to feast this night.'

He suddenly cracked his whip and I was thrown back into the calèche as the horses sprang forward and the coach flew into the night.

'Upton!' Clara uttered a shrill cry of horror and I followed her pointing finger towards the upholstery of the carriage.

Embroidered on the black satin cushions was the image of a white dragon. Underneath it was one word .... *Dracula!*

CHAPTER TWENTY-FOUR

The speed with which the calèche travelled made any thoughts of escape nonsensical and it did not seem long before the grim coachman drew up in some dimly-lit courtyard. We were ushered through a large door, along several stone passage-ways into a surprisingly bright room. A roaring fire crackled in a great hearth at one end of the room, before which a large table was spread, as if for the evening meal. Only two places were laid and the tall coachman ushered us to them, bade us be seated and poured out some drinks.

'I have been expecting you both,' he said softly. 'You must be tired after the distress of your journey, so eat and refresh yourselves.' I looked at him in puzzlement.

'*You* have been expecting us?' I queried. 'Then you are...?'

'I am Dracula,' the man acknowledged with a bow.

It was then that recognition flooded my brain.

The dreams, if such they were, that I had experienced in London, flooded back into my memory. Here stood the same man; the man who had whispered to me in my dreams. Yes, from head to toe he was draped in black; the very same man.

He was tall, elderly it seemed, although his pale face held no ageing of the skin, only the long white moustache which drooped over his otherwise clean-shaven face gave the impression of age. His face was strong - extremely strong, aquiline with a high-bridged thin nose and peculiarly arched nostrils. His forehead was loftily domed and the hair grew scantily round the temples but profusely elsewhere. The eyebrows were massive and nearly met across the bridge of his nose.

As in my vision, it was the mouth which captured my eyes. That mouth set in the long, pale face; fixed and cruel looking, with teeth that protruded over the remarkably ruddy lips whose redness had the effect of highlighting his white skin and giving the impression of

177

an extraordinary pallor. And where the teeth protruded over the lips, they were sharp and white.

Even in this brightly-lit room I could not discern the natural colour of his eyes. They still seemed red in the glow of the flickering fire.

'And so ...' he smiled softly. 'So you have both come to me.'

Clara shuddered.

I forced myself to meet his smile.

'And now you owe us explanations, Count Dracula.'

He chuckled without mirth.

'I do?' he bantered.

He pointed to the table: 'Eat, and while you eat, my friends, I shall talk. You have many, many questions which you want to ask of me. I feel it. But you shall eat and I shall talk.'

I looked across at Clara and tried to smile.

'We had better do as he suggests. It is no good starving ourselves in the midst of plenty ... and we may need our strength.'

I added this last sentence *sotto voce*, implying a deeper meaning.

The count did not appear to have heard and was standing with his back to the fire.

Clara was unable to do anything but pick at her food and I must confess I felt no better an appetite.

While the count seemed to be lost in thought I suddenly dared venture a question.

'What is your connection with Draco? Why do you seek the statuette?'

He looked sharply at me and then smiled.

'You ask me why I seek the image of Draco, the fire breather from the great deep, the giver of immortality?'

He paused as if contemplating how best he should answer.

'Countless years ago, there arose in ancient Egypt a set of earnest enquirers of the sciences, observers, if you will, of all natural phenomena. They followed the cult of the life-giving force of Draco - the dragon god, Draco, the personification of the elemental life force. As they studied and experimented, those ancients found that not only the spirit could achieve immortality but, if a man had courage and possessed the correct rituals and knowledge, a man's body, too, could obtain perpetual life. The ancients found the

178

forbidden secrets of life, discovered ways to release what they called *Ka*, the spiritual body of man. They pursued their science to its rightful conclusion and they prospered. There came the years of the great flowering of knowledge, the days when the Draconian Cult was followed from the shores of the Atlantic Ocean to the shores of the Pacific Ocean.

'But others,' his eyes flashed in vicious hatred, 'puny mortals full of petty prejudice and pretentious morality, others came and condemned without understanding the great achievements of Draconian science. They said it blasphemed against the true gods, against Nature herself and against man. Thus a great persecution of the priests of Draco commenced in the ancient land of Egypt and by the force of that bloody persecution new, weaker gods like Ammon and Ra and Hathor were raised in place of the one true creator of life. In their hundreds, the priests of Draco, keepers of the great secrets of Nature, fled from the land of Egypt. They fled east and west, north and south... to Asia and Persia, to the bowels of Africa, and to the cold north wastes and beyond.

'And some of them took their learning and, in the dark forests or windswept plains, they raised up the image of the dragon god again and once more began their search for the secret of life.'

We sat listening to his amazing narrative, mesmerized by the intensity of his voice, seeing the images which he sketched as vividly as if we were witnessing them at first hand.

Clara reached out a hand to mine for comfort.

'I am a Dracula,' he said, raising himself to his full height. 'Our family is ancient, more ancient than you can ever guess, for we are the very spawn of Draco and our name links us with him. We are descended from the loins of Setek Ab Ra who was his greatest priest and philosopher. The children of Setek Ab Ra fled Egypt with others of the cult and made their way to the fortress of the Carpathian peaks, bastions against the blood-thirst of Amenhotep the Fourth who tried to destroy Draco and set up a worship to Aton, the sun god. And here, my friends, among the defenses of the Carpathians, the seed of Draco prospered.'

He struck himself on the chest with a clenched fist.

'And I, I am proof that his seed still lives!'

A fierce fire blazed from his eyes.

'We Draculas settled this country when the people wore animal skins and hunted with implements of stone. We watched and saw the land become the crossroads of civilisation; we saw the Getae come and settle on the Wallachian plain, saw the coming of the Thracians, Scythians and Celts... each nation mingling its blood with the whole to sire a new race of people.

'And when there *was* a people to command, a Dracula it was who commanded them. It was a Dracula who offered aid to Mark Anthony at Actium. It was a Dracula who held back the Roman conquest, who repelled the Goths and the Huns from the Asiatic steppes when they came like a devouring fire to eat up Europe. Attila himself bowed his knee before Dracula.

'The Draculas are a proud house bearing a proud name. Out of the mingling of the nations of Europe, the house of Dracula springs unsullied, owing allegiance to none save Draco who spawned them.'

He suddenly snarled.

'But what does this new Europe know about such things? What do you - foreigners from some accursed north land - know or care?'

'You have told us that you claim to be a descendant of priests of Draco from ancient Egypt,' I ventured. 'But you have said nothing of...'

I fell silent as his baleful eyes bore into mine.

'Claim?' he spat the word. 'Claim? I *am* descended from Draco. When I was a young man, a prince of Wallachia, I pursued the Draconian path of knowledge, for in knowledge there is power. I contemplated on philosophy, on alchemy and theology and law. With the aid of Draco I wrested Nature's secrets from her. Aye, one by one I looked into the secrets of Nature and they opened to me like flowers before the sun. And the time came when I could dare to challenge the gods themselves and gain immortality as they...

'I took myself off into the mountain peaks and performed the ritual... step by step, line by line, but something went wrong, wrong!'

He smashed his fist into the palm of his hand.

His eyes glared round wildly as if seeking someone to accuse for the error.

'I achieved immortality, true, but not the complete immortality that I sought. I found myself but a mockery of an immortal, an Undead creature with great constrictions upon me. I could only move by night, and each day I had to return to a cursed sleeping-death, hidden from any who knew the secret of my destruction. And each night I was forced to find warm, living blood to drink, to sustain my existence, for in that blood was the essence of life for which I hungered. Without it I would eventually fade into the elemental dust of my creation. And, cursed be my fate, each person that I drank from became as I... and we were called vampires!

'Vampires!' he screeched the word. 'A Dracula, a follower of the true life force, made into a mere creature of the night, little better than a wolf or bat, a prey to those who could stalk me in the sunlight!

'The ritual for immortality was wrong, I knew it. I have been cursed as you see me now for a span of four long centuries...'

'What?' I cried aghast.

Clara gave a cry and sank into merciful unconsciousness.

My eyes did not leave this strange, terrifying being who claimed he had walked the earth for four centuries. God! Could it be true?

'Impossible!' I cried.

The count threw back his head and bared his teeth in a parody of a laugh.

'The only impossible things are those which have not yet been mastered! You cannot conceive of immortality? But I tell you that I am Vlad Dracula whom the men of my time once called Vlad Tepes, the Impaler, who ruled Wallachia for many a year and made it great. Did I not drive out the Turk and the Saxon who came to dominate the Carpathians?'

I felt my body turn to a trembling jelly.

'The seed of my loins ruled Wallachia for near two centuries after - shall I call it my death? Yet the ungrateful Wallachians rose up and drove out Mihail Radu, drove him out of Wallachia and out of Castle Dracula at Arefu. Mihail, as all other Draculas, knew my secret and took me with him, carrying the earth of my burial ground in large boxes so that I could rest at my ease during the accursed daylight hours. We fled from Arefu across the Carpathians to this castle where, for the past two hundred years, I have rested.

'Long have I fretted in my confinement, long have I pondered on my mistake in that ritual. And, at last, I discovered my mistake ... a discovery born of four hundred years of contemplation. Now I know the remedy, the ritual which will set me free of this... this constriction! Soon I shall no longer be restricted by the rising or the setting of the sun. Soon I shall walk the earth freely. True immortality shall be mine!'

I shuddered at the prospect.

'Then the house of Dracula shall rise again!' he was staring into the fire, his voice full of vehemence. 'The fates have decreed it and it would be blasphemy to deny the course already charted in the heavens. I shall go forth into the world and seize what is rightfully mine. The world will be but a bauble at my feet. I have but to bend down...'

It was like listening to the ravings of some megalomaniac... the old desire of world conquest! Yet what chilled me with a sense of dread and awe was that I knew him to be no maniac bent on fanciful dreams. He had a power so terrible, so ghastly, that I knew my poor friends Yorke and Avram had been right. That evil power must be destroyed at any cost! But how?

'Where do we, Miss Clarke and I, fit into your plans?' I ventured to ask. 'And what of the dragon statuette?'

He smiled like some benign schoolmaster to a backward child.

'You will know all about reincarnation, so I will not bother to explain. Let me merely state that your spirit once walked the earth as a priest of Ammon. Many centuries ago you were Ki, Kherheb of Ammon, and you were eventually executed as a foul traitor and blasphemer against the true god, Draco. Miss Clarke,' he smiled thinly at Clara's still insensible form, 'was once Sebek-nefer-Ra, a magnificent queen of Egypt who placed Draco above all else, aye, even though she loved Ki the Kherbeb, she sacrificed the false priest with her own hand because he refused to turn away from his heresy.'

I felt another spasm of shudders run through me as I recalled my early nightmares.

'If you refuse to admit belief in reincarnation, then consider the matter thus: in you there are the same components, the same electrical forces, the same life spark, that dwelt in Ki the Kherheb and in Sebek-nefer-Ra. Then, by accident, there came into your hands the very statuette of Draco that was made by the first worshipper perhaps some six thousand earthly years ago. The very statuette that was placed in the sanctum of the great temple at Thebes.

'Let me explain it this way... the statuette possessed a power, an essence. You were the negative element and she,' he motioned to Clara,' was the positive element. Between you, you comprised both parts of a conductor of the force. When you met, with the statuette as transmitter, the circuit was complete. The force was all powerful and through it I was able to extend my thoughts across the continent to guide your steps hither.

'And why do I need the statuette? As the statuette acted to complete the circuit with you and the girl, so will it complete my circuit...it will allow me to complete the ancient ritual which will allow me to strike off these fetters I have worn for four hundred years. I can strike them off and walk the earth in the sun once more and be, at last, omnipotent in the eyes of puny man. The world shall be mine at last!'

'But what of the girl and me?' I pressed.

'The girl I need for the ritual. As I have said, she is the positive element. You, I do not need now that the girl has brought me the statuette. That was why I tried to prevent you from following her, in case you succeeded in stopping her. That was why I tried to stop you on the ship, on the road and in Bucharest.'

'But you sought me out at first,' I said, not understanding. 'Through the dreams and through the mediums you enticed me to come to you and bring the statuette.'

'That was before I found her,' he said, nodding to Clara once more. 'You were a difficult subject, but she was easier to control and came without trouble. I needed you no longer.'

I suddenly became aware of another presence in the room.

I turned, startled, to a corner of the room where it seemed as if three people had suddenly materialised out of nowhere. I could have sworn that they had not entered by the door, for I had been sitting facing it. A tall, youngish-looking man, bearing a striking resemblance to the count himself, stepped forward and examined me with burning eyes set in his pale face. With him were two voluptuous young women, so remarkably like Malvina that for a moment I thought my eyes were deceiving me. They smiled, nay - leered, at me like hungry cats waiting for their meal.

183

The young man turned to the count. He was dressed in a grey cloak that enveloped him from feet to neck, leaving as a relief only the pale white of his face and the blackness of his hair.

'It is nearly sun-up, lord,' he said.

An anxious frown gathered on the dark brows of the count. He glanced towards the window.

'You are right, Mihail. We must show our guests where they must rest until... until the ceremony.'

One of the women, the smaller of the two, whose rich red lips seemed obscene against the white of her skin, crept closer to me.

'But why, lord,' she breathed in a purring tone, 'why not let us enjoy them... they are so young, so rich in blood...'

I pulled back as she came nearer me. I could feel her dank, putrid breath hot on my cheek.

In two strides the count had crossed the room, seized the creature by her white, gross neck and - with a strength that appalled me - lifted her bodily and sent her crashing across the room.

'These people are mine,' he snarled. 'Mine! No harm shall come to them until after the ceremony! Do you hear?'

'We hear, lord,' the young man answered for the trio.

'Very well. You understand the importance of the ceremony... they must not be touched.'

The two female creatures, hissing terrifyingly in their disappointment, crouched back as the count towered over them.

'Begone you sluts! Begone you vile creatures, back to your lairs. The sun comes!'

He raised a forefinger at the window and, sure enough, I could see the pale cast of dawn against the black sky.

No greater horror was mine when the two creatures vanished as if in a whisp of smoke... dissolving into some vapour-like substance which sped in a tiny stream through a crack in the door.

The count turned and swept up the still mercifully unconscious Clara in his arms.

'Follow me,' he said curtly, and led the way from the room.

I looked back to where the young man, Mihail, had been standing but he, too, had vanished.

The count led the way to a small bedchamber and laid Clara on the bed. Then he ushered me, protesting, from the room and locked the door. An iron grip on my shoulder, he ushered me to another door, opened it and pushed me, none too gently, into a second bed-chamber.

'Tonight!' he said, smiling through thin lips.

Then, with an anxious glance at the light now streaming through the window, he slammed the door shut. I heard the key turn and his ringing footsteps echoing down the passage.

CHAPTER TWENTY-FIVE

No sooner had the count gone than I was at the door twisting the handle this way and that. But it was to no avail. I do not know how many centuries that castle had withstood the storms of war, but the mighty portals were secured with great oak doors many inches thick and intricately fastened with iron hinges and locks. Even as I struggled I knew my task was futile.

My brain now burned with the thought of one endeavour. I must rescue Clara and seek a way out of this vile prison and, before nightfall, must put as much distance as I could between ourselves and Castle Dracula.

My attention focused on the window and, to my excitement, I found that the iron lattice work opened to my touch. I peered out and my excitement gave way to a groan of anguish. It must have been all of fifty feet down to the tiny cobbled courtyard below. Again, excitement stifled my anguish as I caught sight of a ledge, not more than six inches wide but a ledge nevertheless, which ran six feet below my window.

I leaned out of the window and cupped my hands to my mouth.

The sun, now standing well above the eastern horizon, beat hotly down on me as if mocking my endeavours.

'Clara!' I yelled. 'Clara, can you hear me? Come to the window!'
I paused.

Suddenly the next window to mine was pushed open.

A trembling voice cried: 'Upton, is that you? Where are you?'

'At the next window.'

Her face peered out.

'Upton, what are we to do? What has happened?'

'Don't worry,' I cried, full of false courage. 'I have a plan. Look, I shall try to come along to you.'

'But how...?'

'The ledge below. I shall drop down to it. I think it is wide enough to take me. Then I shall come along towards you, but you will have to find some means of giving me a hand up to your window.'

She nodded.

'A bedsheet rope.'

'Clever girl,' I cried.

She disappeared and shortly was heaving a torn sheet out of the window.

I applauded her endeavours.

'Now for the difficult part.'

Taking my courage in my hands, I climbed out of the window and slowly let my body down towards the ledge. For a moment I thought I was slipping and my body hung swaying in the air with only my fingers gripping the window ledge.

Hanging at the full reach of my arms, my fumbling feet found the ledge and I stood unsteadily upon it. I paused for several moments to recover my confidence and then began to edge my way along the ledge towards her window. It seemed an eternity before I was grasping the torn bedsheet and hauling myself up into her prison. I lay a while gasping on the floor while she bent anxiously over me.

'We must escape,' I said, recovering and stating the obvious.

'Yes but how?' she wailed with despair in her voice. 'Even if we can make it down to the courtyard, the castle gates are probably locked. And, look, you can see the great iron bolts shot home from here.'

What she said was true enough.

'Nevertheless,' I insisted, 'we must try.'

But her mind was thinking more clearly than mine. My thoughts were only of physical flight, of placing geographical distance between us and the grim fortress of this evil monster. She, however, was more logical.

'Escape to what, Upton?' she pointed out. 'Did this Dracula not call us here to Bukovina all the way from London in England? If we escape, surely he will merely call us back to him again. We will never be free of him until we have destroyed him.'

She was right. I agreed and, at her insisting, I recounted the terrible story the count had told me while she lay in her swoon. 'He was only able to call us, to control our minds, while the accursed

187

statuette was near at hand.'

'Nevertheless, Upton,' she said firmly, 'he must be destroyed. If he succeeds in his evil plan then no-one in the whole world will be safe.'

How my heart went out to her for her fortitude and courage, a greater courage than any I had witnessed. I seized her hands and kissed them.

'We must find his lair and destroy him and his kind,' she said. 'He has already confessed that he is vulnerable during the day. Let us put the day to good use.'

'Yes,' I replied, recalling my conversation with Avram. 'I have the knowledge of how his kind may be destroyed thanks to my poor friend who was slain by the coachman.'

'Then let us commence this grim task, Upton.'

I tried the door but with as little success as my own.

'The only way out is down to the courtyard.' I told her.

In silence we sat knotting the sheets into a rope which reached into that cobbled courtyard.

The descent was easier that I had imagined. The stones of the castle walls under her window were large and roughly cut and the mortar had by process of time been washed away between them. Thus a secure foothold could be easily attained by an enterprising climber. It was not long before we both stood safe and secure on the ground.

It was true, as Clara had predicted, that the great doors of the castle were closed, bolted and locked by heavy padlocks which might have been centuries old.

Clara squeezed my hand in encouragement.

'We must find his lair,' she whispered.

Squaring my shoulders I pushed at a side door, which opened into one wing of the castle containing bedchambers. But such chambers... most of them were entirely empty, others were barely furnished and all seemed never to have been used in ages, for everything was covered in a profusion of dust and grime.

One room caused Clara and I to gasp aloud for, although empty, there lay in one corner a pile of gold of all kinds - gold coins, from every part of the earth and covered with a thick film of dust as though it had lain long in the ground. None of it was less than three hundred years old. And next to this amazing treasure trove were chains, ornaments, some jewelled, but all of them of incredible age.

I do not know what drew me, but there was a door in a corner of that particular chamber. It was a heavy door, of the same dark oak and iron fittings that were found throughout the castle. With Clara at my side I tried its rusty, screeching handle and, to our surprise, it swung gently open. It led through a stone passage-way to a circular stairway which went steeply down as if driving towards the very bowels of the earth.

I called to Clara to keep behind me and mind her step, for the stairs were dark, although a faint gloomy light spread through a series of loopholes which pierced the heavy masonry to the world outside. Slowly, carefully, we went downwards and came to a dark, tunnel-like corridor.

'Upton, what is that dreadful odour?' gasped Clara, coughing as she breathed in some obnoxious fumes.

The air smelled of a sickly perfume, the odour of musty old earth newly dug. It was quite oppressive and grew in its intensity as we pushed our way down that passage. At the end of the corridor was another heavy door. Surprisingly, the handle seemed well oiled and it swung open quite easily before us.

We found ourselves in a chapel-like vault. Everywhere were fragments of old coffins and piles of dust. We could clearly see them in the dim light which seemed to filter in through cracks in the roof.

And everywhere were piles of earth.

'Upton!' cried Clara in horror. 'Look!'

With a quivering finger she pointed to a darkened end of the chapel vault.

There were several coffins resting on trestles in the gloom, but without lids covering their contents.

'It... it looks like people newly interred,' I said, aghast, as I perceived each coffin contained a body, but a body not yet in the process of decay.

Then I drew nearer and recognised one of the figures that lay stretched on a pile of that putrified earth.

I stifled a cry of terror.

There lay the count in some catatonic trance, or so I judged it to be. His eyes were fully open and stony, but lacking the glaze of death, and his cheeks were not the colour of parchment as in death. The lips were as red as ever but there was no other sign of life.

'This is what they meant, Clara.' I whispered. 'This is what they meant - Avram and the count. He lies confined in this box from sun-up to sunset.'

Clara's face was drained of blood and I could see she was fighting hard to control her twitching nerves.

'They must be destroyed,' she choked the words out.

I searched that terrible vault for some weapons and chanced upon a spade, a wooden shaft with iron blade, and with this I turned back to those gruesome creatures. Firstly, I bent over the count. There seemed a mocking smile upon his pale face, the thin red lips were drawn back, showing those terrible sharp teeth. I felt a revulsion so great that I wondered for a moment whether I should fall insensible. But sanity gripped me from the abyss.

In the other coffins were the two female creatures and the grey-clad being called Mihail.

The sooner I commenced my work then the sooner it would be ended.

The blade of the spade was sharp enough.

I raised it over my head and struck downward. With one blow it split through the white fleshy neck of Mihail.

I was unprepared for what happened.

A great scream of anguish came from that monstrous body, echoing and re-echoing through the close confines of the dank vault. And, horror upon horrors, a fountain of black blood sprayed from that corpse, splashing on my sleeve as I stumbled to escape from its ghastly deluge.

I fell back, near swooning.

Then, as I looked on in naked terror, the body of Mihail, as Malvina's body had done before it, crumbled slowly away into dust.

A strange itching in my skull caused me to turn back to the count's coffin.

Great God! The count's head was turned towards me and the eyes... the eyes were boring into mine in a blaze of basilisk fury.

I dropped the spade from my nerveless hands and stood paralysed in terror.

Clara's iron composure suddenly crumbled at the terrible sight.

190

Hands to her cheeks, she emitted scream after scream and suddenly went stumbling back towards the door, along the passage-way, away from this fiendish nightmare.

Anxious for her safety, I sped after her and finally caught her in the great dining room where we had eaten the night before.

She collapsed senseless in my arms for a moment and, on recovering, gave vent to the most heartrending fit of sobbing that I ever want to hear from a human being again.

I do not know how long she lay sobbing in my arms, and all the while with me trying to offer her reassurance and comfort. I do not know how long it was nor do I remember when the sobbing faded and, not having slept the previous night, we sank into a sleep of sheer exhaustion, comforted by the nearness of each other.

I recall springing awake abruptly, my heart pounding in sudden dread.

'My God, Clara!' my voice rose to a hysterical note as I saw the dark shadows at the window. 'Clara, the sun... I must finish the job before it is too late!'

Wide eyed in terror she, too, peered at the evening shadows creeping round the window.

'Quick, Upton!' she cried, 'we must...'

There was a sudden passage of cold wind into the room. In terror we glanced up.

There, standing before the door, his dark cloak flapping behind him like some gigantic bat's wings, stood the count.

'You are already too late,' his thin red lips curled in a sneer. 'You are already too late. The sun has set.'

CHAPTER TWENTY-SIX

I know not what passed that night in reality nor what passed in my fevered fantasy. I see images of the count, who spoke no word of my destruction of Mihail, and those images will haunt me until the day I die. I recall his tall figure conducting us into a vault, furnished in strange exotic trappings. This time the putrid smell of mouldering earth did not pervade the air but rather that terrifying sickly sweet smell of jasmine, the smell which had haunted my nightmares, hung in the atmosphere. Whether Clara and I went willingly with the count or whether we were propelled by his powerful will and ability of mesmerisation, I cannot be sure.

I do recall that Clara and I, though not physically bound, were held in some kind of bondage.

The vault was like some grim replica of my nightmares. At the end of the room stood a large figure of the accursed Draco, whose dragon features I knew so well. Flickering torches lit the scene. Before the statue stood a black-draped altar on which sat the jade dragon which had been the cause of our ghastly adventures. It seemed to be dwarfed by the bigger replica behind it. Also on the altar, I recall that there were chalices filled with certain flowers and herbs. There was an ancient manuscript, like some papyrus I had seen in the British Museum, as well as other paraphanalia whose function I could not guess at.

The count stood before the altar, hands upraised in supplication, mumbling in a strange tongue.

At his side stood the two voluptuous devil-women who seemed to act as his servers in a terrifying parody of some ancient mass.

The deep sonorous voice of the count began to intone:

'I come from the Isle of Fire having filled my body with the blood of Ur-Hekau, Mighty One of the Enchantments. I come before thee, Draco. I worship thee Draco, Fire-breather of the Great

192

Deep. You are my lord and I am of thy blood.'

I strained my head to look at Clara who was standing opposite me, on the other side of this terrible temple.

Her face was flushed and her eyes were glazed as if she were in a trance.

The count turned and followed my gaze, a smile sneering across his thin lips.

'Sebek-nefer-Ra! Do you hear me?'

To my horror, Clara's eyes were forced towards the count's stare. Her lips opened.

'I hear, lord.'

'Then the time is come when the world must be filled with the *Ka* of Draco. When the spirit of Draco must enter the world through my body and fill it with abundance.'

'It is the will of Draco,' intoned Clara's voice.

I struggled feebly with my invisible bonds.

A strange green fire seemed to be playing over that accursed jade statuette.

A voice was beating in my head, telling me to do something, to stop this evil bursting forth into the world.

And yet what could I do? I was held in the thrall of a force so powerful, so evil ...

'I come before thee Draco,' came the count's voice again. 'I who have been faithful to thy service over the centuries... I come before thee to demand my reward.'

The strange green fire was almost obliterating the statuette.

All about me was a strange drumming sound and I could distinguish in this percussion human voices chanting, chanting to the very beat of the drum, joining and mingling until voice and drum were indistinguishable from each other.

It was like my nightmares.

But I was no longer asleep.

'I call upon Sebek-nefer-Ra to exhort thee, Draco, to bestow on me the reward of thy office.'

The count flung up his arms towards the image behind the altar.

With numbed emotions, I saw Clara walk towards the altar. She walked slowly, like one in a dream; walked forward and genuflected towards the statuette. Then she climbed upon the altar and lay full length upon her back, hands across her breast as if in repose, her eyes closed.

'I am thy servant, Draco. I, Sebek-nefer-Ra willingly do offer myself to thee, creator of life, so that in my blood judgement may be made on this, thy servant Dracula.'

The women harpies, teeth churning at their fleshy lips until the blood trickled down their chins, gave frightful chuckles of delight and drew near the girl's still figure.

The count waved them back.

'To thee, Draco, I take this drink of life...'

I saw his mouth open, the elongated teeth bared, saw him bend slowly forward.

Clara gave a langurous sigh and arched her neck to met the sharp prick of those teeth!

I tried hard to cry out but no sounds would come.

It was then I felt a curious burning sensation at my throat. I felt my hand fused with some strange power, felt it recover its power of movement and felt it come up to my neck to feel the object at my throat.

It was the small silver crucifix that Dennis Yorke had given me for protection. I had worn it every day since that time and forgotten about it completely. It had been Clara's crucifix which I had thrown at that ghastly wolf-beast on the decks of the derelict *Ceres* but I had continued to retain my cross about my throat, under my shirt.

Not knowing exactly what I did, I reached up and snatched it from my neck. Then, mustering all the force I could, I flung it straight into the grinning green-black face of the dragon.

It was as if I had thrown a stick of dynamite at the beast. There was a terrific roar as if from an explosion. The statuette seemed to shatter into a million tiny splinters of green crystal. The blast flung Clara from the altar table.

The count gave a scream of fury and tried to run towards the smashed altar but now great sheets of flame were bursting over it, consuming the splinters of the statuette as if they were merely dried wood, wrapping the accoutrements and ancient papyrus in sheets of hungry flame. Eager tongues licked at the large dragon replica until it, too, cracked and splintered into fragments.

'The formula! The formula! The statuette!' Dracula was

screaming. 'I cannot succeed without them.'

He tried to enter the consuming fire but the flames caught at his great black flapping cloak until he was forced to desist.

Fear sped adrenalin through my frame.

Clara lay at my feet moaning as she seemed to rouse herself from her hypnotic trance. I bent down and seized her in my arms and ran towards the stairs.

I heard a vicious snarl behind me.

'So you think you have thwarted me... thwarted the work of four centuries by a moment's caprice? You will know my revenge now, I shall not spare you!'

The count, his face working in obscene hatred, rushed towards the steps calling to his two screaming harpies.

'Come sisters! Do not let them escape! You have wanted to drink from their young blood... drink then! They are yours! Drink your fill, my sisters, let vengeance be ours!'

They gave cries like wolves on the scent of their prey.

I do not know what lent me strength but, with Clara semi-swooning in my arms, I hurried through the corridors of the castle with those unholy demons of the night shrieking after me.

How I managed to keep ahead of them, whose strength and guidance gave me support, I will leave it to the readers to make their own observations. Somehow I reached the door leading into the courtyard. A joyous exultation filled me as I saw that the ceremonies which the count had performed had lasted through the night. Day was already breaking, the courtyard was filled with grey light and over the eastern walls of the castle, the sun's rays were starting to stream.

With Clara still in my arms I ran out into that light.

One of the female fiends was at the door before her sister and the count and, to my consternation, rushed straight into the courtyard after me.

For a long horrified moment, as she bore down on me, I thought that Avram's knowledge of these phantoms had been wrong. Perhaps they could move in daylight?

The creature, that vile creature of the grave, neared me, a blaze of unholy triumph in her red, burning eyes.

Then I heard the screams of warning from the count and his

companion.

A black shadow passed across her contorted, hate-ridden face. She glanced up and appeared to see the light of dawn for the first time. Her mouth twisted in terror. She made to turn back.

Abruptly, as if her legs had lost their power, she collapsed on the ground. Her black hair suddenly streaked with grey and, even as I watched, turned white. The skin crinkled, became dry and cracked as the rays of the rising sun swept across her body.

'Help me... help me...!'

It was the last plaintive shriek I heard from her decomposing body.

Then, as the rising sun blazed down in its morning strength, that terrible body collapsed into the dust from whence it came and was blown hither and thither in the gentle morning breeze.

I looked towards the doorway where the tall, black figure of the count hovered in the protection of the shadows.

'Puny humans!' he screamed in rage. 'You with your pale, stupid faces. I shall make you sorry yet... you have destroyed the dragon god... you have destroyed the ages-old formula by which I could have attained true immortality... you think that you have thwarted me? You have not yet destroyed me and while I exist I shall find a way to make you pay. You shall yet be sorry. My revenge will be sweet and time is on my side. Though you go to the ends of the earth... though you go to the ends of time... time is my friend and the centuries are mine to control. I shall be revenged!'

With another wild scream of anger the great castle door slammed shut and I could hear the bolts thrown.

I stood for a while unmoving, how long I did so I cannot recall. An insane terror rooted me to the spot and I stood in that courtyard in the golden warmth of the morning sun, babbling and trembling in my fright.

It must have been Clara who, recovering from her swoon, gathered new strength and guided me from that accursed place. I cannot even recall how we managed to open the great outer gates of that grim castle, nor, indeed, whether the outer gates were barred as they had been the previous day.

I know little of what followed. I dimly recall a long walk through some green valley, lit in the bright sunlight, of meeting with a band of strangely clad people - gypsies, perhaps - who gave us food, shelter and warm clothing and on whose strange wagons we eventually came to Bistritz. Clara afterwards told me that my hair had become streaked with white. I kept babbling, I know, as the enormity of the horror of what I had witnessed burst like a flood over my sensibilities. God knows how Clara managed to keep herself sane, perhaps it was my greater need that made her control her shattered feelings, for she nursed me day and night in my deliriums. By easy stages we went from Bistritz to Klausenburg and from thence to Budapest and on to Munich. From there the railway brought us to Calais and thence to Dover. All the while it seemed as if I continued to exist in some dark nether world, only half-realising what was going on about me.

At times I would rave and rant and cry on people to help me destroy the evil before it was too late.

And they would sorrowfully shake their heads and cluck sympathetically as if I were some lunatic.

Some times the terrors seized me with such force that not even Clara could control me.

And now...

How long I have been here I cannot recall exactly. I do not resent Clara allowing them to take me to this place for, though they do not believe me, the doctors have, at least, been able to calm my fears, sedate my terrors so that I am now able to control them and face the future with a more positive frame of mind. No longer do I shriek uncontrollably as the sun sinks below the western hills, nor do I start at the sight and sound of bats, dogs and rats.

Yet they say I am mad.

And at times, mostly at night, as I stand peering through the small iron grille that blocks the window of my room, staring at the ominous black clouds that scud across the death-white face of the moon, I find myself wishing that it *was* so, wishing that I were indeed mad. For at such times, I experience an unearthly chilling tingle that vibrates against my spine; I find my heart beats twice as fast; I feel the blood bursting hotly into my cheeks, roaring in my ears, and a mist begins to cloud my eyes. And through it all I hear *his* voice, mocking, sardonic, telling me that the time is coming... his will shall triumph, his revenge can extend to the tranquil shores of

England ... soon, soon...

God! What will happen to us if he finds a way to escape from the confines of his castle in the Borgo Pass... if he finds a way to come to England! The thought is too horrible.

Even as I look on, in my vision the swirling mists clear momentarily and I catch a glimpse of him - a tall, thin man, all in black. I see his face, that waxen face; the high aquiline nose, the parted red lips, with the sharp teeth showing between them; and the eyes - those red basilisk orbs, burning as if I were staring at the very sunset.

And the voice.

'Soon... soon...'

Oh Clara! How shall we protect ourselves if *he* finds a way to come to England?

CHAPTER TWENTY-SEVEN

At the end of Upton Welsford's manuscript were pasted three yellowing newspaper cuttings. The first read:

The Westminster Gazette, June 10, 1862

We regret to report that Mr. Upton Welsford, a former senior official at the Foreign Office, has been committed to the Netley Heath Sanatorium for the Insane. Mr. Welsford was committed on his recent return from Romania where he had, apparently, suffered a mental breakdown.

Mr. Welsford was one of the British delegation to go to Romania early this year to witness the formation of the new Romanian state. Colleagues said that overwork was probably a contributing factor to his illness. A spokesman for the Foreign Office told our reporter that they have accepted Mr. Welsford's resignation from office.

Following this cutting there appeared a note, written in a precise copperplate, which read: 'Welsford was released in September, 1868. His delusions apparently no longer exist or trouble him. He left this manuscript behind. It is a remarkable example of the imagination of a brainsick individual which students of such disorders will do well to read.'

The other two newspaper cuttings then followed.

The Westminster Gazette, March 10, 1869

The marriage of Mr. Upton Welsford and Miss Clara Clarke took place on Monday last at St. James's Church, Westminster.

Mr. Welsford was formerly personal secretary to Lord Molesworth at the Foreign Office. He resigned due to ill-health which he has suffered in recent years. Miss Clarke is the daughter of...

At this point the rest of the cutting had been torn away.

The Westminster Gazette, September 27, 1890.

ANOTHER HAMPSTEAD MYSTERY*

We regret to announce the deaths of Mr and Mrs Upton Welsford of Devonshire Road, Hampstead Heath. The unfortunate couple were found dead in their home yesterday by a domestic servant. A doctor was called and pronounced life extinct, the cause of death being put down to exposure due to progressive anaemia, a lack of haemoglobin or red blood corpuscles. The servant afterwards recalled that this condition had been prevalent for some days, the couple showing a peculiar spiritlessness and langour. The servant expressed regret and remorse that she had not been able to attribute these symptoms to serious illness.

Our correspondent learns, from a reliable source, that the throats of the unfortunate couple showed tiny wounds of the kind which have been associated with the recent cases of injured children who have been found in a distressed condition on the nearby Heath after disappearing in mysterious circumstances for often as much as twenty-four hours. The facts in these mysterious cases have been reported in the columns of this journal.

The attending doctor has disclaimed any significance or connection between the couple and the children, although a police spokesman suggests that the same animal, thought to be a rat or a small dog, which attacked the children on the Heath, also attacked the couple who lived close by the Heath. The police spokesman told our correspondent that a group of rat catchers will shortly be investigating the vicinity for the animals.

Mr and Mrs Welsford were well known for their charitable work in local circles, especially in their efforts to raise finances for medical research among the insane as well as supporting work for the upkeep of hospitals for the mentally ill.

*Articles from **The Westminster Gazette** *of September 25, 1890, giving an account of 'A Hampstead Mystery' and 'The Hampstead Horror' were quoted by Bram Stoker in his* **Dracula** *(1897) in Chapter XIII.* **Tremayne.**

Mr. Welsford was fifty-five years old at the time of his death. The son of the late Reverend Mortimer Welsford of Gisleham, Buckinghamshire, he graduated from Oxford University and became personal secretary to Viscount Molesworth whose work at the Foreign Office is well known. Mr Welsford accompanied Lord Molesworth to Romania at the time of the establishment of the Romanian State. On his return, an illness forced his resignation from public office.

Mrs Welsford was formerly Miss Clara Clarke, daughter of the late Colonel George St. John Clarke of the Egyptian Brigade of Rifles.

Psychiatrist's Afterword by Hugh Strickland, MD, FACP, FAPA.
In allowing Mr. Peter Tremayne to publish the foregoing manuscript - which was written by Mr. Upton Welsford when an inmate of the Netley Heath Sanatorium for the Insane sometime between 1862 and 1868 - I have stipulated that I, as present director of the sanatorium, be allowed to contribute a few observations to this case.

Mr Welsford's story is horrific; but it is by no means unusual for someone to suffer delusions of being persecuted by vampires and werewolves or, indeed, even believe that they are changing into such mythological creatures themselves. If Mr Welsford were alive in this day and age we would have been able to cure his psychiatric disorder without too much trouble. 'Lupomania', the werewolf or vampire complex, is still known today. In my initial letter to Mr Tremayne, quoted in his introduction, I have listed some modern occurences.

In this post-Freud period the sexual basis of vampirism and lycanthropy has been recognised by psychiatrists. The Jungian psychologist, Robert Eisler, in his excellent study *Man into Wolf* (1949) also advances a creditable hypothesis.

Man was once a peaceful herbivorous ape, living on roots and berries. But as an imitative creature, in his battle for survival against wild animals, he acquired the ferocity and bloodlust of a wild animal. So intense was this experience that man sees the mark of masculinity, a form of behaviour to impress women, as being violence. The great men of history are not usually peacemakers but those who are warriors, conquerors, full of this terrible primitive bloodlust. Soldiers are made heroes by an adoring society because they represent mankind's collective bloodlust. And when man feels frustrated, that frustration usually manifests itself in aggressive behaviour.

Bloodlust in man is often combined with an animal identification-hence the phrase 'as strong as a lion' etc. for it is the hunter-animals, the killers, who are most respected by man.

Respect for the hunter-animals has led man into animal worship. There still exists, in Africa, a leopard cult because the leopard is one of the most bloodthirsty beasts of prey. But the leopard's equivalent in Europe is the wolf. In mediaeval Europe, it was the wolf which was the commonest and most dangerous hunter.

Therefore numerous sexually repressed men identified with the wolf as the hunter and believed themselves to be werewolves as their justification to attack young girls in order to fulfil these repressed lusts. There are many historical cases which one is able to cite. Perhaps the most famous was that of Gilles Garnier who was executed as a werewolf in 1574 at Dole in France. In recent times, in New York as late as 1928, Albert Fish, and in Wisconsin about the same time, Ed Gein, attacked young girls, sucked their blood and ate their flesh because they believed themselves to be werewolves or vampires.

These attacks arose out of a suppressed sexual desire but, unable to come to terms with it, the perpetrators of the deeds seemed to convince themselves that they were victims of a terrible destiny - that what they did was out of their control and attributed to some strange mystic disease called vampirism. And the same basic sexual drive lies behind both vampirism and werewolfism.

It is my belief that Upton Welsford, who admits in his manuscript to a rather narrow Anglican upbringing during the worst excesses of the Victorian Age, had an inverted sexual frustration. The sexual drive is obvious in his descriptions of his love-making to Clara and of his near seduction by the vampire Malvina. These were not so much incidents that happened but incidents that he wished would happen. His whole fear of being attacked by vampires was expressive of a desire to be seduced by women, yet, at the same time, a fear of what that seduction might bring. Victorian society had taught him that sex was something sinful, that it must be repressed. This conflict with his sexual frustrations grew more acute and, with increasing overwork, he suffered a serious mental collapse in which his mind created a fascinating fantasy whose symbolism is now obvious. I find it significant that, having married Clara Clarke, and thus enjoying a normal sex-life, Upton Welsford seems to have undergone a complete cure.

THE END